The Killing of a Shadow

The Killing of a Shadow

J.F. HILLEY

gatekeeper press™

Columbus, Ohio

This book is a work of fiction. The names, characters and events in this book are the products of the author's imagination or are used fictitiously. Any similarity to real persons living or dead is coincidental and not intended by the author.

The Killing of a Shadow

Published by Gatekeeper Press
2167 Stringtown Rd, Suite 109
Columbus, OH 43123-2989
www.GatekeeperPress.com

Library of Congress Control Number: 2021944727

ISBN (hardcover): 9781662918483
ISBN (paperback): 9781662918490
eISBN: 9781662918506

This book is dedicated to my
husband John. Thank you for always
making me feel like I can conquer
anything that I put my mind to.
Love you, my love.

Thank you, Gatekeeper Press,
especially Jessica Bushore for helping
me along with this new endeavor of
writing my very first novel. I hope
this will be a success and if so,
then many more to come!

Contents

Prologue

It's midmorning and everyone on Alpha compound is finishing breakfast. They're all heading to their respective duty sections to begin the day. Everyone, that is, except for Alex.

She intentionally woke up late and decided not to go for her hour-long run, eat breakfast, or show up for mandatory training. Instead, she's drinking vodka and smoking cigarettes in her room, which she knows is against the rules. For her, it's hard to break them. She's known as the "go-to" person who's never late for anything and never gets in trouble.

After the physical altercation with Captain Marcs the night before, she thought, *Why even bother showing up this morning. I'm already in trouble.* The captain is the whole reason she feels like shit and doesn't want to leave her room.

Before this deployment, Alex was the first one to arrive at work or the gym, and she was always ready to go. However, this morning is a different story. When she first arrived on Alpha compound eleven months ago, Alex was excited to be there until Captain Marc's mission changed everything.

As the cigarette smoke billows out of her mouth and the music of her favorite rock band blares in her ears, Alex can only think about the fight from the night before. Her aching eye and cut lip give her the feeling that the captain isn't finished with her yet. Even though her swollen face is slowly starting to heal, she asks herself, *How could I let him do this to me? I fucking played with fire and got burned.* As the music plays in her room, she slowly moves her body from side to side with the rhythm, trying to focus on that and not the fight.

Alex's dorm room is dark, with the blinds fully shut and minimal light coming through them. Her uniform is flung unceremoniously on the chair and her combat boots are thrown to the side of the bed. Her room's a mess, which isn't normal for someone who usually keeps up with proper military standards.

Alex used to care about keeping up with appearances but not for the longest time now. Not since she arrived in Afghanistan, and certainly not since she started training for her mission with the captain.

There's a fully loaded Beretta M9 pistol she keeps on her nightstand and an M4 rifle propped up in the corner. The room is full of cigarette smoke, and the stale smell of sweat and vanilla perfume lingers in the air. As she continues to dance, the music's so loud that she can see the perfume bottle vibrate on the nightstand.

I can't believe I wore that for him, she thought as she looks at the bottle of perfume and thinks about how disgusted she felt when the captain was on top of her the night before. *The things he did to me*, she thought with disgust as she feels the vibration of the music on her skin.

To take her mind off her aching body and face, she takes a long drag from her cigarette. Exhaling slowly, she then takes another swig of the vodka and as it falls down her throat, a sudden wave of euphoria comes over her. Holding up her long dark wavy hair with auburn highlights that catch in the light, she inspects her half-naked body in the full-length mirror on the wall. Even in the dim light, she can see the bruises on her arms and legs, as she's wearing a black lacey thong and nothing else.

From where she's standing, Alex can see how badly the captain marked her face the night before. She walks closer to the mirror and slowly touches her black eye and cut lip. *That son of a bitch*, she thinks angrily as her mind flashes back at how horrible the fight was. All that tension that had built up between them for the past eleven months didn't help.

What the fuck was I thinking and what if my plan doesn't work? she asks herself again in frustration. Alex isn't the type of woman to allow a man to strike her and get away with it, but she had to let him hit her this time.

At that moment, she imagines how the wounds she inflicted on him are feeling, and with that thought, she grins with satisfaction. She never hated anyone as much as she hates the captain. Not even her father could compare to him.

Growing up, she suffered an abusive father who drank too much and then hit her if she got too close or crossed his path. The moment she met the captain, he instantly reminded her of her father. Specifically, during training when the captain would yell in her face or degrade her in front of everyone.

As the music continues to blare off loudly for the entire building to hear, she continues to stare at her battered face. Then her bright green eyes, smeared with last night's eyeliner, move to the reflection of the photos on the wall. The captain gave her those photos when she first arrived on Alpha compound eleven months ago. They reveal the blood-stained and beaten bodies of so many girls who were left for dead. The man responsible is known throughout the country as someone whose own shadow would terrify the devil himself.

Months ago, she placed the man's photo in the middle of the photos of all the dead girls to remind her of what he's done. Looking at them now, those photographs haunted her dreams and it's about time they come off her wall. She gazes into the man's eyes as his careless stare looks back at her. It's as if his eyes follow her around the room, which still gives her chills up her spine. *Just five more days and it'll all be over,* she thinks to herself as her favorite rock star's voice continues to sing loudly in her ears.

As she stands there in front of the madman pinned to her wall, she takes another long drag from her cigarette and blows the smoke in his face. *I can't wait to see your blood hit the floor*, she thinks before glancing at the calendar pinned to the wall next to the photos.

When she found out the date of her mission, she placed a red X marking October 15, the day of the total solar eclipse. Looking at the date, she feels a sudden rush of adrenaline in her system. Alex has trained all year for this and is finally ready to take on the most dangerous mission she'll ever be part of.

But for now, she just wants the pain to stop, so she picks up the bottle of vodka on the vanity and downs the liquid. That same euphoric feeling runs through her body as sweat slowly runs down her neck. Dizzy from the overwhelming and blissful feeling of the vodka, she decides to lay back down. *Just go to sleep and don't wake up until the day of the solar eclipse*, she thinks as she lets the cigarette smoke billow slowly from her lips.

Suddenly, she hears loud, aggressive banging on her door, and even through the loud music, the noise still makes her jump. She looks at her alarm clock and realizes she's late for training. *They can bang on my door all they want, I'm not going*, thinking she doesn't want to see anyone right now. She just wants to be alone with her thoughts and let her body heal in time for her final mission.

She takes another long drag from her cigarette, hoping they'll go away. Letting the smoke fill her lungs and then exhaling slowly, Alex closes her eyes again and only focuses on the music.

As the person behind the door continues to knock loudly, Alex suddenly realizes the inevitable fate she'll be facing soon. Once she faces it, there'll be no turning back.

Chapter 1
The Arrival

Eleven Months Earlier

Staff Sergeant Alexandra Foster arrives for her 365-day deployment at the international airport in Kabul, Afghanistan. Alex found out the day after Christmas that she was leaving, and since she'd volunteered for this deployment, getting the call so soon after the holiday didn't bother her. Since she doesn't have a family and doesn't celebrate the holidays at home with her dad, she was excited to leave.

After receiving the call, she was sent to combat skills training, or CST, first for a month to train on things like land navigation, hand-to-hand combat, and convoy training. It was miserable since it was the dead of winter and training in the snow in Washington State wasn't fun. Alex was exhausted after traveling from the States, to Germany, to finally flying to the main hub in Manas, Kyrgyzstan.

Standing there in her clean and pressed uniform, with her long dark hair placed in a perfect tight bun, she waits patiently for her contact to pick her up. Traveling alone this time, she struggles with all her bags. With her military-issue C-bag on her back and one on each arm, she feels excited that she finally made it here in-country. She watches as the local Afghan people walk past her as they rush to make their flights. The airport isn't what she's used to coming from the States. It's not as clean and the smells of sweat and fuel are overwhelming to her.

This is Alex's third deployment in her seven-year career. However, it's her first deployment to the Middle East. She's heard stories of how different the culture is here and what a great opportunity it is to learn and get to know the people. Usually, she deploys with a team of three to four other military members, but she volunteered for this deployment, so this time she's on her own. *I can't believe I'm finally here*, she thinks as she looks around the airport. Being twenty-five years old and on her own in a foreign country makes her feel adventurous like she's ready to take on anything.

As she continues to stand by waiting for her contact to pick her up, local Afghan men walk past her. She notices that some of them turn and look back at her with confusion, seeing that she's a woman in uniform and by herself. Alex suddenly feels nervous being that she's alone and that she's a woman in a country where women are considered second-class citizens.

As they stare, she notices that the men don't look away like the men back home normally would do. Feeling even more uncomfortable, Alex realizes that she's completely exposed and has no idea how to get to her assigned unit. *Shit, why do they keep staring at me like that*? she asks herself as she starts fidgeting with her bags, feeling their eyes on her.

Alex starts to look around for anyone who might speak English when she sees a local man watching her as if he wants to tell her something. She hesitates for a moment then walks over to ask him where the phone is. Not knowing how to speak in Dari, she places her thumb and pinky finger on her cheek simulating the handle of a phone. This gesture instantly changes his look from confusion to disgust as he looks at her up and down and then points toward the end of the airport.

Red faced and embarrassed, Alex suddenly realizes how stupid that was of her as she quickly picks up all her gear and starts walking in the direction he pointed. *That's just great Alex. Your first day in-country and you insult the guy*, she thinks as she finds her way down toward the end of the airport only to find one old phone that looks broken. Luckily, when she picks up the receiver it has a dial tone. She quickly reaches in her cargo pocket and pulls out the paper with her contact's phone number written on it. As she starts to dial, a black armored SUV comes up. A soldier from the passenger side window leans out and asks, "Hey, are you lost?"

Alex looks up to see a guy in an Army uniform and instantly feels at ease. *Oh, thank God*, she thinks as she places the half-broken receiver back onto the base of the phone and turns around to respond to him.

"Kind of, I'm supposed to report to Alpha compound, which is near the embassy and the main headquarters. I'm replacing Sergeant Kushner and he's supposed to pick me up today," she said to the Army guy, who's leaning out the window.

He looks at her, shakes his head, and scoffs, "Sergeant Kushner's an idiot. He forgot you were getting here today and asked us to come and get you at the last minute," he says as he gets out of the vehicle to talk with her face to face.

Alex notices how tall and good-looking he is as he walks closer to her, and how the light hits his jawline. His blue-grey eyes come across as sincere and genuine, which makes her feel instantly attracted to him. Alex doesn't want him to notice her looking at him like that, and so she quickly looks away. *Don't stare*, she tells herself as he walks closer to her.

"Sergeant Kushner didn't tell us you're a woman traveling here alone. I hope you weren't waiting here too long?" he asks while looking around at all the local Afghan men in the airport standing by and watching them.

"No, it hasn't been too long of a wait. I'm just not used to deploying by myself. I'm usually with a team," she says. "And with a name like Alex Foster you probably thought I was a guy you were picking up," she says with a slight grin.

"Yeah, actually I did!" he says as he laughs a little, noticing her bright eyes and warm smile.

Alex slightly tilts her head to the side and says, "Yeah, I get that a lot with a name like Alex. It's actually Alexandra, but I'd rather be called Alex. Nice to meet you." She reaches her hand out for him to shake.

The first thing he notices about her are her bright green eyes. They have a hint of light brown when the sunlight hits them and seems to take him in. He notices how attractive she is and tries not to make her feel uncomfortable by looking at her for too long. *Stop staring you idiot and shake her hand*, he tells himself as he extends his right hand to shake hers. "I'm Sergeant Anderson, but call me Liam," he says as he gently lets her hand go.

Why did she come here? he thinks as he looks at her with concern.

Alex briefly catches the worried look he gives her and wonders why. It's as if he knows something about her that she doesn't. As she moves closer to the SUV, she sees the driver sitting there waiting for her and Liam to get in.

"Tate, help me with her bags," Liam says to the young sergeant sitting in the driver's seat.

"Coming Sarge," Sergeant Tate says as he runs around the SUV to meet with them.

"This is Sergeant Tate, the driver and communications specialist of my team," Liam says.

Sergeant Tate is five-feet, six-inches tall, skinny, and looks like he's still in high school. He has a baby face, and when he smiles, his dimples come out, making him look even younger.

"Hey, I'm Staff Sergeant Foster, but just call me Alex," she says as they both shake hands.

"Staff Sergeant, what is that in the Air Force, an E6?" Tate says as he grabs one of her C-bags and throws it in the back. He never met a member in the Air Force and isn't used to the Air Force rank structure.

"No, I'm an E5 like you, we just add the Staff in front, don't ask me why," she says as she rolls her eyes and grins.

"Come on, let's get your bags so that we can make it back in time for dinner. We don't want to get caught outside the green zone after hours because if Captain Marcs finds out he'll give us hell," Liam says.

"Yeah, he can be a real prick," Tate replies.

"Is he in charge?" she asks.

Unfortunately, Liam thinks as he slightly rolls his eyes.

"The captain's in charge of a smaller team that Tate, myself, and two other guys are part of, so let's hope you don't run into him," Liam says as he gives her that worried look again. He opens the door behind the driver's seat to let Alex in as if he is her chauffeur.

Alex thinks it's cute when Liam opens the door for her, then says, "Thanks, but I think I can open my own door."

Liam looks back at her with a playful smile. "Yes, but these doors weigh about four hundred pounds each, and I didn't want you to get hurt on your first day."

Well shit, she thinks and instantly feels foolish for even mentioning it, but grateful at the same time that the door didn't crush her. This is her first deployment to the desert, and with her last two deployments, they didn't have armored vehicles with bulletproof glass.

"Oh, sorry I didn't know, thanks Liam," she says apologetically.

He doesn't get offended by this and says, "No problem. Just make sure you lock your door after I shut it okay. If we get into some trouble on the road, we don't want *them* getting in the vehicle."

Wait, what? Who's them? she wonders while trying not to look worried at his comment. "Roger that, let's get out of here," she says as she locks the door and puts her seat belt on.

Alex looks out the window of the black, armored SUV and sees the sun starting to set. Despite the heavy pollution in the air, she can see the light orange and pink colors streaking across the sky. The streets are full of garbage, and the smell in the air is of burnt rubber and metal. The air is heavy with black smoke from the burn pits and the people are dressed in tattered clothing. Most of them are without shoes as they walk along the side of the highway, while others huddle around a lit fire from an empty oil drum.

Oh my God, these poor people, she thinks as Tate continues to drive down the narrow highway past buildings that look like they're about to fall apart. When Alex went to combat skills training last month, they set up mock villages with actors portraying the local Afghan people. The instructors did this to help the trainees deploying to the desert have a better understanding of what it will look like. After seeing the real thing, Alex is in shock at how much the instructors got it wrong.

To get back in time, Sergeant Tate speeds down the road, bobbing and weaving through traffic. He frequently glances back at Alex through the dashboard mirror with the same worried look on his face that Liam gave her earlier. As the communications specialist of the team, Tate is highly knowledgeable about passing intel from compound to compound. He's been in-country a couple of months now and already knows every road and back alley in Kabul.

Looking through the rearview mirror back at Alex, Tate asks, "Hey, are you okay back there? I'm sorry that I'm driving this way, but I have to make sure not to get caught on this road after curfew," he says.

Alex realizes that she has a scared look on her face due to his erratic driving. She's also gripping the passenger assist handle above the window, which was referred to as the oh-shit handle, so tight that her knuckles are turning white.

Jesus, calm down or they're not going to respect you, she thinks as she quickly corrects the look on her face and replies, "No, I'm okay. I just didn't realize how Afghanistan looked compared to the mock villages in CST," she says.

Liam nods his head in agreement. "Yeah, I went to CST at Fort Dix in New Jersey before coming here and you're right. It's not at all what I expected either, but you'll get used to it.

"And the smell. The instructors didn't mention that either," she says as she covers her nose in disgust.

"You think this is bad? Just wait until Thursdays," Tate replies as he gives her a look like someone just shit themselves.

"Man, don't tell her that or she's not going to want to stay," Liam says to Tate.

"Wait, what happens on Thursdays?" Alex asks with curiosity.

Liam laughs a little and says, "It's the day the septic trucks come and suck all the waste out of the tanks."

"Yeah, if you like running outside, don't go after they show up!" Tate says.

"Oh shit, thanks for telling me," Alex says with a smirk on her face. "I'll be sure to remember that."

Even though she deployed there without a team, she suddenly feels at ease with them, knowing that she isn't going to be alone. Feeling hungry and tired, all she wants to do is make it to the compound before dark, check in, eat, and then go to sleep. Then she's going to take each day one at a time and take in all the exciting experiences she's heard about.

In no time, they reach the compound's front gate before curfew, safe and sound. As the front gate closes for the night, they get out of the armored SUV. While Tate and Liam clear their weapons in the clearing barrel, Alex stands by and looks around Alpha compound. She notices that the military members and civilian contractors just ended their shifts and are heading to the chow hall to eat and go back to their dorm rooms. As she looks around, she also notices that the compound isn't that big. There're a few buildings in the middle of the compound for office work and a few two-story buildings that are the dorm rooms.

"Are you hungry?" Liam asks as he watches her look around at her new home for the next twelve months.

"Yeah, I've been traveling all day and I haven't eaten," she says as she holds her stomach.

"Okay, let's take you first to the J1 office where you can in-process and then get your room assignment. Once we get that, we can drop your bags off and then get something to eat," he says feeling a little hungry and tired himself.

That's nice of him, she thinks as he escorts her from the front gate to the J1 office, which is no more than fifty feet away. As they walk there, many of the military members and contractors start to look back at them. They know that she's the new girl because of all her bags and for the fact that the ratio of women on this compound is twenty men to one woman.

Liam helps her carry two of her bags while he walks her over to get in-processed. The J1 office consists of both military members and civilian contractors, and they handle all the finances, awards presentations, and accountability for everyone there on the compound. Alex is going to be assigned to this office and take over for Sergeant Kushner, the guy that was supposed to pick her up but forgot about her.

Liam sets her bags down and introduces Alex to Captain Tracy Goodfellow, who's the officer in charge.

Alex can tell right away that Captain Goodfellow is a nice person by seeing her welcoming demeanor and gentle smile. She's tall and thin with short brown hair and light brown eyes. When she speaks, Alex picks up a hint of a New England accent that reminds her of those cozy winter days sitting in front of a fire.

"Hello Staff Sergeant Foster, I am so happy to meet you. I apologize that Sergeant Kushner didn't pick you up at the airport today. It's been a hectic afternoon," she says while extending her hand out for Alex to shake.

"Nice to meet you too ma'am. It's okay. Sergeant Anderson and Sergeant Tate saved the day," she says as they both turn and look at Liam with gratitude.

"It's no problem," Liam says giving her and Goodfellow a warm smile.

Captain Goodfellow's staff in-process and give her a room key. They already knew she was coming and had everything ready for her when she arrived.

"Looks like you got the nicer building right next to the gate," says one of the office clerks.

"Why's it nicer?" Alex asks out of curiosity.

"It's one story and only a few people are staying there right now, which means it's quiet and nobody bangs on the bathroom door in the morning," the desk clerk says with a slight smile on her face.

At this point, Alex doesn't care. She just wants to get some food in her stomach and go to sleep.

"Well, it's nice meeting you all and I'll see you tomorrow morning," Alex says with exhaustion.

Captain Goodfellow looks at her and Liam as they leave and says, "Have a good night you two, and see you tomorrow, Sergeant Foster."

As they make their way toward her assigned dorm room, Alex says, "She's really nice."

"Yeah, she in-processed me when I got here too and showed me around," Liam says as they reach the inside of the one-story dorm building.

The hallway is about forty feet long with three doors on each side and three full bathrooms at the end of it. Alex's door is the second door on the right and as she goes to open it, she realizes just how small it is.

The room is about ten feet long and seven feet wide. It has one window with a twin bed, a nightstand, and a wall locker for her uniforms and clothes. There's a full-length mirror affixed to the wall and a small chair to sit in. The room isn't much but at least she has it all to herself. With her last two deployments, she had to share rooms, which sucked, especially if your roommate was on the same shift. At least with this room, she'll have some privacy.

"Home sweet home," she says as she throws her C-bag on her bed.

"Yeah, it's a little small but at least you don't have to share it with anyone," Liam says lightheartedly as he slowly puts her other bags down on the floor.

Smiling back at him she says, “I was just thinking the same thing.”

I can’t believe she’ll be staying right next to me, Liam thinks as he feels a sudden flutter of delight in his stomach.

“Come on, let’s get some food,” he says seeing how tired she looks.

As they leave her room, Alex watches as Liam opens the door right next to hers.

“Where are you going?” she asks and then realizes that he lives there.

“This is my room,” Liam says as he walks inside and grabs a DVD from his nightstand. “I forgot to give Tate his movie back and he’s been nagging me all week about it.” Liam shows her the bootleg DVD copy of *Superbad.*

The cover of the DVD reminds her of a guy in CST who made a name tag that read “McLovin’” and wore it during training. It was the name of one of the characters in the movie. She never saw the instructors laugh so hard when they saw that name tag.

We’re going to be living next to each other? she thinks while looking around his room. She notices that he hasn’t been there long because his room isn’t as lived in. There’s nothing on the walls and some of his bags are still packed.

“When did you get here?” she asks.

“Almost a month ago. Yeah, sorry, my room’s a little messy,” he says embarrassed.

“I don’t think it’s that messy,” she says while thinking how nice it’s going to be having him close by. From the moment they met, she felt drawn to him, but then thought it’s not a good time to get too close to someone in a place like this. She also doesn’t want to get hurt again.

"Come on, let's go to the chow hall before they close," he says as they walk out into the hallway toward the entrance door.

"Hey, maybe I can ask Tate if I can borrow that movie. I brought a laptop with me, and I've been wanting to see that one," she says with a slight smile.

"There are so many bootleg DVDs floating around this compound it's not even funny," he laughs. "Echo compound, across the street, has vendors that sell so many bootlegs and other things too. We can go tomorrow after you settle in if you want." Liam asks, hoping she'll say yes to hanging out with him.

Alex thinks about it for a minute. "Sure, I'd like that." Deep down she's excited about this but doesn't want to show him that. She wants to make friends while she's here, but she doesn't want to get too close and get hurt.

The sun's almost completely gone and all that remains is the dim light of the horizon as they walk together to the chow hall. The sound of their footsteps on the gravel echo softly as they slowly walk together side by side in silence. Suddenly, Alex hears a man singing and doesn't know where it's coming from. His stunning voice booms loudly for the whole city to hear and Alex stops so she can listen to it. He's singing in Dari, which is the native language of the Afghan people. Each word is drawn out in a soothing harmony that makes Alex's hair on the back of her neck stand. The melody is awe-inspiring, and she wishes she understood the words.

Liam stops to listen as well and can see her reaction. He says, "It's the call to prayer. There are loudspeakers all around the city and a man will sing five times a day letting the people know it's time to pray. When the people hear him sing, they face Mecca, kneel, and then bow in that direction until he's done."

Alex stands there in silence listening to the Afghan man sing with such compassion in his voice. As the sun finally sets and the light is completely gone, Staff Sergeant Alexandra Foster thinks it's the most beautiful thing she's ever experienced.

Chapter 2
The Nightmare

Breathing hard, shaking, and hiding under the bed, she hears those dreaded footsteps coming toward her room. The sound is deafening as each step he takes grows louder in her ears. Frozen in place, she can't move for fear that he'll find her.

The door suddenly slams open with such force that pieces of the wall come off as he yells at her to come out.

"Come out you little BITCH! Get over here!" he says through gritted teeth and with anger in his voice.

Suddenly, she feels a hand grab her by the hair and violently drag her from under the bed. She feels her head throb and his foot repeatedly kicking her stomach.

She screams, "No daddy please! Stop it please!"

He kneels and grabs her hair once more then yells in her face, "You worthless piece of SHIT!"

She smells the alcohol on his breath, and she feels the spit from his mouth hit her face. He punches her hard on the side of the head and Alex instantly wakes up, in her bed, in Afghanistan. For a moment she forgets where she is until she hears the final call to prayer outside her window. *It was just a nightmare*, she thinks as she remembers her dad hitting her that hard once after her mother died.

Laying there, she thinks about all the years away from her dad and how she still fears him and his shadow that lives deep in her mind. *Let him go. He can't hurt you anymore*, she tells herself as the man continues to sing outside her window. She listens as his voice vibrates out of the loudspeakers and echoes into the quiet night sky. *How's this deployment going to turn out?* she asks herself as she starts to think about how this deployment will be compared to the other two she went on.

This deployment is going to be twelve months long, and Alex doesn't have any family to call, no boyfriend, and zero friends back home. She joined the Air Force at eighteen, right after her high school graduation seven years ago because she didn't want to spend another moment in that trailer park with her dad.

Despite her upbringing, Alex managed to keep her head on straight all those years by doing what she was told and staying out of trouble. At her first duty station, she made promotion to staff sergeant on her first try. Her leadership awarded her for all her efforts, and they told her that volunteering to go to Afghanistan for a year would do wonders for her career.

And now here I am, she thought as the call to pray ends and Alex realizes that it's late with an early morning ahead. As she lays her head back onto her pillow and closes her eyes, she hears a small knock at her door.

What the hell? she thinks as she slowly gets up and presses her ear to the door. "Who is it?"

"It's me, Liam. Are you okay? I heard you scream," he whispers back from the other side of her door.

Shit, she thought. She didn't realize that she made any sounds while she was sleeping. Alex opens the door to see Liam leaning against the doorway with no shirt on. He's wearing dark sweatpants that lay low on his well-defined hips and with the dim light in the hallway, she can see the contours of his abs and arms.

Jesus, she thinks as she tries not to stare at his body and says, "I'm so sorry, I didn't mean to wake you up."

"It's alright, the walls are really thin, and I just wanted to make sure you're okay," he says in a low and concerned voice.

From the dim light of her window, he can see the outline of her hourglass figure. He notices how different she looks out of uniform. How her hair hangs down in long curvy waves to her waist and the pleasant smell of her vanilla perfume. Liam does his best not to stare at her as she stands inches away from him in the doorway.

"Thanks, I'll be okay. And I'll try to keep it down," she says with appreciation in her voice.

"Please don't apologize. My first night wasn't great either, but you get used to it after a week or so."

"Thanks Liam, I really appreciate it."

"Hey, how about tomorrow, after your shift, I take you around the compound and show you where everything is. Then we can grab some food," he says.

After a few moments she replies with a warm smile, "Yes, that would be nice."

As his eyes adjust to the dim light, he can see her warm smile and smiles back at her. "Okay, get some sleep, I'll see you tomorrow," he says as he turns to go back into his room.

As Liam returns to go back to bed, he can hear Alex getting into her bed right behind his wall. Taking a chance, he lightly taps three times on the wall above his pillow to see if she responds.

A few seconds later, Alex lightly taps her wall three times in the same spot above her pillow. To her, that gesture alone makes her feel at ease and in no time, she falls back asleep unencumbered by bad dreams.

The morning light is coming through Alex's window shades, and she can hear the morning call to prayer. This time, Alex can tell that it's a different man singing because his voice isn't as passionate as the man from the night before.

She gets up, takes a shower, brushes her teeth, and puts on a fresh ironed uniform. She double-checks herself in the mirror to make sure her hair is in regulation and her boots and uniform are up to standard. Alex feels that first impressions are important when meeting new people, especially Captain Goodfellow and the coworkers she'll be around for a year.

She hears a light knock on her door and already knows it's Liam coming to take her to breakfast when she says, "Come in."

Liam opens the door but doesn't cross into her threshold. He's a gentleman and doesn't want her to feel uncomfortable by entering without her permission. He notices how clean and neat her room is and how professional she looks in her uniform. Liam's never met anyone from the Air Force but heard from his Army friends how sloppy and lazy they are and how they thought they were better than everyone else around them. He, however, doesn't see this in Alex, just her well-behaved demeanor and professionalism.

Why did she come here? he asks himself again as he watches her from across the room. Liam starts to get that worried look on his face again but quickly changes his expression. He needs to make sure nothing happens to her while she's here.

When Alex turns to face him, he straightens up. "Ready to go?"

"Yes, I'm starving. I hope breakfast is good." She grabs her M9 and places it in her thigh holster.

"It's hit or miss with this chow hall, but you get used to it," he says as he looks at how that M9 looks on her thigh.

"Yeah, well right now I could eat a horse," she says as they leave, and she shuts her door.

As they make their way down the hallway, the rest of the building is quiet. The desk clerk Alex met the day before was right; this is the best building to live in.

"What's there to do around here after shift is over?" she asks.

"I'm happy you asked. So, me, Tate, and a couple of the guys on my team play Spades two nights a week. Do you play?" he asks, hopeful that she does.

Alex does know how to play Spades. She learned from Sydney, who was her high school boyfriend's dad. His dad was in the Navy and when they played together, he would tell her stories of when he was on ship for months at a time. Sydney taught Alex all the tricks and they would always win against Jacob, her now ex-boyfriend, and his older sister, Tammy.

"I play, and I'd love to be partners with you," she says, giving Liam a sideways grin before nudging him on the shoulder.

Shit, why did I just do that, she thinks as she quickly composes herself. *Don't get too close*, she orders herself as they continue to walk down the hall.

"Perfect! And on Saturday nights we use the projector in the back building and watch bootleg movies that Tate picks up when he goes out on missions. We have the kitchen staff whip up some popcorn for us too. It's always nice to look forward to something in this place."

Alex thinks about it for a minute. "That sounds like a lot of fun. Count me in for the next movie night too."

Walking side by side to get their breakfast, the rest of the compound is already up and starting their shifts. While standing in line for breakfast, Alex notices many people giving them odd looks. She catches a couple of the civilian contractors giving her and Liam dirty looks, which kind of pisses her off a little.

Why are they looking at us like that? she thinks just as both contractors look away.

"What's up with the looks we're getting from everyone?" she whispers to Liam.

"It's probably because you're new here," he says as he plops runny eggs onto his plate. "Or it could be that they're looking at me walking around with *you*." Without looking at her he gives her a slight smile.

Alex doesn't like it when people stare at her, specifically strange men, but she doesn't let this incident bother her and moves on. As they sit down to eat, an Army officer is sitting by himself in the corner and is also watching the two of them. He's not giving them dirty looks like the two contractors from before. Instead, he looks at Alex with intent, like he's been waiting for her to show up.

When Alex catches him, he doesn't look away like the two contractors. His piercing eyes look right through her as if he can read her thoughts. It seems that he knows Liam and is waiting for him to turn and look in his direction.

"Hey, don't look right now but there's an officer in the corner that's looking at us. Do you know him?" she asks as she watches the officer casually drink his coffee.

To Alex, he looks stern and abrasive with his piercing eyes and intimidating demeanor.

Liam didn't notice him at first when they sat down. He slowly turns his head to look in that direction, then turns back toward Alex before letting out a breath of frustration.

"Fuck. It's Captain Marcs, my team leader and the man that I told you about when I picked you up from the airport. I don't want to deal with his ass right now, and I know he's going to come over here," he says in frustration. After a few moments, Liam says, "Let's go outside and eat at the picnic table away from everyone."

"Shit, he's that bad?" she asks as she follows him out the door and to the side of the building. As they sit down, she can see the J1 office she's assigned to with Captain Goodfellow about forty feet away.

"It's just how he is, you know...intimidating," Liam replies.

"Oh, okay," she says. *He's not telling me something*, she thinks while sitting there and eating the same type of runny eggs Liam put on his plate. Nobody on the compound eats at the picnic table. They prefer to eat inside where the TV is on and where there's air conditioning. Alex likes the outdoors better since the chow hall is small and crowded during shift change. She also likes eating alone with Liam and getting to know him better. So far, he seems like a nice guy and easy to talk to.

As the sun slowly comes up, she looks at her watch and notices that she has thirty minutes before her shift starts at J1. As they're sitting there, she can feel that it's getting closer to springtime due to the air being slightly chilly in the morning. For a moment, it feels like she's back home at the trailer park where she used to sit at this old picnic table next to her trailer and listen to the crickets as the cool air hits her skin.

She watches Liam eat his runny eggs and wonders what's going through his mind. Alex can tell he's deep in thought but doesn't want to be nosey and ask him. She tries not to look at his smoldering eyes or his lips as he takes a sip of water. *Don't let him see you looking at him like that*, she thinks as she moves her eyes to her plate.

Since she met Liam, he's been nothing but kind and welcoming to her and she isn't used to that when it comes to guys. Normally, they'd be nice at first and then only try to get in her pants, which is a complete turn-off. She hopes to get to know him better and maybe, possibly, become more than just friends during her time here in-country. But for now, she doesn't want to get too close to him or anyone else until she feels right about it.

"Thanks again for coming to see if I was okay last night," she says while watching his light blonde hair blow slightly in the wind.

Liam suddenly comes out of his deep thoughts and looks into her bright green eyes. With the morning sunlight hitting them, he can see the caramel color, mixed in with the green, and quickly looks away.

"Anytime," he says lightly as he finishes his breakfast.

After breakfast, Liam walks her over to the J1 office when her shift starts and smiles, saying, "I'll see you tonight for cards."

"Yes, I can't wait to meet the team," she says back. As she closes the door, she can see Captain Marcs staring at her and Liam again as he's leaning against the picnic table. This instantly makes her feel uncomfortable.

What's his problem? she asks herself as she moves away from the glass door and toward her new desk.

This is her first day and already someone is giving her the creeps. Luckily, Captain Goodfellow and her coworkers make her feel at home right away. Throughout the day, the captain is showing her the ropes and what her duties are going to be. Alex's duties consist of typing up reports for the colonel as well as processing the new and departing members. She also must leave the compound to get new members from the airport when they arrive from time to time.

Sergeant Kushner, the guy she replaced, had already left the country. She's sitting at his old desk, which he didn't bother to clean up, and starts going through the piles of paperwork he left for her to finish. Seems he wasn't just forgetful, but also awful at his job.

Alex doesn't mind though because she likes busy work. It makes the days go by faster and all she can think about is hanging out with Liam and his team tonight to play cards. She told Liam that she knew how to play Spades, but it's been many years since she played. To solve that issue, she Googles the rules to refresh her memory.

"How are you doing, Sergeant Foster?" Captain Goodfellow asks with a cup of coffee and a warm smile.

She speaks with the softest voice, and Alex knows they are going to get along just fine. The Air Force officers Alex encountered over the years weren't so friendly at times. They believed that the enlisted needed to stay in their place, which was below the officer ranks. Captain Goodfellow, however, is prior enlisted and became an Army officer later in her career. She knows how difficult enlisted life can be since that was one of the main reasons she decided to become an officer.

"I'm doing good, ma'am. I'm still trying to get used to the time difference and being in a new place. Sergeant Anderson is going to show me around after my shift tonight," Alex says.

"Oh yes, I in-processed him not too long before you showed up. He works under Captain Marcs and is a great sergeant," Goodfellow says.

Alex noticed the grimace Captain Goodfellow made when she mentioned Captain Marcs' name. Goodfellow doesn't seem to like him much, and from what Liam told Alex about him, she probably won't like him either. The way Captain Marcs stared at her reminds her of a guy who lived in her trailer park where she grew up. Every time she'd play outside, her creepy neighbor would lean against his trailer and watch her play.

Alex's shift is finally done and her first day wasn't too bad. She walks back to her room and, after getting ready, she watches the sunset from her dorm room window in silence. She waits patiently for Liam to knock on her door to take her to meet the team and play Spades. As the first note of the call to prayer starts, Alex hears footsteps coming down the hallway toward her room. She turns and sees the shadow under the door of someone standing there who's about to knock, and she already knows it's Liam.

I hope the guys like her, Liam thinks as he stands in front of her door. He takes a quick breath and lightly knocks three times, hoping that Alex didn't fall asleep from being jet-lagged. Relieved, he hears light footsteps quickly approaching the door when he hears her say, "Coming." She opens the door and there she is, dressed in tight, dark blue jeans and a white, low-cut V-neck shirt that reveals the curvature of her body. Her dark-brown hair is down and has touches of auburn highlights that match the caramel color in her bright eyes.

"Hey Liam. Man, I've been looking forward to this card game all day," she says with excitement.

Not expecting to see how good she looks in normal clothes, Liam does his best to keep his eyes on hers and not on her body. "Good," he replies as he suddenly feels his stomach flutter with delight again. "The guys are ready to meet you too and see just how good you are at playing. Tate's normally my partner when we play, but he's just a young kid and sometimes doesn't catch the signals I'm giving him."

Alex tilts her head back and lightly laughs at this. "Oh yes, the signals like, 'Hey I got the ace of Spades,' or 'My hand is loaded with Spades' kind of signals," she says.

"Yes, exactly that!" he says. "Well, I think we're going to do just fine, and seeing as how the other team always wins, I need your skills."

He walks with her to the back building at the edge of the compound. "Building seventeen was once used as a transit dorm for members coming and going, and then it transformed into a recreation center that nobody used. Now it's used for my team to train for missions," he says as they walk side by side.

They head down a long narrow pathway that leads to the back of the compound where no one else is around. As they approach, Alex looks at the building. To her, it seems abandoned as Liam opens the door for her to go through. She walks down the dark, narrow hallway and into a bigger room that's around twenty feet long by thirty feet wide. There's a slick wood floor that would be found in an old yoga studio or basketball court.

The room is empty except for some blue workout mats rolled up in the corner, a large mirror that covers the entire back wall, and a fold-out table where two guys and Tate are sitting, waiting for them. It smells a little stale, like it hasn't been used in a while, and the small bathroom in the back has an old sink, toilet, and stand-up shower.

"Yeah, it's not the greatest, but we like to use it. Plus, nobody uses it anymore since everyone has their own rooms to hang out in now," Liam says as they walk up to the table.

Both Sergeants Thompson and Castillo stand up to meet Alex while Tate shuffles the deck.

"Guys, this is Sergeant Alex Foster who works up at J1 with Captain Goodfellow," Liam says.

Sergeant Thompson is the first one to shake Alex's hand. "Nice to meet you," he says in a deep southern accent.

Sergeant Thompson is a medical specialist and is medium-built with short brown hair and brown eyes. He looks to be in his late twenties. When he speaks, he has a deep southern accent that feels warm and welcoming to Alex. His accent reminds her of the time she got a flat tire on the I-95 in North Carolina and a sweet local guy helped her change it. He too had that southern accent and acted like a complete gentleman to her.

Sergeant Castillo then stands and shakes her hand, laughs, and says, "I heard you know how to play Spades and you're here to *try* and kick mine and Thompson's ass."

Sergeant Castillo is the demolitions specialist of the team. He's short and stocky and looks like he lives at the gym. He also looks to be in his late twenties with brown hair and dark brown eyes. Sergeant Castillo sounds like he's from the upper East Coast like New Jersey or New York City.

When she hears Castillo talk, it takes her back to her last duty station where this sergeant from Brooklyn had the same accent. Every time the guy from Brooklyn talked, she couldn't help but laugh at the way he pronounced certain words. They would playfully argue all the time about how he thought he didn't have an accent when clearly, he did.

Alex scoffs slightly while shaking his hand and says with sass, "You bet your ass I'm here to play and win!"

"Ohhh shit! You're gonna win, huh?!" Castillo replies. "Well don't be so sure *girl*. You don't even know who you're dealing with! And hey, call me Cast, okay? I don't wanna hear none of this Sergeant Castillo shit," he says as he tilts his chin up toward her.

Tate sits there laughing, just wanting to watch them play this time. He feels that maybe he could learn a thing or two by watching instead of playing.

"And you already know this guy," Liam says while putting Tate in a playful headlock.

"STOP, you dick!" Tate says as he breaks free from Liam and punches his arm. Then he realizes he used the word dick in front of a girl and quickly apologizes to Alex.

"Sorry, Alex," Tate says.

"For what? Calling him a dick? It's cool Tate, I'm not offended by that word," Alex says with a slight grin on her face.

She looks at Tate like he could be their little brother. He's the youngest of them all and he still has a baby face. He's a little shorter than her and has dirty blonde hair and dimples when he smiles.

"Where do you come from Tate?" she asks because she can't place his accent.

"Shit, he doesn't know where he's from! His mama spent too much time in those hippie communes before he was born!" Cast says as Liam and Thompson laugh their asses off.

"I'm from Orange County you dick," he says while chasing Cast around the table so that he can hit him.

"Oh, Jesus!" Alex says as she barely makes it out of the way as Tate catches up to Cast and tackles him to the ground.

They start roughhousing for what seems like an hour, but only a few minutes go by. Cast manages to get Tate in a chokehold with his meaty arm as Tate's face starts to turn red, and it takes Liam and Thompson to break it up. When they've had enough, Thompson reaches over and grabs Cast by the arm while Liam grabs Tate and pulls them off each other.

Out of breath and red-faced, Tate says, "You heavy-ass motherfucker," to Cast, but he says it with a smile on his face. Apparently, this kind of thing happens all the time between them.

"Aw, did I hurt you, bro?" Cast responds with humorous sarcasm.

“Oh, don’t worry, you’ll get yours,” Tate says with a devious smirk as he sits down at the table and starts shuffling the cards again.

“Are you two finished? Can we play cards now?” Thompson asks loudly with annoyance.

“I bet you miss the beaches, huh?” Alex asks Tate as she sits next to him at the table. She envies people who got to grow up near the ocean. The first time she saw the ocean was when she got stationed in Florida.

“Yeah, I miss it. I would cut school sometimes and go surfing with my friends,” he says as he continues to shuffle the cards.

“Why did you leave?” she asks out of curiosity.

“One of my friends joined the Army and said I should go with him. It sucks cuz, we thought we were going into the same career field, but he wound up working in intelligence and I got into communications. It’s been a long time since we’ve seen each other or even talked,” Tate says.

“Aw, that sucks. I’m sure you’ll run into him some time,” Alex says.

Tate’s a good kid, Alex thinks as she watches him take interest while they play the game.

While he’s watching, Tate talks about how much he loves going to the movies back home and going to see his favorite actors. He also mentions that he has two older sisters that used to constantly pick on him the same way Cast picks on him. According to Tate, joining the Army right out of high school was a great decision. He wanted to be the first one in his family to get out there and make something of himself.

The hours fly by, and everyone agrees that the night turned out to be great. Alex and Liam beat the two sergeants in cards but don’t gloat about it. After playing Spades, they sit around and talk about themselves for a couple of hours. Alex doesn't want to open up too soon with them, so she only talks about her past deployments. By the end of the night, the guys instantly like her and she also likes hanging out with them.

Thompson tells them he's from Tennessee and has a little girl and wife back home. He reaches in his wallet and pulls out a picture of them that was taken during Christmas time. He and his wife, Melissa, and four-year-old daughter, Christy, are sitting in front of a mantel wearing matching Christmas sweaters. He also talks about their yearly fishing trips and how he's going to miss doing that with his family this year.

Cast also has a wife and two little boys back home. He talks about his wife Maria like they're best friends. His oldest son, Jimmy, is six years old, and Vincent is four. He talks about how his kids are his whole life and how he married Maria right after high school. "I'm the luckiest guy in the world," he says as he shows them the photo he pulls out of his wallet. The photo is of Maria holding Vincent when he was born and Jimmy sitting next to her smiling at his little brother.

It's getting well into the night and Alex can feel herself starting to get tired. Liam notices her stretch her arms into the air as she yawns. When he sees her yawn, it makes him yawn too, so he gets up to stretch as well. This is the cue for the rest of them to start to get up and head back to their dorm rooms for the night. As they walk toward the door, they hear the main entrance door to the building slam shut. They can see the shadow of a man standing there looking down the narrow hall at them. Alex notices the rough exterior of the man's silhouette and the intimidating stature of his body.

The man starts to walk down the hallway in his loud combat boots, and it reminds Alex of the sound her father's footsteps made before he'd come into her room and beat her.

The shadowy figure of the man suddenly yells, "What the fuck is this!" as his voice booms down the hallway toward them.

Liam and the guys say nothing because they already know who it is. The man approaches the room. As soon as the fluorescent light hits his face, Alex realizes that it's Captain Marcs. The same man who stared at her in the chow hall and outside her office.

He's just as tall as Liam and his uniform is pressed to perfection. His hair is short and tight to military standards and his eyes are bright blue. He stands there looking at Liam and the guys with fierce intent but doesn't say a word. He just stares at them with an icy glare like it's a bad thing to hang out with friends in a place like this.

The captain's glare makes Liam uncomfortable, so he stands at attention and says, "Sir, we were about to leave and go back to our dorms."

Captain Marcs turns his body toward Alex, and even up close he's very intimidating to her.

Despite being out of uniform, Alex also goes to attention and doesn't look him in the eyes.

Captain Marcs positions himself right in front of her and continues to glare while Alex does her best to keep her composure. She doesn't look down at the floor but straight down the hallway and focuses her sight on the door he came in.

"So, this is the new girl," the captain says in a low and calm yet intimidating voice.

"Air Force, huh? They always have the pretty ones," he says again in a whisper.

Alex starts to feel uncomfortable by his remarks and shifts slightly. She keeps her composure and continues to focus her sight down the hallway at the entrance door.

"I've never come across one as pretty as this one though," he says to Liam and the guys as he starts to move closer to her. This is his way of using intimidation to make himself feel powerful. He especially likes to intimidate young, enlisted women this way because he likes the feeling he gets when they are afraid of him.

Thompson, Cast, and Tate all have shocked looks on their faces as Liam starts to get pissed off.

Alex has enough at this point and decides to take her gaze off the door behind him and looks straight into his striking blue eyes. She doesn't blink or say a word, she just keeps staring right back at him without showing fear. She's tired of men like him who only see her from the outside. It's always about the way she looks and not about her intellect. Alex continues to stare at him with a back the fuck off look on her face.

Catching the icy glare, she's giving him he asks, "Where are you working?" The captain is fully aware that she's working in the J1 office with Captain Goodfellow. He did, after all, stalk her when Liam took Alex to her new office. He asks because he wants to hear her voice when she says it. He wants to know if she's the sassy type or the obedient type.

Alex continues to look back at him without fear and responds, "In the J1 office with Captain Goodfellow, *sir*," in a tone that the other branches of service call Air Force sass.

The captain slowly nods his head at her remark. *Good, I've been waiting for a challenge,* he thinks as he makes his mind up of what type of girl he's dealing with. He looks at her with a slight smile on his face, turns, and walks down the hallway and out the door.

Alex lets out a sigh of relief as Liam and the guys continue to look at the door down the hallway where the captain departed.

"What the hell was that about?" she asks relieved he's gone.

Liam looks at her with dread, then asks the question he's been asking himself since he picked her up from the airport. "Why did you come here?"

She looks at him with confusion to such a question and responds, "What do you mean? Because, I volunteered, that's why."

They all slowly turn and give her a look of worry, which makes her feel uneasy.

Liam slowly shakes his head and says with apprehension in his voice, "I wish you hadn't."

Chapter 3
The Request

It's just after daybreak and Alex notices Liam sitting quietly by himself at the picnic table eating his breakfast. She doesn't feel hungry this morning, so she grabs a cup of coffee, brings it out, and sits with him.

"Hey," she says lightly while sitting across from him. "I didn't hear you get up this morning."

"I didn't want to wake you up," he says as he looks at her apologetically.

She watches Liam for the longest time and wonders why he hasn't talked with her in the last couple of days. Since the night of the card game and her encounter with Captain Marcs, he hasn't mentioned why he thought she shouldn't be here. *Did I do something wrong?* she asks herself while taking another sip of her coffee.

But she didn't do anything wrong. Liam can feel her apprehension, but he feels as if he can't talk to her. Captain Marcs had pulled him aside after the card game and ordered him to bring Alex to his office by today. Liam already knows what the captain is up to and is furious that he would even consider Alex for his bizarre and obsessive mission.

When the captain met Alex the other night, he knew she was the right person for the mission he's been planning for years. He just needed a couple of days to find out about her background. Since her arrival at the compound, the captain found out where she's working and what her duties are.

Liam doesn't want to talk about the captain's mission with her because he's a part of the captain's team. Tate, Thompson, and Castillo got to Alpha compound a week before Liam and were briefed by the captain as well. Liam didn't want to believe it then, but now that Alex has arrived, he knows what the captain is going to ask her to do and he's not happy about it.

I can't do this. I don't want her to be around that asshole, he thinks as he looks up at her with worry. *I have to follow his orders though and let her know that she is to report to his office this morning*, he thinks with dread in his heart for having to be the one to tell her.

Finally, he looks up at her from across the table and says, "Captain Marcs wants you to report to his office today after breakfast." He takes a sip of his coffee and watches her reaction.

After she takes a few moments to process what he just said she asks, "What's going on? Why does the captain want to see *me*?" *What did I do?* she thinks as she waits for Liam to reply.

Liam hates seeing her this way and regrets not talking with her about it. He's sitting there trying to think of the best way to explain to her why the captain wants to see her.

"Please say something. You haven't talked to me in two days, and I want to know what's going on," she says with frustration.

Liam looks up at her and is about to answer but Tate, Thompson, and Cast sit down at the table to eat their breakfast.

Tate sits next to Alex and nods his head toward her, "Morn'n, Alex. Hey, great game the other night!"

Both Thompson and Cast sit down on either side of Liam, and each gives him a light punch on his arms. It's their way of saying good morning without saying a word to him.

"Morning, Alex," Thompson says.

Alex nods with a look of frustration. She still wants to know why the captain needs to see her when she did nothing wrong.

"Hey," she says while still looking at Liam for an answer.

Cast doesn't look up when he says, with a mouth full of scrambled eggs, "Hey, Alex."

Even though she's pissed off now, Cast makes her smirk at the way he's eating his food. It's like they're in a prison cafeteria and he's guarding his plate like someone's going to reach over and take it from him. He must've just gotten back from the gym and is famished.

She looks back at Liam again, who continues to stare at the table and not give her an answer. Then she looks at Thompson and Cast to see if they may know why the captain needs to see her.

"So, I've been summoned to Captain Marcs' office, and Liam won't tell me why," she says to Thompson and Cast who are busy eating their breakfast.

They both stop eating and look up at her but don't say a word. Then they look at Liam with a what the fuck look on their faces.

"I thought he wasn't going to do this shit anymore?" Thompson asks, clearly annoyed.

"Yeah, I thought so too, but the night of the card game, he pulled me aside and said to bring her to his office after breakfast this morning," Liam responds.

Cast looks over at Alex and shakes his head. "Oh man, that's fucked up."

Alex starts to get annoyed by this and asks, "Can someone please tell me what the hell is going on? Am I in trouble or something?"

Liam looks at her apologetically and whispers, "No, it's not that. It's just that the captain wants to see you because he's going to ask you something and you can say no."

What the hell? Alex thinks as she looks at Liam and the rest of them with confusion.

Tate looks over at Alex and says, "Yeah, you don't have to agree to do it if you don't want to."

Alex is completely confused by this point and replies, "Why would he ask me to do anything? It's his job as an officer to give me orders instead of asking, right?

Cast gives her a sympathetic grin and shakes his head again before saying, "It's not like that. It's something you have to choose to do."

Liam starts to feel frustrated by this back-and-forth conversation. "Basically, it's something that we can't talk with you about. It has to be the captain that explains it to you and then you have to decide from there."

Everyone suddenly gets quiet.

First, he ignores me for the past couple of days, and now he's yelling at me, Alex thinks. When she looks up at his face, she can see how much this is weighing on him. She sits there in silence as she takes a sip of her coffee and can feel them looking at her to see what she's going to say next. After thinking about it, she lightly puts her coffee cup down and says, "Okay, take me to his office so I can get this shit over with."

"I'm sorry Alex, I didn't mean to raise my voice at you," Liam says.

"No, I understand, the captain put you in a difficult position and honestly if he wanted me to report, he should've just told me himself," she says giving Liam a look that she's not upset with him.

"Don't worry. He's probably going to ask you to be part of our team, that's all," Thompson says with optimism as he gets up to leave for his first mission outside the wire.

"Yeah, that'll be cool," Tate says as he empties his uneaten food in the trash can.

"Don't let that prick intimidate you when you're in his office okay," Cast whispers as he starts walking off toward the SUV with Thompson.

After Cast said that to her, Alex suddenly feels the pit of her stomach turn. She normally tries to come off as a tough girl, but on the inside, she gets anxious when it comes to overbearing and dominant men. Contemplating what Thompson said earlier about the captain possibly asking her to join his team, she's curious as to what that entails. With just her and Liam left at the table, she asks, "What do you guys do exactly?"

Not sure how to answer that, he tilts his head to the side. "Sometimes, we go outside the wire and do special missions that no one knows about except for leadership. The captain needs certain members of his team to make it function, like a communications specialist, a medic, a demolitions specialist, and a weapons expert." He can see her reaction as she starts to understand what he's talking about.

Alex thinks back to her last two deployments and remembers that she wasn't allowed to ask about the small teams of military and civilian contractors that would leave in the middle of the night and not get back until morning. She was told by leadership that those members were called ghost teams and didn't exist, not even for accountability purposes.

At that moment, Alex realizes why the captain wants to see her so soon after getting to Alpha compound. She can feel it in her gut that the captain is going to ask her to be part of his ghost team. In her mind, if something were to happen to her on a mission, there is no one back home to mourn her. No husband or children, no mother, and her father wouldn't care. She's considered a disposable asset that nobody would miss if she's killed during a secret mission.

As Liam and Alex walk together to Captain Marcs' office, Captain Goodfellow sees them and comes over to talk.

"Good morning you two," Goodfellow says to Liam and Alex. She looks at Alex with concern and asks, "May I speak with you for a moment?"

"Yes ma'am," Alex replies as Captain Goodfellow escorts her to the side of the chow hall while Liam waits for them at the picnic table.

Captain Goodfellow has a look of disappointment on her face and Alex can tell she doesn't have something good to say.

"I'm sorry to say that you'll no longer be working with me in the J1 office for the remainder of your time here. Captain Marcs has requested that you move to his team and already got approval from up the chain of command. You'll be starting this morning with him, and I wanted to let you know that if you need anything, and I mean anything, that you do not hesitate to come see me okay," Captain Goodfellow says with a stern but motherly tone.

It feels like Goodfellow knows that working with Captain Marcs will be no easy task, and the way she offers her support to Alex makes her feel like a mother would support her daughter during a difficult time. Alex looks at Goodfellow with gratitude and says, "Yes ma'am. I'll come to you if I need anything." She watches as the captain walks past Liam and into the chow hall.

"Are you okay?" Liam asks as Alex sits next to him at the picnic table. While sitting next to her, his thigh lightly brushes hers from under the table. He feels bad for treating her the way he did the past couple of days by not keeping her in the loop on what the captain is planning.

He says, "I'm sorry for not talking with you. It was wrong of me to keep you in the dark."

"It's okay. I understand your frustration with Captain Marcs. It seems that he told Captain Goodfellow that I'll no longer be working with her in the J1 office and that I'll be on his team from now on. So, it looks like you and the guys are stuck with me," she says with a slight smile.

Maybe he won't ask her. Maybe she's just reporting to him this morning, and that's it! Liam thinks as he gives her a light smile but still feels worried about the whole situation. He doesn't trust the captain. It's something he feels when he's around him that makes him uneasy, like the captain is up to something. Liam wants to just tell her not to say yes to any of his requests and just go back to the J1 office. Before he can say anything, she gets up from the table.

"Okay, I'm ready to report to Captain Marcs," she says with a little more optimism this time.

Liam walks with her to the doorway of the captain's office. Before he knocks, he turns and looks at Alex and says, "Remember, if you're not here to just report in, then you don't have to say yes to what he asks you to do. You have a choice."

Alex can see the worry in his eyes, and with a smile she says, "Don't worry, I'll be fine. I promise."

He looks at her and wonders how she's going to handle what's behind that door. He questions if she's going to come out of that room just as innocent as she is now, or is she going to accept the captain's proposal, which could change her life forever.

Liam pauses for a second in front of the captain's door and then knocks three times. On the other side, he hears a stern voice say, "Come in." He opens the door for Alex but doesn't enter the room. This meeting is only meant for her and Captain Marcs.

As Alex steps into the room, Liam closes the door behind her. She quietly approaches the front of the captain's desk and immediately goes to attention then does her reporting statement.

"Sir, Staff Sergeant Foster reports as ordered," she says as taught to do from day one.

He looks at her with curiosity and optimism as she stands there tall and professional at attention waiting for him to put her at ease.

"At ease, Sergeant Foster. Please sit down," he says in a calm tone while motioning his hand to the chair to her right.

She notices how his demeanor has changed from the first time she met him after the card game. Alex takes the seat near the corner of his desk and places her hands on her lap with one hand on top of the other. She then plants her feet no wider than a few inches apart, as she was taught to do when ordered by an officer to report to their office. She keeps a straight face to hide her nerves and waits for him to talk. Alex can feel him observing her and wonders what he's thinking at that moment. She doesn't want to be the first one to talk, so she starts to look around the room.

His office is exceptionally clean, well-kept, and doesn't have many things. However, he does have a picture of a young girl on the shelf behind him, which Alex assumes is his daughter. The little girl looks to be around nine or ten years old and has long curly blonde hair that is put up in little pink barrettes on each side. She's smiling in the picture and Alex can see that she's missing her front tooth. His desk is extremely neat and to the right of him is a stack of folders with one thick red folder on the top.

He notices her observing his office while she waits for him to speak first. *She's perfect and I need her to say yes to this*, he thinks.

Finally, after a minute of observing her long neck and feminine jawline, he asks, "Do you know why you're here?"

Alex has an idea but doesn't want to tell him for fear she may be wrong. She looks at him with curiosity and says, "No sir, I don't."

He gets out of his chair, picks up the thick red folder from the top of the stack, and walks around the desk to where she's sitting. He sits at the edge of the desk that's closest to her and where his legs almost brush hers. "You're here because I need you to do something important." He holds the red folder in his hand like it's something precious to him.

Alex notices the way he's sitting across from her on the edge of his desk and how he looks directly down at her, which makes her feel like a little girl that's about to be punished. She still can't figure out why the captain needs her for anything. But when she looks up at him, she can see the desperation in his eyes.

"I spoke with Captain Goodfellow to let her know that she's going to need to acquire another sergeant for the duties you were brought here to do. That's if you agree to my request," he says. "What I'm about to show you does not leave this office. Do you understand me?" he asks in a calm but stern tone.

What the hell is going on? What is in that red folder and why is he talking to me like this is a life-or-death situation? Alex thinks as she looks at the red folder. She looks back at him and says, "Yes sir."

He slowly opens the folder and takes out several eight-inch by ten-inch photographs then hands them over to Alex. The look on his face as he hands her the photos is the look of disgust and anger. It's as if something smells bad or when there's a dead animal on the side of the road.

Alex reluctantly takes the photos from his hand, knowing she doesn't have a choice. She stares at the first photograph with wide eyes and a gaping mouth.

Captain Marcs can see the look of terror on her face and begins to speak to her calmly. "These little girls were victims of a madman who needs to be stopped," he says.

Alex doesn't look at the captain as he speaks. She just continues to stare at the photos one by one with shock, as if she's watching a horror movie.

He continues talking even though he can see that she's preoccupied with the images of the girls. "They were kidnapped, raped, tortured, and ripped apart by his dogs when he was through using them."

The photos don't lie. She can see all the blood and half-eaten faces of the girls and how many of them are unrecognizable. Feeling dizzy, Alex does her best to compose herself and tries to not vomit on the floor. The room suddenly becomes extremely hot, and she starts having a hard time breathing. The photos start to stick to her hands from her sweat as she closes her eyes and takes in a few deep breaths.

Captain Marcs watches her reaction and hopes this doesn't scare her away from what he's about to request of her. He's patient with Alex and gives her a few moments to compose herself before he continues. Leaning over her, he hands her another photo of a man.

"They call him 'the Shadow,' and right now he's staying in a heavily guarded palace right here in the country. He throws parties almost every day and requests girls be brought in from all over the world for him to rape, torture, and then kill. He also is known for crashing weddings and stealing the brides so that he can rape them and sometimes murder them in front of their families. This madman needs to be stopped," the captain says as he looks at her with furious intent. He tries to control his anger, but the images of those girls and the image of the Shadow's face always make him feel this way.

Why is he showing me these pictures? What does this have to do with me? she asks herself. As she looks at the photo of this man, she instantly feels dizzy again. Those dead, dull eyes look back at her and suddenly give her chills up and down her spine. She looks at his face in the photo and gets the courage to look at the dead girls again. This time she's able to focus and take in what he's done to them. Many of the girls look like they were in their mid-teens. Others look like they may have been no more than twelve years old.

Alex can feel the captain patiently watch her as she continues to look at the horror that's on those photographs. Her face feels hot, and her shirt is soaked through with sweat. Every time she takes a breath, it feels like the hot air gets even hotter and that she's going to vomit. Finally, she looks up at him, and with a broken and shaky voice, she asks, "Why are you showing these to me, sir?"

Captain Marcs looks down at her. With his head tilted to one side and a questionable look on his face, he replies, "Because I want you to kill him."

Chapter 4
The Decision

Alex can hear what the captain is saying but can't focus on what's going on around her. It's as if the particles in the air have stopped moving and all the sound has left the room. Trying to snap out of it, she looks back up at him and says, "Sir?"

He looks at her incredibly still and slowly repeats, "I…want…you…to kill him."

Sitting there, with her mouth slightly open but unable to speak or make a sound, she suddenly feels like this is all a joke. *They're fucking with me. It's because I'm Air Force and they're seeing if I'll fall for it,* she thinks as she continues to sit there unable to respond. Still not saying a word to him, she can feel the pulse in her neck throb from her heart beating so fast.

"Are you not upset with what you saw in those photographs? I mean, I figure you of all people would be upset," he says in frustration. The captain thought that any woman would want the chance to kill a man like the Shadow.

Holy shit. He's really serious. He wants me to kill this man, she thinks as the captain continues to look at her with frustration. Alex is upset to see how those girls were treated but she still can't understand why he wants her to kill this man.

"Sir but aren't their Special Forces teams that handle situations like this?" she asks as she sees his expression change from patient to angry.

He sits there for a moment, thinking about the question she just asked him. Then he quickly gets up from the corner of the desk and picks up another folder from the pile. This time the folder is brown and has six parts to it. He walks back around the desk, sits on the corner in front of her again, then opens the folder and starts to read out loud.

"Staff Sergeant Alexandra Foster, born 15 September 1984 in a small town in Missouri. Mother passed away from a car crash at age 7. Father worked as a janitor and was arrested for being drunk and disorderly on several occasions. This file also states you attended many mental health counseling sessions due to being raped at age 10 and attempted rape by your father as well. You joined the Air Force right after your high school graduation and never returned home. You don't have a husband or children and no other family that you're aware of. Does that all sound accurate to you?" he asks as he waits patiently for an answer from her.

Alex looks at him in shock that he has a file on her with all that personal information. She can even see her photograph from when she won Airman of the Year a few years back. *Where the hell did he get that picture of me?* she asks herself. She can see that he's waiting for her to answer him.

"Sir, how did you get all that information on me?" she asks.

Looking back at her with a sly grin he says, "I've been searching for months for the right person that could actually pull this off and I think I finally found her."

Watching her reaction closely, he realizes that she's perfect for the mission. She's attractive, smart, athletic, and she has no one back home if the mission fails or if she dies in the process. After waiting a few moments for her to respond, he can see that she still will not accept. He continues to read out loud.

"Fitness shows top scores, firing range shows top scores, and the best part is that you never get in trouble, which means you follow orders, which also means you have a hard time saying no. Is that accurate, Sergeant?"

He can still see the look of doubt on her face and decides to move closer to her. Very gently, he says, "Sergeant Foster, you'll be training every day for this. You'll learn hand-to-hand combat and Muay Thai and I'll be there every step of the way." He looks into her bright green eyes that are full of worry and doubt.

As she sits there and thinks about his request, she remembers the month she spent at combat skills training where she learned hand-to-hand combat. To Alex, the hand-to-hand combat training was the toughest part. The instructors didn't hold back, and even though the training wasn't that long, she still remembered some of the moves she learned. The training wasn't as extensive either since there were too many other students there for the instructors to focus on. With what the captain's proposing, she will at least be the only one in training, which means she'll learn even more. She still feels some doubt about his request and continues to sit without saying anything for fear of making the wrong decision.

He patiently waits for her to respond but notices that look of doubt on her face again. It's starting to upset him because he's wondering if she just wasted his time. Instead, he thinks of a different approach to convince her. He suddenly stands up and turns away. He tries to think of something that will make her understand what he wants her to do and why. Finally, he turns around to look at her and calmly says, "Sergeant Foster, close your eyes and listen to my voice."

What is he trying to do now? She thinks as she reluctantly closes her eyes for him.

"Now, picture a little girl walking to school one day and two men come up, grab her, throw her in the back seat of a car, then drive away. The little girl finds herself in a strange place and a man is standing in front of her naked."

Alex keeps her eyes closed and slightly shifts in her seat as the image starts to develop in her mind.

What the hell? she thinks as the pulse in her neck starts to pound harder again.

"The man grabs her, rips her panties off, and forces himself inside her over and over again, and the little girl screams but no one's there to help her. Then when she looks up, she sees another man filming the rape with a video camera."

Alex finds it hard to breathe at this point but continues to keep her eyes closed.

The captain can see her starting to feel uncomfortable and says, "After the man is finished raping this little girl, he starts to smear her naked body with honey and ties both her arms above her head. You see, the man who raped her didn't feed his dogs in two days. He lets the dogs into the room to tear her to shreds, while still filming the whole thing."

Alex's hands are covered in sweat, and she's interlaced her fingers tight to keep herself from passing out. With her eyes still closed, Alex opens her mouth to breathe and wants to vomit. She controls herself as the captain watches her reaction.

Calmly reaching toward her, he says, "Now open your eyes," as he hands her another photograph.

When Alex opens her eyes, she sees the face and the half-eaten body of the naked little girl he described. She can see part of the little girl's jaw was ripped open and most of her intestines were splattered on the floor.

The captain looks at Alex once more as tears stream down her face and calmly asks, "Now will you do this? Will you kill this mad man they call the Shadow?"

After some time, Alex leaves the captain's office and sees Liam is there waiting for her. He takes one look at her face and can see that she's going to be sick. Her skin is pale, and her hair looks wet from her sweating so much.

Oh my God, what did he do to her? Liam thinks as he reaches out to stop her from passing out.

"Alex, are you okay?" Liam asks with concern.

She looks at him with panic and asks, "Where's the bathroom?"

Liam quickly holds her by the arm and helps her down the hall to the bathroom.

When she sees it, she runs in and slams the door shut so that he can't see her hurl the only thing that's in her stomach. The coffee she drank earlier mixed with her stomach acid isn't a good combination coming back up. Afterward, her stomach feels better but unfortunately, she still has those images stuck in her head of those poor girls and of that motherfucker who did that to them.

"Alex, do you need anything?" Liam asks with concern from the other side of the door. He knows what she's seen in that room, and hopes she turned the captain's request down. He remembers hearing about the last two recruits the captain asked. Those women didn't make it far enough through the training and were sent home early because they couldn't handle the trauma.

Alex finally comes out of the bathroom looking a little better after washing her face and rinsing her mouth out with water. It takes her a few moments to think about what happened in the captain's office. She can't believe someone that evil exists and gets away with all that he's done. Alex thinks about some of the horrific testimonies the captain mentioned about the Shadow and his treatment of women and little girls. As she leans her head against the cold wall, Liam starts talking to her, but his voice fades away as her mind takes her back into the captain's office when he told her everything he knew about the Shadow.

His real name is Asim Barzan Majid, and he's the eldest son of a notorious political leader in the country. If the American military were to kill Asim or his younger brother Akram, then their father would wage war, and the situation in the country would get worse for the American troops. "This mission must be done in secret, and it must look like the Americans are not involved in his death," the captain had said to her.

Asim got the name the Shadow because once he finishes raping, torturing, and killing his victims, he disappears for months and then resurfaces to do it again. His father imprisoned him for a short time due to Asim killing important political members and their families during a wedding because they didn't comply with his father's political agenda.

One of the testimonies mentioned that Asim once threw a party at his palace and forced all the women there, at gunpoint, to have sex with each other while he filmed it. If they didn't comply or please him sexually, then he ordered his guards to execute them on the spot. Sometimes he'd let his most loyal guards rape the women while filming it and could be heard laughing on the videotape during the act.

Asim also enjoys women dancing seductively in front of him in private. If they perform poorly, he'd slash the bottoms of their feet with the long, double-edged sword that he keeps hidden inside the top of his cane. He uses a cane because of an assassination attempt where he was shot five times. One of the bullet fragments lodged in his spine couldn't be removed for fear that Asim would become paralyzed. People say that the cane makes him look even more fierce and intimidating than before.

The captain told her that Asim had the cane specially made of black mahogany wood with a black leather-bound handle. The 22-inch blade hidden inside is Ikazuchi-forged with 2,048 layers of folded steel, double-edged and razor-sharp. Any time he pulls the blade out, it makes a distinctive sound that makes everyone in a room stand frozen in fear.

The Shadow's known for his wild temper and violent outbursts, and many say that this is due to his father executing people right in front of him when he was a little boy. Once at a party, Asim found out that one of the guests was making fun of his cane and his slight limp. He found the guest, removed the sword from his cane, and sliced both ears and the nose from the man's face. Then had his dogs eat them in front of the man. The rest of the guests watched in horror and feared for their lives. They knew when Asim loses his temper that he'll execute whoever is standing nearest to him.

"Alex, are you listening? Please say something," Liam says with concern as he gently touches her shoulder.

Liam was talking to her the whole time and Alex didn't hear a word he'd said. She was going over in her mind what the captain had told her in his office about the Shadow. *Did I make the right choice*? she asks herself.

"I'm sorry, I was just thinking about what the captain told me in there," she says apologetically.

I wish I could help her, he thinks as he looks at her. He wants to hug her or comfort her in some way. "Did you still want to walk around the compound, get some food, and then watch a movie later tonight? That might help you feel better, and we can talk about what went on in there," he asks her calmly.

"Yeah, I need some fresh air first," she says as she places her hand on her forehead to indicate how hot it is. Suddenly, she feels grateful to have Liam with her, especially after what she saw in the captain's office.

She needs to talk to someone about it, but not right now. All she wants is fresh air and a moment to collect herself.

As they walk together around the compound, he introduces her to some of the local guards like Hamid. Liam can see that Alex is preoccupied with her thoughts, so he takes her to the chow hall to get some food in her stomach. On the way, they run into Captain Goodfellow and she stops them both to talk. She can see Alex's pale face.

"Sergeant Foster? Are you okay?" she asks out of concern.

Alex looks up at her and says, "Yes ma'am. I just need some food," which is a lie.

"Did Captain Marcs talk to you about working with his team?" Goodfellow asks.

"Yes ma'am, he did," Alex says without looking at her. She doesn't want Captain Goodfellow worrying about her or knowing about the mission since it's on a need-to-know basis.

"Remember what I said earlier. If you ever need anything, please don't hesitate to ask me, okay?" Goodfellow says as she leaves and walks to the J1 office.

Liam opens the door to the chow hall for Alex as she steps in. She silently stands in line and fills up her plate with cut up strawberries and pineapples while Liam grabs a premade turkey club sandwich with a small bag of chips and a can of Coca-Cola. Staying inside to eat this time, they head to the corner table where no one can hear them talk and sit down.

Alex looks down at her food and suddenly doesn't feel like eating. It could be because of her throwing up earlier or of the images of the dead girls that are stuck in her head. Instead, she runs the fork over the food in silence.

Liam watches her and suddenly feels bad. He doesn't want to ask what decision she's made until she's ready to talk about it. He can see the worry on her face and wants to know what's going through her mind. But he doesn't want her to feel uncomfortable or get sick again, so he leaves her alone.

Alex can feel the silent tension and looks up at him and into his eyes for the longest time without saying a word.

Liam can see her pain and frustration and knows what she's feeling. He felt it himself when the captain approached him after the card game. Liam remembers how frustrated he'd felt knowing what the captain was going to ask her but couldn't tell her. He doesn't want to see her go through this alone and he wants to be there for her every step of the way.

Finally, after a minute of silence, Liam says, "Let's go see what movie Tate brought." *Hopefully, that will cheer her up*, he thinks.

They both leave the chow hall and walk together in silence to the back building where Tate, Thompson, and Cast are already there setting up the projector.

"Hey guys," Liam says as Alex follows behind him into the room.

"Where's the popcorn?" Tate asks with his arms out in frustration.

"Sorry, I forgot to get some," Liam says while looking at Alex with concern.

The guys can tell that Alex isn't feeling right and they also know what the captain showed her because it's written all over her face.

"Here Alex, I got you the comfortable chair," Tate says as he sets down one of those armchairs one would find in a hotel room next to a TV set.

"Thanks man," she says lightly as she sits and curls both of her legs inside of it.

Liam grabs one of the foldout chairs they sit in when playing cards and places it next to Alex. "So, what's the movie going to be tonight, Tate?" Liam asks as he sits down to get comfortable.

"It's an oldie but a goodie," Tate says. He pauses for effect, then says, "Ridley Scott's, 1979 film…wait for it…*Alien* with the illustrious Sigourney Weaver," he says as he waves his hands out then gives them all a bow.

Everyone but Alex claps with agreement that Tate picked a good movie. As Tate bows in front of them all, Alex sits there not listening and is preoccupied with the decision she's made about the Shadow.

As the movie plays on, the guys are fixated on Ms. Weaver trying to out-clever the villain in the film. Liam looks at her and can see that she isn't watching the movie at all, so he takes a chance and gently places his hand on top of hers. As she turns to look at him, he can see it in her eyes that she's ready to talk. He gently takes her by the hand and quietly leads her outside where no one can see or hear them.

Liam finally asks the question that he's been dreading to ask since she left the captain's office.

"So, what have you decided? Are you going to kill the Shadow?"

Alex turns and looks at Liam with fear and frustration, like maybe she made the wrong decision. She remembers the man who raped her when she was ten years old and what she saw today in the captain's office didn't help. She doesn't use words to answer him. Instead, she answers him with her eyes in a way that makes him look away from her with sorrow in his heart.

As the sun starts to set and the pinkish hue begins to fade from the sky, Liam continues to look away from her so that she can't see his watery eyes and the regret on his face for not telling her sooner about the captain.

He finally looks at her and says, "No matter what, I am here for you Alex, and I'll be with you every step of the way." He reaches over to hold her hand again.

She smiles slightly back at him and looks at him with gratitude that he's here for her. In a low, tired voice she replies, "I know."

Chapter 5
Innocence Lost

Alex and Liam decide not to go back in to see the rest of the movie and instead slowly walk back to their dorm. On the way, they stop by the picnic table they usually eat breakfast at and lean against it for a while to talk. The compound is completely quiet while everyone is either still on night shift or in bed sleeping. The air is cool on their faces and the sky is full of bright stars.

"Are you okay?" she asks, knowing that he doesn't agree with her decision to kill the Shadow.

"Yeah. It's just that you're not the first girl he's asked to do this, you know," he says as he looks up at the stars. "There were others and they failed."

"I know. He told me right before I left his office. He's convinced that this mission will work and has confidence in me to make it through. I'm hoping to get the same support from you and the guys," she says as she watches his eyes move away from the stars and into hers.

Calmly he replies, "I do support you, Alex. I just don't trust the captain. Please believe me when I say that I have your back."

"I know the captain's an asshole but I know I can do this. I'm here for a year and I start training tomorrow for this mission," she says.

"Can I just ask what made you agree to do something like this? I mean, you could die Alex," he says in a way that lets her know that he genuinely worries about her.

"Liam, my whole life I've been told that I'm not good enough, most of all from my dad. This man they call the Shadow *needs* to die. So far, many men have tried to kill him and failed. There were many times in my life where men took advantage of me, and I wish someone was there to protect me when it happened," she says as she watches Liam look down at the ground.

"I understand," he says while feeling bad for pressing her about the mission.

They decide to stay at that picnic table for most of the night talking and getting to know each other. Alex tells Liam about her dad and when her mom died when she was seven. About how her dad changed for the worse when he drank and how the only person that would stand up to him was her high school boyfriend Jacob. It was hard for her to open up sometimes because she was afraid to get too close to people for fear of getting hurt or judged. With Liam, it's different. He's easy to talk to, and when she talks about her parents and her past, he doesn't judge her.

"Growing up without a mom was hard," she says. "My dad started drinking and he lost his job and the house and we wound up living in this rundown trailer park where everyone lived on welfare. When I graduated, I couldn't wait to leave."

Liam lets her finish then says, "Shit, I'm sorry to hear about your mom. My mom left me, my dad, and four brothers for another guy. I miss my brothers and I never thought I would until I got here."

"Four brothers? Jesus," she says. "I'm an only child and can completely understand how you feel. It was so lonely growing up by myself. I loved going to school because I had some friends to hang out with and they'd let me stay at their houses for a few days at a time so I could be away from my dad," she said.

"Your dad was that bad, huh?" Liam asks.

"He would hit me in the face just for getting in his way. Sometimes, he would get so drunk that he'd come into my room while I was sleeping and try to…you know…" Alex says with embarrassment. "But I would push him out of my room, and he would pass out on the couch. Jacob, my boyfriend at the time, tried once to convince my dad to let me stay at his house, but my dad slapped him hard in the face. When Jacob's dad found out, he came to my trailer and threatened him. I felt like Sydney, Jacob's dad, was more of a father figure. Every time I would run away from home, he and Jacob's mom would take me in without question. They would feed me, and Sydney was the one who taught me how to play Spades," she says as she looks up at the bright stars.

"Oh shit, that was nice of them to take you in like that. So, what happened with you and Jacob?" He asks out of curiosity, and a slight bit of surprising jealousy.

"I think he got over me after he graduated from high school. We started dating when I was in the ninth grade, and he was a year ahead of me. He was my world, and I gave him everything. We had so many plans for after my graduation to travel the country and never go back to that small town."

"So, what happened? Did he leave without you?" Liam asks.

"No, it's worse. I caught him cheating on me the day before my graduation. I showed up at his house earlier than normal after school. When I went up to his room, I caught him having sex with another girl. I couldn't believe he did that," she says as she shakes her head. "Then after I joined the Air Force, I met Kyle. He was in the Air Force too and we went out for about a year until he got orders to go to Iraq and then Germany right after that. He was a good guy, nothing like Jacob, but at least he told me he was breaking up without cheating on me first."

"Man, Jacob sounds like a real dick."

"I mean, if he didn't do that then I would've never joined the Air Force right after graduation and I wouldn't be here now. I feel that everything happens for a reason," she says as she looks up at the stars again. "I don't mess with fate either. Besides, after Kyle broke up with me, I realized that I needed to start focusing on my career and make promotion. I want to become successful, get recognized for my hard work, and make something of myself. You know what I mean?"

"Yeah, I know exactly what you mean. I'm sorry about the way your dad and Jacob treated you. Not all men are like that, you know that right?" he asks her, subtly letting her know that he would never treat her like that.

"I know. I just have to keep my guard up, that's all, because I don't like getting hurt," she says.

As they're sitting on the picnic table, Liam watches the guards at the front gate do shift change. "Oh shit, what time is it?" he asks. He lifts his sleeve to check the time. "Shit, no wonder I'm tired, It's midnight," he says as he laughs a little.

"I need to get some sleep. I start training tomorrow morning with Captain Marcs," she says with dread in her voice.

They walk back to the dorms in silence and Alex thinks about what Liam said to her about him not being like other guys. She wants to believe that's true, and after talking with him tonight under the stars she decides that it probably won't be a bad idea to get closer to him during her time here. When she reaches her door, she turns and says, "Let's have breakfast tomorrow morning before my training starts."

Liam can feel his heart beat a little faster and replies, "Yeah, I look forward to it. Hey, it was nice talking with you tonight."

"Thanks for listening," she says with an appreciative smile.

"I'm here for you, Alex. You don't have to worry about me leaving or not being there for you. I'm right here," he says as he points his finger at his door.

"I know," she says lightly. "Good night."

"Good night," he says back.

The day was long, and as Alex lays in bed, she thinks about what the captain showed her earlier that day about the Shadow. She'd never thought she'd see such images in her lifetime but realizes that's the reality of the world she lives in. The room is quiet, and she can hear Liam moving around in his bed through the wall.

Liam's such a good guy and I'm happy he's here with me, she thinks to herself as she lays there wondering how she's going to train to kill someone like the Shadow. *How do you kill a man like that?* Suddenly, her mind takes her back to the many times her dad would beat her, degrade her, and make her feel small and worthless. After closing her eyes, she suddenly feels the worry and doubt drain from her body as she drifts off to sleep.

A couple of hours go by and it's the dead of night when Liam suddenly hears Alex's bed frame lightly hit his wall. He can hear her move violently in her bed as she starts to make suffocating sounds. Instead of waiting until the next day to ask her if she's okay, he gets out of bed and runs into her room. Kneeling beside her bed, he gently touches her shoulder to try and wake her up.

"Alex, wake up, you're having another nightmare," he says while lightly shaking her shoulder again.

Alex sits straight up in her bed and lets out a small gasp. "Goddamn it!" she says slightly out of breath and places her hand on her forehead.

"It's okay. It's me. You're okay now," he says as he reaches out and hugs her.

Oh no. Don't get too close. Not yet, she thinks as she stays frozen in his arms. *We had a great talk at the picnic table. Don't ruin it.*

As he continues to hug her, he can feel that her shirt is soaked with sweat and that she's slightly shaking.

I've never had someone be there for me after having a nightmare. Do I lightly push him away? Do I tell him to stop? she thinks as Liam continues to hug her in silence. After a few moments, she remembers what he said to her during their talk, that he's here for her. She decides to relax her shoulders and slowly wrap her arms around him. She doesn't want this feeling to end no matter the consequences of getting hurt. It feels good to have someone there to finally open up to and connect with.

Liam holds her tighter but doesn't say anything. He can feel her light, warm breath on his neck and her body against his.

She starts to slowly move her mouth up against the side of his neck and up to his ear. She whispers, "Thank you."

Not letting her go, Liam softly says, "I told you I'm here for you."

Alex finally lets him go and looks at him with tired eyes.

"I haven't had that nightmare in years," she says.

"I didn't want to ask but it seemed like a really bad one," he says while sitting next to her.

"Well, it's more of a memory about something that happened to me when I was a kid and I thought I was over it."

"Do you want to talk about it?" he asks out of concern.

"Liam, I don't want to burden you more than I already have about my past. I think it's because the captain showed me those pictures of the dead girls and it brought back memories of what happened to me when I was a kid, that's all."

"I want to help you, but it's okay if you don't want to talk about it," he says to her reassuringly.

"No, I feel like if I don't get it out then it's just going to keep happening. I also want you to understand why I would make such a decision about killing the Shadow," she says.

"I didn't see the pictures of the dead girls or the Shadow, but if it's giving you nightmares, I want to help you through this," he says as he waits patiently for her to talk.

Alex can see that he's ready to hear her talk about the one memory that's like a dark shadow living in her mind.

"When I was ten, a guy raped me at the summer county fair. My dad took me to the county fair once a year just outside the small town I grew up in. This was only if he wasn't drunk or passed out on the couch. He'd let me play some of the games, and during one of the games I turned around and he was gone. I remember feeling scared as I waited for him to come back, but he didn't."

"Then a man came up and asked if I was okay. He looked normal and talked with me in a gentle voice, and I told him that I couldn't find my dad. He put out his hand and said that if I went with him, he would take me to the lost and found to find him. I know I shouldn't have gone with him, but I thought he was going to help me," she says with embarrassment.

"He was an adult, Alex. You didn't know any better," Liam says. "So, what happened next?"

"I went with him and as we walked toward the lost and found, he kept going toward the parking lot instead. I remember that he didn't look down at me, just straight forward as he tightly held my hand. I thought that maybe he knew my dad and that he was taking me back to my dad's car. When we got further into the parking lot, he grabbed me by the hair and threw me in the back seat of his car. I landed face down and this is when he tore my underwear off from under my dress and slid his fingers inside of me. I couldn't move or understand what was happening to me," she says as she put her hand on her forehead.

Liam reaches out and holds her hand and says, "Alex, you don't have to go on. It's okay."

She looks back at him with appreciation for letting her get this out and says, "It's okay. I can talk about it now."

"When he put his fingers inside me, he yelled out and removed his hand with disgust. I got my period the year before, which was rare for a nine-year-old girl. I guess he never thought a girl so young would have her period. He was so angry and disgusted with me that he grabbed my legs and violently dragged me out into the dirt, got in his car, and sped off."

Liam looks at her with horror and disgust that a man would do such a thing to a little girl. "I'm so sorry that happened to you," he says.

"That's not even the worst part. I was more afraid of my dad than the guy who raped me. I had to get up, clean myself off, go back, and look for my dad then pretend that nothing happened," she says.

"Why were you more afraid of your dad?" he asks.

She sighs. "He's a drunk, and at that time he was pissed off at the world for his wife dying. He terrified me when he got drunk because nobody was there to stop him from beating or trying to rape me himself as I got older."

"Oh my God, what the fuck!" he says in horror.

"When I was in high school, I started to look more like my mom. So when he got drunk, he thought I was her. I had to start sleeping with a knife under my pillow to defend myself against him. In my senior year, I remember when I pulled out a knife, put it against his throat, and told him that if he ever came in my room again or put his hands on me that I would end him."

"What an asshole, and good for you for standing up to him like that," he says as he smiles at her.

Alex smiles back and says, "Right after graduation, I signed up to go into the Air Force and I never saw him again."

"I'm happy you did because if you didn't, I would never have met you."

She's so strong and been through so much and still turned out to be a decent human being, he thinks. Liam realizes that he wants to get to know her better, become closer to her, and keep her safe from the captain and anyone else who'd do her harm.

They sit there for a while and talk about growing up in broken homes and how things may have been different if Liam's parents were together and if Alex's mom didn't pass away.

Liam shares about growing up just outside of Denver, Colorado, in a household with four other brothers and no sisters. He mentions how he never saw his dad so brokenhearted after his mom left. Even at the age of ten, he could feel how distant his parents were from each other.

"I was the middle child, and we were each two years apart in age," he says. "Sometimes, I wish I was the only child. With my dad working at the mill, I had to take care of my two younger brothers."

"Yeah, but at least you had each other. I was completely alone with a man that lost the love of his life and took it out on me when he got drunk," she says sensitively.

"I'm so sorry. I didn't mean it like that," Liam says as he got off the bed.

"No, it's okay. I know what you meant. You had to grow up fast like me," she says, trying to make him feel better. She gets up and walks with him to the doorway. "Listen, thanks again for coming to see if I was okay. And remember we're hanging out tomorrow with the guys," she says as she tries to change the subject to a lighter mood.

"Yeah, that sounds good," he says as he walks out into the hallway. He turns around to say, "Alex, remember what I told you earlier that I'm here for you. I want you to know that you can come to me if you ever have a hard time with the captain or anyone else."

"I appreciate that. I really do," she says as she watches him go into his room and slowly close the door.

Liam gets back into bed and remembers the first time he knocked on her door her first night in-country. She didn't open up to him then, but now that she has, he feels better about getting to know her.

Just as he starts to close his eyes to go back to sleep, Alex taps her finger a few times on the wall above her pillow. It's their way of saying good night or I'm here if you need me. He remembers when he did that to her the first night they met, and the feeling he has for her now are already growing into something more. Liam hopes she feels the same way. As he pictures her face and warm smile, he lightly taps the wall back to her to say good night and sweet dreams.

Chapter 6
The Schedule

Alex gets up early the next morning and tries to not wake Liam. She feels bad for waking him the night before due to her nightmare, but she also feels grateful to him for coming to see if she was okay. She goes outside before the first call to prayer and walks around the compound to get fresh air. The buildings look old, and she notices that Alpha compound is small and has tall pine trees that surround the area. Many of the local guards, including Hamid, are starting to change shifts as she watches them process out of the gate to head back to their homes before daybreak. Hamid sees her and waves goodbye and Alex does the same.

Alex finds this compound to be incredibly quiet this early in the morning, which wasn't the case with her last two deployments. There was always some noise outside with the new deployers coming in and out and the loud C-5 airplanes flying in all the time. This place, however, is eerily quiet, which she isn't used to.

She can see that the chow hall is open, so she decides to get a cup of coffee before it gets crowded. When she walks in, she sees the back of Captain Marcs' head as he's sitting at the table in the far corner by himself. Alex doesn't want him to notice her, so she quietly gets her cup of coffee. As she tries to leave, she hears him say, "Sit down Sergeant Foster. We have some things to talk over."

What the hell. Does he have eyes in the back of his head or something? She thinks as she reluctantly sits down in front of him. She still won't look at him because he intimidates her, especially when he looks straight into her eyes.

In the background, the TV is set to play music videos all day. On the screen is a new singer playing something Alex has never heard before. The video caption at the bottom reads, Lady Gaga's "Bad Romance." Alex keeps watching the bizarre video while the captain slides a piece of paper across the table to her.

She shifts her gaze from the music video to the piece of paper.

After waiting for her to look it over he says, "I made this schedule of your day-to-day training," while finishing his black coffee and slightly burnt toast. The captain watches her closely, thinking about the last two girls who tried to accomplish this mission but failed. Then he thinks about another young female soldier he was fucking before his tour started here. Her name was Miranda, and she was new to the unit back home.

She reminds me of her, and she even looks good this early in the morning too, he thinks while watching the stern expression on Alex's face as she reads the schedule.

Alex looks at it for some time.

0430 – 0530 hours: Physical fitness and running

0600 – 0900 hours: Convoy to surrounding compounds for delivery pickup and drop-off

1000 – 1300 hours: Hand-to-hand combat training, Muay Thai, and Krav Maga

1400 – 1600 hours: Exotic dance (on your own)

Alex knows that hand-to-hand combat and mixed martial arts training play a vital role in this mission however, she looks at the last item and asks, "Why exotic dance, sir?"

"That's why I wanted to sit down and go over the details with you. The way I need you to execute the Shadow is by going in disguised as an exotic dancer. When the moment is right, that's when you kill him. He'll never see you coming, and his men will never suspect that it was the Americans that did it."

Is he fucking joking? I'm going to dance my way in there and kill him? she thinks as she looks at him with wide eyes and a gaping mouth. Suddenly, Alex realizes one important fact. "So, I won't have a weapon on me?"

"*You'll* be the weapon. That's why we're teaching you hand-to-hand combat and martial arts," he says in frustration. He's starting to get the feeling that Alex probably isn't going to do well with the exotic dance portion, which is the key element to this entire mission.

The captain notices that people are starting to enter the chow hall for early breakfast. He gets up and says, "Report to the back building in the next thirty minutes ready to go and I'll introduce you to your trainers."

He's such an asshole, she thinks to herself. "Yes sir," she says.

Without saying another word, he turns and leaves her there just as Liam comes in.

Liam looks at the captain but doesn't say anything to him. The captain walks out, completely ignoring him. Liam slightly rolls his eyes and comes over to the table where he sees Alex is covering her face with her hand as she holds the schedule.

"Hey, you. I didn't hear you get up this morning. What's going on?" he asks after seeing the frustrated look on her face.

"I just had an interesting conversation with Captain Marcs," she says as she hands him the schedule.

Liam takes a few moments to look it over and says, "Wow, what is this?"

"Oh, it's my crazy schedule for training, including exotic dancing," she says as she rolls her eyes and scoffs with sarcasm.

"Exotic dance is probably going to be your toughest part of the day," Liam says. "But I think you're going to be okay."

Alex looks at him and laughs a little. "Seriously? Does it matter that I can't even dance to begin with?" she asks with zero confidence.

He looks at her with optimism and says, "Alex, I think you can do anything you put your mind to."

As they walk outside, they can see that the compound is starting to wake up. People are heading to their buildings to work, and some are rushing out of the compound to do missions for the day.

"I'm supposed to report to the back building in a few minutes. You wanna walk me there?" She asks him.

"Yeah, let's go," he says, noticing that she's starting to feel better.

"Do you think we're going to see much of each other since I have this crazy schedule now?" she asks.

"Yeah, you know those convoy missions you'll be taking from 0600 to 0900 hours. You'll be going with Tate and the rest of the team, including me," he says grinning at her. "So, we'll be out there in the shit together."

"Good morning, Sergeant Anderson, Sergeant Foster," Captain Goodfellow says to them as she walks toward the chow hall for breakfast.

"Good morning, ma'am," Liam and Alex reply in unison.

"She's so cool," Liam says as he and Alex watch Goodfellow walk past them.

"Yeah, she and Captain Marcs are on the opposite ends of the spectrum."

When they arrive at the back building as instructed, Captain Marcs is already there waiting for her.

When he sees that Liam is with her, the captain looks at him and says degradingly, "Don't you have somewhere you need to be, Sergeant?" implying that Liam doesn't belong in there even though he's part of the team.

What a dick, Liam thinks as he looks at the captain. "Yes sir," he responds.

As Liam is leaving the room, Alex lightly touches his arm, thanking him again for being there for her. When the captain sees that gesture, he's not pleased.

She needs to concentrate on the mission, not him, the captain thinks as he watches Liam leave the room.

Ignoring the captain, she starts to stretch in front of the wall-sized mirror at the back of the room. For training, Alex decided to wear workout clothes instead of the required Air Force physical training, or PT gear as it's called. She hates the material and the swooshing sound it makes every time she moves. Instead, she's wearing a pair of tight, black yoga pants and a grey V-neck T-shirt with the Air Force symbol printed on the top left corner.

The captain can see her black sports bra under her shirt as she moves her body to warm up and stretch. As she bends down, he glances at the curvature of her ass and thinks to himself, *The other girls wore tight yoga pants like that*, while pretending to look at the schedule and not her. His heart starts pounding faster as he thinks about the previous girl he asked to do this mission. She was athletic like Alex and had the same ass and esthetically pleasing face to look at. *I wonder if she'll be easy to control like the others. But first, she needs to train,* he thinks.

After a few minutes, the captain stands in the middle of the room and says, "This morning you're going to meet a couple of guys that are going to train you on different variations of hand-to-hand combat, and then *if* you get better, you'll move onto Muay Thai and Krav Maga. They're going to work you hard and there are going to be days where you're tired and want to give up. You'll leave here with bruises and possibly fractured bones, but the harder you train, the better you're going to get," he says sternly to her.

The captain's voice booms in the room as he speaks. Through the door come two well-built men in black workout pants, tight black shirts, and black sneakers. Their muscles are so big that their shirts look two sizes too small for them. They stand on either side of the captain with their arms folded and with a don't fuck with me look on their faces. The guy to the right of the captain is Brock and the guy to the left is Decker.

How the hell am I supposed to train with these guys? she thinks, suddenly feeling nervous before quickly composing herself. With a hint of confidence but also uncertainty she asks, "Okay, so, what do you need me to do?"

Decker curls his lip to an almost grin, eyeballs her, and asks, "Did you learn the basics of what we're about to teach you at combat skills training?"

"Yes, but it was only for a couple of days. But I think I remember what to do," she says with uncertainty. Before she can say another word, Brock moves behind her and puts her in a chokehold.

Decker watches her eyes widen. He stands there looking at her calmly with his arms still folded and asks, "So, how are you going to get out of this situation, Sergeant?"

She's already out of breath as she tries to use her arm to punch at Brock. The more she struggles the worse it feels as the walls start to close in. Alex starts feeling dizzy from the lack of air and from across the room, she catches a glimpse of the captain watching her intently as she falls to the floor unconscious.

In the next ten seconds, Alex wakes up and yells, "What the fuck just happened?!" Her voice echoes in the room.

"You died, that's what just happened. Never…ever…let some strange guys come up to you like that without being prepared," the captain says. "When you're standing in front of the Shadow, you must not drop your guard at any time. If he or his guards catch you, they'll kill you. Understand?"

On the floor, cradling her neck, Alex suddenly contemplates her decision for this mission. As she watches Captain Marcs circle her and continue to lecture her, she knows that this is going to be just one of many hard lessons she's going to learn in that room.

Two months go by, and each day of training is just like the last. Her schedule is like the workings of a perfect Swiss-made clock. Alex wakes up at the crack of dawn, runs for an hour, gets cleaned up, has breakfast, and heads out with the guys on convoy missions. Then she returns and trains with Brock and Decker in hand-to-hand combat before she practices exotic dance by herself. Sometimes, if Liam doesn't have to leave early for a mission, he'll go for a run with her, and then they have breakfast together. On the days that Liam is sent on an early mission, the captain runs with her without even asking her first.

She'll be running along and then out of nowhere Captain Marcs will pop in and run right next to her. This always makes her feel awkward because even though he's the officer in charge of the team, she doesn't like him or his attitude. She knew from the moment he intimidated her after the card game that he's not right. To make it worse, sometimes she'd catch him glancing at her breasts bouncing up and down from under her T-shirt while running side by side with her.

Fucking creepy asshole, she thinks every time she catches him looking at her breasts. Alex would try to run faster but he'd catch right up to her and continue to run next to her. *I wish he would find another time to work out and let me run in peace.*

The first two months of training are a blur to her and the only way she keeps track of it all is by keeping a calendar in her room. She tracks when movie and card nights are going to be with Liam and the guys. To her, it's nice to take a break from her crazy schedule, let loose, and have fun. She's also never slept this hard either. Luckily, she doesn't have any nightmares, but she's stressed out from the captain constantly yelling at her to get the moves right during training. What gives her comfort in all this is that Liam's always there afterward to make her feel better, and even Tate, Cast, and Thompson sometimes show up to give her support.

On one of her grueling training days, Tate decides to play a joke on her and playfully put her in a chokehold from behind while she's talking to Liam. Poor Tate goes flying across the floor because Alex reacts so quickly now.

"Oh my God, Tate! What the fuck!" she says pissed but also worried that she hurt him.

Hunching over from the pain in his back, Tate laughs a little and says, "Jesus, Alex. Fuck, I was just playing around."

Both Thompson and Cast shake their heads at Tate and laugh at him for underestimating her.

Cast snorts under his breath and says, "Man, that looks like it hurt, you fucking idiot!"

Thompson also snorts with laughter and says, "Yeah, don't mess with Ms. Krav Maga over here," in his deep southern accent.

As Cast reaches over to help Tate, they hear the door to the training room slam. The captain yells, "All right, knock that shit off!" as he walks in with Brock and Decker. "The last thing we need is one of you hurting her and then she's out for a month recovering over something stupid. Now get the hell out so we can train!" he yells again.

The guys, including Liam, all look at each other thinking the same thing they always do when it comes to the captain and silently leave the room. Before they leave her there, they each look at her apologetically and nod. Then Liam flashes her a look indicating that he'll see her later for dinner.

You're an asshole, she thinks toward the captain as she watches him speak with Decker about her training progress. *Who the fuck does he think he is, talking to them like that*? she thinks as she stretches silently in front of the large mirror. She goes to eyeball the captain with disdain when she catches him staring at her as she stretches. *Really asshole? Take a picture already,* she thinks as she turns her body away from him, so she doesn't have to look at his face.

Training day is just like any other as Alex endures a few hours of being thrown around the room by Brock and Decker, then gets yelled at by Captain Marcs for not getting the moves right. Finally, the worst part of the afternoon is exotic dance by herself. During this time, it's only her in the room as she tries to figure out how to learn to dance on her own. By that time of the day, she just wants to lay on the cold, slick floor and fall asleep but she knows better for fear of getting caught by the captain.

She notices that sometimes, he'll come in the training room out of nowhere just to make sure she isn't just laying around and then tries to talk to her like they're friends. Little does he know that in her mind, they are not friends. Alex hates when he does this because when it's just her in the room, he'll try to make small talk and ask her personal questions like how many boyfriends she's had in the past and if she's ever dated older guys.

Other times, she's noticed that he'd send the guys out on a mission during her scheduled dance time so that he can be alone with her. He treats her differently in front of everyone so that they don't suspect anything.

The captain has a thing for young, enlisted girls and knows just how to manipulate them into sleeping with him without anyone knowing about it. The last girl he manipulated left the country after he forced himself on her. She tried to tell leadership when he threatened her career and told her that no one would believe her. She then backed off and asked to be sent home due to stress.

With Alex, he needs her to concentrate on the mission first and then he'll make his move. The thing is that he wants her to feel the same way he feels about her. To show support, he helps her out with the exotic dance portion of her training by bringing her an old CD player and some CDs people left behind. Then he brings her some DVDs that were confiscated because they're considered unauthorized items and are banned in the country.

It's after lunch and Alex is stretching in front of the mirror, dreading the last part of training for the day. Going through the CDs, she tries to find something to listen to that'll help her learn how to move her body. She recognizes a few bands like Nirvana, Radiohead, The Offspring, and Alex's favorite band, Deftones. During the first and second months of training, she'd put a CD in and would just stretch on the floor. Now that she's in her third month, it's time to get serious and start practicing.

How the fuck am I supposed to convince the Shadow that I'm an exotic dancer? she thinks as she's standing there in front of the mirror without any confidence to go on.

Suddenly, the captain comes into the room and brings her a box with DVDs of exotic dancers that he confiscated from a guy on the compound.

Alex remembers when she in-processed she was instructed to read General Order number one that stated the following: According to General Order number one, anyone stationed in any deployed location shall not possess drugs of any kind, alcohol of any kind to include mouth wash, or any pornographic or sexually explicit material of any kind such as videos, magazines, photographs, and movies.

Alex starts stretching before she attempts to dance and notices that the captain won't leave. *Why's he just standing there?* she asks herself as she catches the captain's eyes moving toward her ass again.

"So, how are you feeling about this deployment so far? Are you making any friends?" he asks as he leans up against the mirror where she's stretching.

Just answer him so he'll go away, she thinks while politely replying, "I'm doing good and yes I've made some friends," without looking in his direction.

"Yes, I've noticed how you and Sergeant Anderson look close," he says waiting to see her reaction.

Don't react. That's what he wants you to do, she thinks. She replies, "Sergeant Anderson's on my team and he's helping me get through all of this, sir."

"Oh, I see. I thought that the two of you were dating or something. You ever date anyone older?" he asks out of curiosity.

What the fuck does that have to do with anything? she thinks as she stops stretching and looks directly at him. Feeling uncomfortable while rolling her eyes at him she replies, "I don't know sir, I haven't thought about it," seeing that he's trying to get her to open up to him.

The captain can sense that she's not up for talking at the moment and says, "Make sure you put that box of DVDs away before you leave. I wouldn't want you to get in trouble." He gives her a coy smile then leaves the room.

"Finally, he's gone," she says aloud as she rummages through the box and pulls out one of the DVDs. She puts it in the old Sony television set that's sitting on a rolling cart. It has an old DVD player on the bottom shelf and looks like something one would find in a classroom from her high school days.

Alex watches the video go straight to a half-naked girl dancing on a stage by herself. She looks like she's performing in a Vegas strip club. The dancer moves her body so seductively that it makes Alex blush with embarrassment. *She makes it look so easy,* Alex thinks as she wishes she had someone here to walk her through it step by step.

In the video, the dancer uses a chair as her prop and it reminds Alex of the 1980s movie *Flashdance*, where Jennifer Beals uses a chair as part of her routine and then water comes splashing down on top of her. Alex remembers how provocative that was and the confidence the actress portrayed.

She watches as the dancer sits in the chair and twirls around in the seat with her clear stilettos on. The dancer did this without letting her legs and feet touch the floor or the back of the chair. She then starts to seductively dance by moving her body around the chair and slowly removing her clothing but not her stilettos or her thigh-high stockings.

Alex can't believe what she sees next when the dancer sits with her back in the chair and lifts herself up with the palms of her hands.

She plants her hands on the seat between her legs then she slowly brings her ass up in the air and does a handstand while remaining in the chair. She uses her legs that are in a perfect split above her head. *Jesus, that must've taken years to accomplish,* Alex thinks in amazement.

There's an old wooden chair in the back storage room, so Alex decides to give it a try. She watches the video again and pauses it each time she tries a move. She knows it's too soon to try the handstand in the air, so she puts on some music and starts moving her body around the chair like the dancer in the video.

Feeling embarrassed, Alex looks at herself in the mirror and isn't aware of how attractive she is. All her life she was treated like garbage. Her dad betrayed her in so many ways and he was supposed to raise her to be confident and independent. Instead, Alex finds herself to be timid around men and doesn't understand why they look at her the way they do.

She knows that she needs to get her confidence up and learn exotic dance since it's the most vital part of the mission. If she doesn't learn how to dance, then she can't go in front of the Shadow.

Alex gatherers herself and places the wooden chair in front of the large mirror. Then she takes her hair out of her ponytail and lets it cascade down her back as she ties the bottom of her T-shirt into a knot, exposing her stomach. She then rolls down the waistband of her sweatpants exposing her hip bones. Alex doesn't have heels to dance in, so she decides to take her socks off to give her more traction on the slick floor.

The CD player has an AM-FM radio. However, the radio stations in the country aren't worth listening to, so all she has to work with are the old CDs. She reminds herself that on the next mission outside the wire, she would look for some better CDs.

She picks up a few of the CDs and starts looking through them. *Which one should I start with*? she asks herself as she picks up the Deftones' White Pony album from the year 2000. She loves them but doesn't have this one, so she flips it over to look at the song titles. She puts it in and listens to each song for ten seconds to see which one will work. She decides that the song "Change" is slow enough to start with.

Standing behind the chair and facing the mirror, she hears Chino Moreno's voice singing slowly to the lyrics. As the beat echoes loudly in the empty room, Alex closes her eyes and slowly moves her shoulders one after the other to the beat of the music. Then rotating her hips, she bends down into a squat position behind the chair and pushes herself up as her hair flips back behind her. Starting to feel the slow rhythm as she moves her body, she copies the girl in the video and lightly caresses her breasts then slides her hands down to her exposed stomach.

With her eyes still closed, she lightly touches the back of the chair as Chino continues his ballad before slowly walking around to the front of the chair and facing the mirror again.

The girl in the video straddles the chair, rotates her hips, and arches her back letting her hair touch the floor.

Alex tries this move and it's a little difficult at first since she's still sore from Decker body-slamming her into the floor earlier that day. She closes her eyes because she feels that it's easier to move her body while listening to the beat. Alex repeats the moves until she feels comfortable arching her back toward the floor. After many attempts, she does it. Not as good as the girl in the video but she manages to do the same moves without hurting herself.

Suddenly, Alex hears slow, hard clapping coming from the door and immediately stops dancing. She doesn't need to turn around to know the captain was watching her most of the time. Alex quickly turns the music off and stands there in embarrassment.

"Very nice...not bad for a small-town girl," Captain Marcs says with his lip curling up on one side while eyeballing her up and down.

I can't believe he's been watching me. What the hell is wrong with him? she asks herself, feeling awkward before quickly composing herself.

Standing there looking at her with that same grin on his face, he says, "Oh, don't let me stop you. Please continue."

She looks at him but doesn't say anything. Even though he's a creepy asshole, he's the officer in charge of the team. If she pisses him off or doesn't measure up to complete the mission, then he's going to find someone else.

Just do it, she tells herself as she watches him lean against the wall with his arms folded and waiting for her to continue dancing. She takes a few deep breaths and starts the song over again. Then she closes her eyes and continues to practice her dance routine. *Just make pretend that asshole isn't here*, she tells herself as the rock star's voice fills the room again. Alex starts picturing the girl in the video moving and touching her body, so she pretends the wooden chair is a man she's seducing and repeats her routine over and over until she gets the moves right.

Captain Marcs quietly watches Alex sway her body from side to side and likes how she arches her back in the chair, exposing her stomach and her tits toward him. "Look at me," he says under his breath while watching her body flow with the rhythm of the music. He notices that she won't open her eyes to look at him. It's as if she's purposely forgetting he's there. As she flips her hair and arches her back, he gazes at her long neck and her ass as she squats to the floor.

Out of breath, Alex finally hears the last note of the song and opens her eyes. She can see how the captain is staring at her and wonders what's going through his mind. She notices that he's still leaning on the wall and looking at her in awe.

After a few seconds pass, he slowly walks toward her and puts his hand on the back of the chair where she's standing. Looking into her eyes, he thinks back to the night of the card game and how frightened she was. She's changed from scared to then confident toward him. That night was the main reason he chose her for this mission. He's amazed at how far she's come in such a short amount of time. He thought her dancing was going to be the worst part of her training, but after watching her, she proves to be a quick study.

Continuing to look at her he softly says, "You've come a long way Sergeant, but may I make a suggestion?" Not waiting for her to answer he says, "If you're trying to *picture* a man sitting in that chair, it'll probably be better to actually have a man sitting there when you dance so that it feels real. When the time comes for you to dance for the Shadow, you don't want to make any mistakes." He can see the expression change on her face as he moves in closer to her and says, "Let me know if you ever want *me* to be that man in the chair." Giving her a sly grin, he then turns and walks out of the room.

Watching him leave the room she says, "Holy fucking shit," under her breath while standing there in shock about what he'd just said to her. She thinks about all the times he'd stared at her and then looked away when she caught him. Then all the times he ran beside her without asking and glanced at her tits as they bounced up and down. Now, he's proposing that she give him a lap dance in the chair and pretend he's the Shadow.

The nerve of that motherfucker, she thinks as she cleans up and puts the box of unauthorized DVDs away in the back room. Suddenly, she hears the door open again. Nervous it's the captain, Alex quickly relaxes as she sees that it's just Liam.

Smiling at her, he says, "Hey you." He can see how tired she is from training all day. Her hair is back in a ponytail and her shirt is stained with sweat. The wavy auburn highlights within her dark hair stand out from the beam of sunlight coming through the window.

"How was training today?" he asks.

"It was okay, the captain made a surprise visit during my dance training and made a disgusting proposal," she says with revulsion.

"What did he say?" Liam asks.

"First he comes in right as I'm dancing and then makes me continue as he watches. Then when I finish, I'm expecting him to do what he always does and make degrading remarks about my moves. But instead, he tells me that I should have someone sit in this chair while I dance for them."

"What did he mean by that?" Liam asks.

"He said I should let *him* be the guy in the chair. Like I would *ever* ask him to do that!" she says with disgust.

Liam also looks at her with disgust and says, "What does he think he's doing talking to you like that? You should report him."

"To who, Liam? Nobody will believe me because he's a well-respected officer who went to fucking West Point and I am just a staff sergeant from a small town," she says out of frustration. "I just need to train for this mission and stay out of his way."

"I know you want to do the right thing by killing the Shadow, but you don't have to put up with that asshole," he says as he touches her hand.

Alex looks down at his hand touching her then into his blue eyes and with a warm smile says, "That's why I have you here to protect me."

Kiss me, she thinks as she gives him a look of wanting and desire for him.

Liam reads the look on her face and accepts her invitation by leaning in to kiss her. Before their lips meet, Tate, Cast, and Thompson come busting into the room.

"There you are," Tate says to Liam as Liam and Alex quickly move away from each other.

"What, why are you looking for me?" Liam asks with a slight hint of frustration.

"It's movie night bro. Did you forget? We need popcorn, which is your job to get from the chow hall," Tate says with attitude as he starts setting up the projector.

Slightly laughing at how Tate and Liam bicker like two brothers, she asks, "What's the movie tonight?"

"I'm not saying until I see some popcorn, because last time you didn't bring it," Tate says annoyed.

"Come on, Liam. I'll go with you. We'll be back guys," she says as they leave the room together.

"And make sure you bring enough for *all* of us!" Tate yells out to them.

They return with enough popcorn for everyone. As Tate is announcing the movie of the week, Alex thinks about how she and Liam almost kissed. *I hope I'm not making a mistake getting too close to him*, she thinks as she looks at him.

While watching one of Quentin Tarantino's masterpieces, Liam slowly reaches over and puts his hand on top of hers. He doesn't look at her and waits to see if she's going to move her hand away, but she doesn't.

Giving him a slight grin, she flips her hand over and interlaces her fingers with his as they continue to watch the movie.

Chapter 7
The Shadow

It's Saturday evening at the palace and the party Asim is hosting is no different from all the other events he's thrown in the past. He's already drunk from his made-up concoction of brandy, beer, and vodka. The more he drinks this, the more violent he gets by the hour. After yelling at one of his guards for not bringing his drink to him fast enough, he lazily sits on his throne while watching three underaged girls dance half-naked in front of him and his guests.

The room is extravagant with marble statues of naked women and a large tapestry on the back wall of men and women during an orgy. The tables are full of lavish food and drinks and there's a large Persian rug on the floor made of silk and cashmere. The large fountain in the middle of the room was imported from Italy and portrays a bare-breasted mermaid laying on a large rock with water shooting out of her nipples.

All the guests there are part of Asim's father's political party and are considered the wealthiest people in the country. Some of them help Asim's father gain favor with the rest of the country to help keep his father in power. However, tonight is about Asim's soon-to-be rise to power. He's trying to gain favor with them and make them respect him like they do his father.

This is my night, not my father's. And they will respect me, he thinks as the cup full of his mixture of alcohol fill his stomach. The throne he's sitting in was handmade to his specifications out of black mahogany and black leather for the seat and back cushions. It has a seventy-inch-tall wing-back made of elaborate engraved wood designs. Each armrest has a carved lion head where his hands rest. The seat is so wide that he can fit himself and a naked girl on each side of him.

Asim's sitting there with his right leg propped up on the armrest and his cane resting in his left hand. He shifts his gaze from the dancers over to the guests which are scattered around the room and talking amongst each other. He notices them periodically look at him drinking on his throne, trying not to draw his attention. *They will respect me as much as they respect my father*, he thinks as the alcohol starts to take effect on his temper.

An Afghan man is singing in the corner and was invited to the palace at Asim's request. This singer is well known throughout the country and highly regarded by Asim's father. Jealous of the man, Asim can see how the guests admire his talented voice.

He's here because of me, Asim thinks sternly as he starts to feel the anger and jealousy for his father swell inside him. He tries to listen for any misplaced notes in the man's singing so that he can humiliate the man. If Asim notices a missed note or if the singer doesn't sing to perfection, then he'll beat the man in front of everyone for embarrassing him. Luckily for the singer, he performs perfectly for Asim and his guests.

The guests are fond of Asim's father. However, they aren't completely aligned with how Asim conducts business, and he knows it. Many of the parties the guest attended in the past were decent when Asim's father was present. However, when it's only Asim, they know the rest of the night is going to be interesting. They also know if any of them try to leave the party early, then there will be consequences like a raped wife or daughter. Trust isn't Asim's strong suit. Neither is loyalty to his father. He wants things done a certain way and he doesn't like waiting for the things he wants.

At tonight's party, Asim makes sure to post a guard at each corner of the room with two guards placed outside the main double doors and another two behind Asim's throne on either side of him. Each guard carries a fully loaded AK-47 assault rifle, which is a popular weapon in Afghanistan.

The AK-47 is used by Asim's guards because they're considered reliable under harsh conditions. However, they jam quite frequently if the ammunition is defective or substandard.

At times, when anyone disappointed him, Asim would threaten them with the barrel of one of his guard's AK-47s. First, he'd beat them to the ground and then point the assault rifle in their face until they complied. If they didn't, then a bullet met their skull, and anyone else who stood too close was killed as well.

As he's drinking heavily on his black mahogany throne, Asim starts looking around the room to humiliate some of his guests out of boredom. His father isn't present at the party, so Asim decides that it's time to have some fun.

He suddenly lifts his cane and points it at three men standing together talking. In a demanding voice that booms across the room, he yells, "You three, come." Everyone suddenly stops talking amongst each other, turns, and looks at Asim and the three men.

The guests watch as the three men reluctantly go to Asim. The men know better than to displease him, so all three stand in front of his throne while Asim speaks again in Dari.

He stares at them in contempt and says, "Get down on your hands and knees, dogs."

The three men, dressed in fine silk suits, are reluctant to listen to Asim. However, they slowly get on their hands and knees.

Asim motions one of his guards to bring over the Turkish-made pitcher of his alcoholic concoction. He then stands up with his cane in his left hand and the pitcher of alcohol in the other. In front of the three kneeling men, he begins pouring the liquid on the floor in front of them and says, "Drink, dogs," while smiling at the sight of them.

The men look up at him in confusion as he pours more on the ground.

Mockingly, Asim shows them his tongue to suggest licking the liquid off the floor.

The room falls silent, and all the guests watch in horror at what's happening. They know because his father isn't at the party that this is the start of Asim's boorish rants.

Two of the men comply and start to lick the liquid off the floor as commanded while the man to Asim's right refuses and remains on all fours with a look of defiance on his face.

Asim sees this betrayal and removes the twenty-two-inch blade from his cane and places it at the back of the man's neck. Bending slightly toward the man's ear, he says in a whisper, "If you do not drink my friend, then I am afraid your blood will be the last thing you see."

Pausing in fear, the man finally swallows his pride, and then reluctantly puts his head to the floor and laps up the liquid with his tongue.

Yes, obey me you sons of whores, Asim thinks as he looks down at them in disgust. "Look, everyone, at my beautiful dogs," Asim says loudly while taking several swallows from the pitcher.

Many of the guests reluctantly clap their hands despite the embarrassing scene in front of them. They also don't want to be his next victims, so they smile at him as well.

Look at them. They love me, he thinks as he sees the room start to spin. Not wanting the feeling to end, he calls the three dancer girls over and makes each girl climb on the men's backs like they're donkeys to ride. He laughs watching the men crawl on their hands and knees with the girls on their backs throughout the remainder of the evening.

The man who was reluctant to kneel and drink from the floor is so angry that he's sure to tell Asim's father of this horrible treatment. He's the right-hand man of Asim's father and should never be treated in such a way by a spoiled, arrogant little brat of a man.

By the next morning, many of the guests are still laying on the floor and hungover from being made to drink from Asim's pitcher of alcohol all night. The dogs are licking vomit that's all over the Persian rug, and there's a smell of piss and dog shit that lingers in the air.

Asim is upstairs in his massive suite, laying on his enormous round bed that is also custom made of black mahogany like his throne. The three underage dancer girls from the night before are naked and laying on the bed passed out with Asim in the middle of them.

He lays there on his back looking at himself in the mirror installed in the ceiling above his bed. Asim thinks about the party and what he did to some of his guests and then smiles at his reflection. *They will bend to my will once my father is gone*, he thinks. *I made them crawl at my feet*, he thinks further, suddenly feeling powerful and invincible like no one in the world can stop him.

In his reflection, he can see his black hair is disheveled, and his almost black eyes are red from dehydration and partying all night. His well-groomed mustache and beard make him look distinguished and just like his father. The only difference between him and his father is

Asim's eyes. Behind those dead, lifeless eyes is an entitled and privileged man who'll stop at nothing to get what he wants. Even if that means upsetting his powerful father.

Asim hopes to follow in his father's footsteps and become a powerful political figure. He believes that fear is the only way to win the hearts and minds of the people around him. His father has used fear to get where he is and Asim wants the same thing, but better.

Laying there in the middle of the passed-out girls, his back suddenly starts to hurt from the bullet fragment that's still lodged in his spine. Asim's recent assassination attempt was due to him trying to pick up some young girls in the city when one of his enemies fired at him. The doctors couldn't remove one of the fragments from his spine, so now he has to walk with a cane.

To stop the pain, he pulls a small glass vile of cocaine from under his pillow and spreads the white powder on one of the girl's breasts as she sleeps. Then he snorts the cocaine and licks the rest of it off the girl's hard nipple. This instantly makes him hard, so he climbs on top of her and forcibly starts fucking her.

The girl suddenly wakes up and screams but Asim covers her mouth hard with a pillow and continues to ram himself deep inside of her over and over.

*No...no...*she thinks in a panic as she's having a hard time breathing. *Where am I? I don't remember*, she thinks as she kicks her legs and flings her arms around. She can feel him penetrate inside her and tries to scream from under the pillow but the only sound coming out is muffled.

Yes, scream little girl, he thinks as he closes his eyes, enjoying how violently her body is moving with every thrust he makes. It excites him more, so he pushes the pillow down harder and continues to fuck her.

The other two girls wake up from this and try to get off the bed, but Asim instantly commands them to lay next to him and have sex with each other.

The girls know better to defy him, so they do as he commands, and reluctantly start to kiss each other. The girl with the black hair gets on top of the girl with red hair and begins to kiss down her neck and then to her breast.

Asim watches the two girls as he continues violating the girl under the pillow. He watches as the black-haired girl seductively licks and then sucks on the girl's nipple while slipping her fingers into the girl to get her wet.

She hears the red-haired girl moan with delight and starts kissing down to her stomach toward her belly button. She knows Asim is watching intently. To not displease him, she spreads the red-haired girl's legs open and thrusts her wet tongue into her while pinching the girl's nipple hard with her fingertips.

Asim is incredibly pleased with this and continues raping the girl under the pillow who, by this time, has stopped screaming and struggling.

The red-haired girl closes her eyes, bites her bottom lip, and arches her back as she's about to come. She continues moaning with pleasure as the girl on top continues to roll her tongue back and forth inside her.

Asim finally comes with violent gratification into the girl from under the pillow, who's suffocated to death. Without a second thought, he leaves her lifeless body to be with the other two girls. At first, he lays there and watches them pleasure one another, listening to the delightful sounds of sexual agony coming from them.

Pulling out the vile of cocaine, he gets behind the black-haired girl, whose ass is fully exposed in front of him, and spreads the powder on her lower back. After licking the remaining powder off her, he pulls her by the hips closer to him and spreads her cheeks open. Watching her eat out the red-haired girl, he slips his fingers inside her to get her wet and starts licking her from behind. This and the hit of cocaine gets him hard again, so he thrusts himself inside her as she continues to pleasure the other girl.

High from the cocaine, Asim watches the three of them from the reflection of the mirror above the bed with ecstasy. When he comes into the girl, he pushes her aside as she lands next to the lifeless girl from under the pillow. Asim takes a third hit of cocaine and starts stroking himself to get hard again but that doesn't work so he looks at the black-haired girl and points where to put her mouth.

Still hungover from the night before, she looks at Asim reluctantly, which displeases him.

"NOW!" he says with wide eyes and then slaps her hard in the face. He then grabs her by the dark hair, shoves her mouth on his cock while tilting his head back and forcing her head back and forth. He can feel her warm, wet tongue slide up and down and suddenly he gets hard again. Pushing her aside, he grabs the red-haired girl and forcefully thrusts himself inside her.

Laying there next to the dead girl, the red-haired girl looks up at Asim in horror but doesn't cry as he violates her. *It'll be over soon*, she thinks as she tightly closes her eyes and grips the sheets with her hands.

Asim wants to feel her move violently like the dead girl under the pillow, so as he's looking down at her, he places his hand around her throat. *I want to feel her heart racing as I fuck her*, he thinks maliciously as a violent grin appears on his face.

The girl quickly opens her eyes in horror and looks up at him in shock. She uses her hands to try and remove his hand from her throat, but she can already feel her life slipping away as he continues to ram himself inside her.

The black-haired girl tries to move Asim's hand away from the girl's throat, but he backhands her hard in the face as she lands on top of the dead girl that's laying there, under the pillow.

Asim looks down and can see how red the girl's face is from choking her and how her eyes look glazed over. She's no longer moving violently, and this displeases him. So, mid-thrust, he starts slapping her, but she doesn't wake up, so he slaps her again. *Another dead girl*, he thinks dismissively as he continues to fuck her faster and harder while playing with the other girl's nipple.

Am I next? Is he going to kill me too? The black-haired girl thinks as she lays there in horror beside both dead girls.

When Asim finally comes, he gets off the bed and doesn't feel too much pain in his back. It could be from the three hits of cocaine or maybe his mind is preoccupied with fucking three girls in one morning and then killing two of them. He tells his guards outside the room to bring the girl downstairs and to burn and dispose of the other two girls. While taking a long, hot shower, he feels his body hum with delight while thinking that this was the perfect start to a perfect day.

Chapter 8
Hamid

Preoccupied with her thoughts, Alex thinks about the movie last night with Liam and the guys. *He almost kissed* me, she thinks as Brock and Decker circle around her in the training room. Today they decide to tag team and face her head-on at the same time, which is going to be a challenge since both men outweigh her by about sixty to seventy pounds each.

Fuck, this is going to suck, she thinks as they get closer to her. She sees them surrounding her, but her mind keeps thinking about Liam, which is a bad idea at the moment.

Decker can see that Alex isn't paying attention and decides to swipe her legs from under her. When she tries to get up, Brock pins her down and puts all his weight on her shoulders and chest. He can see the panic in her eyes and yells at her to fix it.

"Come on Foster, get out of this!" Brock yells in frustration.

Standing over her, Decker says, "Remember to use your hips not your legs."

Goddamn it, she thinks. It takes everything left in her to push her hips up and throw Brock off balance. As soon as that happens, she takes advantage and uses her leg to roll him to the side so that she can get up.

"Good job. Okay, we're done for the day," Decker says, patting her once on her shoulder.

It's after one o'clock and Alex is so tired that she goes straight to her room and takes a nap instead of going to exotic dance training. At that point she doesn't care if the captain gets upset. Hell, King Kong can bust in the door to yell at her, and she'll not hear a thing.

Liam comes back early from his mission outside the wire and rushes to Alex's room to see if she's there. He lightly knocks on Alex's half-open door to find her dead asleep on her bed. He'd got her some food and thought she'd be hungry after training all morning. Watching her for a moment as she sleeps peacefully on her side, he thinks about kissing her softly on the lips but is afraid to wake her up. *I missed my chance last night before the movie*, he thinks as he sets the food on her nightstand.

Hearing something move on her nightstand, Alex opens her eyes and sees Liam standing there. In a restful tone, she says, "Hey you," to him while rubbing her eyes to wake them up.

"Hey, sleeping beauty. I brought you some food to eat before your next training session," he says softly.

Alex props herself up on one elbow and picks up the ham and cheese sandwich. "Thanks, you're so sweet. Hey, sit down. Let's talk," she says while patting her hand on the bed beside her.

Liam sits down next to her as she lays upright on her pillow watching him. He can see how tired she is from all the training but at the same time how beautiful she is to him. Even with her messy hair and the slight bruise marks on her arms, he can't resist her. Since the moment they met, he can't stop thinking about her. After all these months, he wants her more than ever.

God, I want to kiss her so bad right now, he thinks as he lightly brushes a piece of hair from her eyes. He never looks into her eyes for too long because he finds it hard to look away.

Alex can sense by the way he's looking at her that he wants to kiss her. *I wish he would just kiss me already*, she thinks as she catches his gaze.

She's had feelings for him since the day they met but was afraid to get too close for fear of being rejected, abandoned, or cheated on. But she can't help it and decides right then and there to take a chance.

Okay, here it goes, she thinks and then takes his hand and moves closer to him.

Accepting her invitation, Liam doesn't say another word as he gently places his hand on her waist and leans in. Coming in slowly, he feels her soft lips on his as she slips her tongue into his mouth. Her warm, wet tongue caresses his as their lips touch and their breaths collide with one another. Moving in closer, he slowly lays on top of her as they continue to kiss long and deep.

Wanting him, she moves her body in sync with his as she takes her hands and places them on his hips to pull him in closer. She quickly rolls him over and lays on top of him as they continue to kiss deep and slow. Feeling a sudden rush of heat overcome her body, she sits straight up, straddles his hips, then arches her neck back as her hips move slightly. She can feel his erection between her legs get harder as she continues moving her hips back and forth.

Wanting her now more than ever, he lets out a small moan and wants to make love to her but doesn't make the first move without her permission.

Alex lays down on top of him as they continue to kiss. She wants to make love to him too but feels that it's going too fast, so she slowly moves off him. She knows that if she doesn't stop, that it'll be harder to if they keep going.

Liam feels her slowly move off him and gently lets her go. He understands that she doesn't want to move too fast in their relationship, so he places his forehead on hers and lightly kisses her lips as he gets off the bed.

"I better go, before the captain comes looking for me," he says.

"Okay, I'm right behind you," she says from her bed as she watches him start to leave her room.

Looking back at her and giving a sexy grin, he says, "Don't lay back down sleeping beauty," in a whisper.

Seeing his grin, she gets the sudden urge to kiss him again and says, "Wait!" She rushes off the bed and runs over to kiss him again.

Their bodies intertwine and their mouths connect with desire for one another. They kiss for what seems like ages. When Alex finally lets him go, she says, "You better get going."

Liam smiles and says, "I'll see you later." He opens the door and looks at her one more time before he leaves.

Alex slowly walks back to her bed, lays back down, and stares at the ceiling. She touches her lips with her fingers as she imagines the kiss they shared. Her whole body is buzzing with delight and nothing, not even the captain, can ruin what she's feeling.

Suddenly, her ears start ringing as her entire bed lifts and then slams back on the floor. Alex's door comes flying off the hinges with force as the room slightly moves back and forth. *What the fuck just happened?* she thinks as she suddenly sees a couple of people running past her door in a panic toward the hallway exit. She quickly gets off the bed to follow them. Her ears are still ringing, and everything sounds muffled as she reaches the exit door.

When she makes it outside, she notices that the front gate was blown up by a vehicle-borne improvised explosive device, known as a

VBIED. The vehicle was destroyed by the explosion and there's pieces of the car and the front gate scattered all over the compound. The bodies of those who were hit with shrapnel from the blast are also scattered.

Alex can hear faint screams despite her ringing ears and can see people running around frantic from the aftermath of the explosion. As she gets closer to help those who are hurt, she sees an Afghan gate guard laying on top of someone with black sweatpants. *No, it can't be. Please no*, she thinks in a panic as she runs over to the bodies on the ground. She screams Liam's name while trying to move the lifeless body that's laying on top of him and screams again, "Somebody! Help!" She holds Liam, who's unconscious with pools of blood that have soaked into his shirt.

Fearing that he's dead, she says, "Liam, please wake up!" as tears form in her eyes. Touching the blood on his shirt, she notices that there're no wounds on his body. She continues to shake him awake when, finally, he sits up and starts coughing.

Placing her hands on his face she says, "Oh my God, Liam."

As he sits up, cradling his head he asks, "What happened?"

"We got attacked," she says as she looks over to the Afghan guard that was laying on top of him. Alex notices that the man has several pieces of shrapnel in his body. When he landed on Liam, the man's blood must have pooled onto him.

Liam looks over to the man and notices his name tag on his uniform and screams, "Hamid!" in horror. Overwhelming grief and emotion come over him as he covers his eyes in frustration. "Fuck!" he says as he tries not to look at his friend laying there dead in front of him.

With sorrow, Alex says, "Oh no, Hamid." She didn't recognize him at first from all the shrapnel in his body. From the looks of him, it seems that Hamid was standing right in front of Liam when the blast hit. He took all the shrapnel, leaving Liam alive and unharmed.

"Hamid was a good guy just trying to survive and take care of his family. What's going to happen to his wife and daughters now?" Liam asks.

Medics from Echo compound heard the blast and came across the street to help the injured people. One of them comes over to Liam and says, "Sir, do you need help?"

With tears slowly running down his face he replies, "No, help Hamid!" He points at Hamid lying there next to him.

In a sympathetic tone, she says, "I'm sorry sir. I can't help him. He's gone."

Alex can feel Liam shaking as he puts his head between his knees and wraps his arms around his legs. She places her head next to his and says, "Let me take you to get cleaned up while they take Hamid away."

Without saying a word, he looks up at her with red, tear-stained eyes, and decides he no longer wants to be there in the chaos. He takes Alex's hand and they slowly walk away together.

She helps him back to the dorm building and down the hall to the bathroom. Slowly removing his blood-soaked shirt, she takes it and throws it away so that he doesn't have to look at it anymore.

Even though they can faintly hear the commotion outside, Liam is quietly sitting there in shock as he lets Alex take care of him. He watches her take a small wet hand towel and place it on his chest to clean off Hamid's blood. Her hands are warm on his skin and the wet towel feels comforting to him. Slowly reaching out, he holds Alex's hand and places his forehead on her stomach.

Standing there in front of him, she slowly caresses his hair. She can hear his broken breath and feel his body shake. "Shhh," she says as she gently lifts his head to see his face. She notices that he wasn't injured from the blast and the only thing she finds is a small cut on his forehead.

"You're okay," she says lightly while gently cleaning the small cut with the towel.

Liam watches her as she looks over the rest of him to make sure he isn't bleeding anywhere else. He brings her closer to him and lightly kisses her lips.

"I'm sorry about Hamid," she whispers.

He doesn't say anything. He just places his head back onto her stomach as she continues to hold him close and caress his hair.

A week after the explosion, everything has gone back to normal on the compound. Sitting at the picnic table, Alex can see Liam speaking with Hamid's wife. He told Alex that morning that Hamid's wife, Fahima, was coming to pick up her husband's belongings and bring her two young daughters with her. Then she's going to live with her brother and his family, outside of the city.

Fahima is a beautiful young girl, maybe in her early twenties. From what Alex can see, she looks sad and worried as Liam speaks with her. She can also see that Liam is trying to reassure her that everything is going to be okay as he wishes her and her daughters well. At that moment, Alex sees Fahima give Liam something as she leaves the gate.

Watching Liam slowly walk back over to her, she asks, "Is she going to be okay?"

"I hope so. She's going to be with her brother and his family now," he says sadly.

Alex is curious about what Fahima gave him and asks, "What did she give you?"

He holds a patch in his hand, "This was the patch that Hamid wore on his uniform," he says as he hands it to Alex to look at.

The round patch has a brick castle with a flag coming out the top. There're words stitched in black around the edges that read *People first, Readiness now, Partnerships forever*. She hands the patch back to him and can see the sadness of losing his friend on his face.

Looking down at the patch, he says, "You know, Hamid was teaching me some words from his language, and I was teaching him some English words. It's something we would do when he had time to sit and talk with me.

"That's awesome! Teach me something," she says trying to lighten the mode.

He smiles at her and says, "Okay, say, Salam Alaikum," as he takes her hand and places it over her heart.

"Salam Alaikum," she says softly and then asks, "What does that mean?"

"It means peace be with you, and when you say it, you place your hand over your heart."

"That's beautiful. Can you teach me more while we're here?" she asks.

"Of course. That's if you're not too busy with everything else you're doing," he says sympathetically.

"No, I want to learn so that when I talk with Jabar on Bravo compound, he'll be impressed," she says eagerly. "I love his store and all those pretty rubies of his. Remember that one we saw a few weeks ago?"

"Yes, I remember it. I remember how much you liked it too," he says while looking down at the patch.

Sitting together at the picnic table, they watch as the rest of the people walk to their workstations when Alex suddenly remembers they have a mission outside the wire this morning. She was so preoccupied with Fahima and Liam that she forgot about not having training this morning and being assigned to a convoy mission with the guys. She loves when training is canceled for the day and she gets to convoy with the team.

"Shit, it's after seven and we're late going to drop off those medical supplies at Bravo compound," she says as she quickly gets up to get her gear.

The past five months on the open road was grueling, but she's already getting used to it. When she first started going on convoys with the team, she was assigned to be the lookout in the passenger seat. Her job is to make sure anything suspicious is reported back to the compound and to tell Tate which roads to take to avoid any suspicious activity. With Tate driving and Cast and Liam in the back seat, she sits in the front looking out for anything suspicious. Depending on the mission, Cast and Thompson take turns riding in Tate's vehicle since Liam always rides in the same vehicle with her.

"I'm not going with you today to Bravo because I'm tasked for something else," he says, hoping she doesn't get upset.

"What?" she asks in concern. "Well, when will you be back?"

Liam can hear the worry in her voice and takes her behind one of the buildings where they can talk in private.

"I'm sorry. I just found out and I should be back before the sun goes down," he says as he feels the sudden urge to kiss her. Leaning her up against the wall, he places his lips on hers. They're soft and he can taste the strawberries she had for breakfast. His heart starts beating faster as he wraps his arms around her not wanting to let go.

Wanting him more than before she feels a wave of emotions come over her and doesn't care who can see them kissing. Deciding that she's ready, she whispers to him, "Come to my room tonight when you get back."

Waiting patiently for her to say that, he looks into her eyes again, holds her tighter, and whispers back, "I will."

Chapter 9
The Secret

On the convoy ride to Bravo compound, Alex can only think about Liam and giving herself to him tonight for the first time. She's quietly looking out the window as Tate is driving with Cast and Thompson in the back seat. Feeling flush, she's picturing Liam's body on top of hers as they kiss and make love. She can't wait to feel his hands on her as he slips himself inside. Their naked bodies entwine, and their lips meet each other's in bliss as he…

"Hello…Alex," Cast says loudly to her from the back seat.

Quickly composing herself, she says, "Oh…sorry. What's up?"

With a huge grin on his face, Cast asks, "What's up with you?"

Grinning back at him she replies, "Nothing…why?"

Out of curiosity, Tate asks her, "Then why's your face red?" His dimples come out while trying not to laugh at her. He too seems to know what's on her mind.

Staying quiet she thinks to herself, *Shit, do they know about me and Liam?* Trying to change the subject, she looks at Tate, "You need to watch the road and not worry about my face," she says as she laughs a little.

"You can tell us, Alex. Why are you being so secretive?" Thompson asks.

Scoffing at these questions she asks, “What are you guys talking about?” She’s trying her best not to look embarrassed while staring out the window and hoping they’ll leave it alone.

“We already know, so stop trying to keep it a secret,” Cast says in his upper East Coast accent.

Alex scoffs again. “You don’t know shit!”

“Ohhhh, so you’re *not* thinking about Liam right now…yeah okay…” Cast says sarcastically as he rolls his eyes.

She feels her face get hotter. “Oh my God. It’s none of your business,” she says as a grin appears on her face.

The guys in the back seat can’t see her face blush but Tate can.

“Girl, your face is so red right now!” Tate says as he points and laughs.

“Tate! Stop it or I’m gonna put your ass in another headlock when we get back!” Alex says as she playfully points her finger at him.

Tate doesn’t look at her finger, but he knows it’s there, so he smiles and says, “I think you two are cute together.” He weaves his way through the slow-moving traffic on the highway, grinning at how Alex and Liam thought the rest of them didn’t know.

Finally, after thinking about it, Alex says, “Yeah…it’s true. Liam and I are a thing. But we don’t want everyone to know about it, especially the damn captain.” She’s relieved she doesn’t have to keep it from the guys anymore.

Lightly laughing, Cast replies with, “Well, that wasn’t so hard now, was it?”

“We kind of already knew,” Tate says like it was no big deal.

Alex looks from Tate to Thompson and then to Cast in disbelief, “Wait…What? How?” They’re incredibly careful not to be affectionate with each other in front of everyone else, especially when the captain is nearby.

Tilting his head to the side, Tate says, "It's so obvious Alex. He always comes to make sure you're okay after training. He brings you food, and we can see how you two look at each other."

"Yeah, and then disappearing during the movie…Come on, girl. Do you think we didn't notice," Thompson says.

Afraid to ask, she says, "Does the captain know?"

The guys fall silent.

"Oh, NOW you guys stop talking. Does the captain know or not?!" she asks loudly.

Finally, it's Cast who answers her and says, "Yeah, I think the captain knows." He realizes what the captain is capable of doing if Liam interferes with the mission.

Feeling her stomach drop she says, "Shit!" under her breath at the thought of Liam being sent away.

They finally arrive at Bravo compound, which is a nice change since it's much bigger than Alpha and has vendors and places to eat like Subway and Pizza Hut. They also like leaving Alpha because it gets them away from the captain.

Alex quickly drops off the medical supplies at the medical tent so that she can have more time to see what the local vendors have in stock. Tate likes to venture off after he double-checks the engine to make sure everything is good for the ride back. While Thompson and Cast go to get food and catchup with some of their friends.

After her assigned drop-off, she quickly heads over to her favorite jewelry vendor, Jabar.

The last time she came to Bravo compound with Liam, Jabar showed them a stunning six-carat ruby that was set on a long silver necklace. She remembers how the red color shined in the light and how it looked on her when she tried it on. Unfortunately, she couldn't afford it, but she liked seeing it on herself even for just a minute or two.

I hope he still has it, she thinks as she reaches Jabar's tent. Ducking her head as she enters the front part of the tent, she sees him behind the counter looking at precious stones through a magnifier. Months ago, when she met him for the first time, he showed her how to use the magnifier so that she could see the stones up close. He let her look closely at her favorite ruby and she remembers not finding any flaws or cracks.

Jabar is a kind and gentle man who looks like he could be the head elder of a local village. He's tall and thin with a long white beard and wears an Afghan Pakol hat. He looks frail in his old age and speaks English very well for a man who's only been around Western culture since the war started. Jabar is always nice to Alex every time she comes to his shop and doesn't treat her like many others would. Jabar sees Alex as a strong woman with potential and enjoys telling her stories of when he was a young man and how different things were back then.

Walking toward him, Alex places her hand over her heart and says, "Salam," to greet him.

Jabar also places his hand over his heart and says, "Salam," and gives her a slight bow of his head. "How are you, my friend?" he asks, giving her a warm smile.

"I'm good. How are you and the family?" she asks. Alex remembers the last time she came and spent some time in Jabar's shop. They sat for a while and exchanged stories about their families' well-being.

"My family is good, and my wife is feeling better from the last time you and I spoke," he says as he picks up the teapot and pours Alex a cup of freshly brewed Kahwah tea.

Accepting the cup of tea she says, "I'm very happy to hear she's feeling better." Then she sits down next to him behind the counter. She instantly smells the soothing aroma of cinnamon and suddenly feels relaxed.

Kahwah is a traditional tea of Afghanistan and is made of green tea leaves with cinnamon bark, saffron, and cardamom pods. Sometimes the tea is served with Kashmiri roses to give it a nice aroma. However, Jabar doesn't have any today. She can hear the large Samovar copper kettle percolate as she tastes hints of crushed almonds, honey, and sugar in the first sip.

"I've come to see that six-carat ruby you showed me and Liam the last time we were here. It was the round ruby on the long silver necklace. Do you still have it?" she asks.

"Oh, my apologies my friend. That piece was purchased," he says with a slight smile. "But I have others if you like to see them." He puts his teacup down and hurries to show Alex some nice stones.

Alex takes the magnifier and looks through some of them, realizing they aren't the same, but she still likes to look at them anyway. As she sits with him for a while longer, Jabar offers her some homemade flatbread and hummus to go along with the Kahwah tea. Alex was told by Captain Goodfellow during in-processing that if offered tea and bread, one should accept it out of respect. Alex always accepts the tea and bread because she enjoys sitting with Jabar and talking with him. It's usually only for thirty minutes since she's only there to drop off supplies and then head back to her compound for training. Her favorite thing to do on Bravo is to come to his tent, spend time with him, and hear his stories.

Taking a bit of bread and sipping her tea she asks him, "So, anything new going on?"

"Oh, my poor neighbor lost his daughters to insurgents last week," he says as he shakes his head in disgust. "Men with AK-47s came into my neighbor's house while they slept and forced the two girls into a vehicle at gunpoint."

"What…why would they do that?" Alex asks in horror fully aware of what happened to those poor girls. She doesn't say anything to Jabar about her mission and the training she goes through every day. She can't tell him that she's training to kill the Shadow, so she only says how sorry she is for his neighbor and that she hopes his daughters will be brought back to him and his wife unharmed.

After visiting with Jabar, she heads back to the SUV and sees that Tate is sitting in the driver's seat eating a Subway sandwich while the other two are leaning against the vehicle, each eating a slice of pizza.

"Hey, we got you a slice," Thompson says as he hands Alex a small to-go box with a slice of pepperoni pizza inside.

"Thanks, I'm starving," she says as she sits on the ground with her back against the tire, enjoying the slightly warm slice of pizza.

"How's Jabar? Did he tell you any more stories about girls going missing?" Cast asks as he wipes his hands on his pants to get rid of the pizza crumbs.

"Two more little girls were taken at gunpoint by that motherfucker's men," she says with disgust.

None of them respond to her comment because they know it's true. Reports of missing girls in the country are getting worse, and every time the captain gets briefed about it, he tells her. Sitting there, enjoying the last bit of crust, Alex thinks about the last time the captain briefed her on three underage girls who were taken by the Shadow's men at gunpoint using AK-47s.

"The villagers didn't see them coming," the captain said to her after she completed training with Brock and Decker the other day. "When the elders came out to confront the Shadow's men, they were shot to death and the girls were taken." She realized the captain didn't have to tell her anything. He wanted her to know that all her training was for something and to keep moving forward with it.

As they finish eating their lunch, they get in the SUV and head back to Alpha compound. This time, instead of thinking about Liam and tonight, she thinks about her talk with Jabar and the little girls being taken. She can't imagine what the parents are going through. She's also bummed about the ruby being sold to someone else, but she lets it go since there are worse things going on to worry about.

Before she knows it, Tate gets them back to Alpha safe and sound. After clearing their weapons, they each head to their assigned duties. Tate reports back to the captain while Thompson and Cast report to the security office to talk about the upcoming bazaar the compound is holding in a few days.

"Hey, don't forget about the movie tonight," Tate says to Alex and the guys as they walk away.

"Oh, shit is it Saturday already?" Alex asks before offering them a devious smile. "Sorry guys but *we* won't be going tonight, so enjoy the movie!"

"Oh…well shit!" Cast says sarcastically while smiling at her.

"Don't have too much fun," Thompson says.

As she waves her hand behind her at Thompson's comment, she no longer cares that the guys know about her and Liam. She only worries about the captain finding out. Which, apparently, he somehow already knows. Even after all this time, he still intimidates her, mainly because she's encountered men like Captain Marcs her whole life. He's the type of man that doesn't know how to take no for an answer and does whatever he can to get what he wants.

As she heads to the back building for training, she thinks about the captain knowing about her and Liam. Suddenly she gets that feeling in her stomach one gets when an elevator stops suddenly, or when riding a rollercoaster and the sudden turns make you want to vomit.

Training that day ends up being just like any other day. Brock throws her around the room until she learns not to let him, while Decker stands there from the sidelines, instructing her how to move her body. Sometimes both Brock and Decker double up and fight her at once, but today she's getting the feeling that they're taking it too easy on her and she doesn't like it.

"Hey! I know you can hit me harder than that so just DO IT!" she yells at Brock as she picks herself up off the floor. Alex doesn't want to be treated like a scared little child. When she kills the Shadow and his men, she needs to be at her best and ready for anything.

Brock looks at Decker and then back at her with a look of determination and says, "You got it. If you want full strength, then that's what you're gonna get." He rubs his hands together, ready to take her on.

"Hold up, stop!" Decker says. "We'll pick this back up tomorrow. Oh…and Alex…be ready, okay," Decker says dismissively.

At that moment, Alex hears stern footsteps coming down the narrow hallway toward her and already knows it's Captain Marcs.

Fuck. Don't look at him or he'll know about me and Liam tonight, she thinks as the captain enters the room. Now that the captain already knows about her and Liam, she's worried that he'll see her secret written all over her face.

Watching Alex put her things away, the captain looks over at Decker and asks, "Training done already?"

With a proud grin he replies, "Yes sir. She's coming along, and right on schedule too."

Captain Marcs looks over at Alex and walks slowly toward her. He notices that she refuses to look at him as he stands in front of her. *What is she hiding*? he thinks as Decker and Brock leave the room. Continuing to look at her and remembering how she danced the last time he watched her in this room, he tries to get her to look at him with her green eyes, but she still refuses.

Reaching in a paper bag he softly says, "I brought you something." Looking around the room to make sure no one is there, he hands her a black shawl with sequence patterns sewn on the edges and something that's wrapped up inside.

So now he's giving me gifts? That's just great, she thinks sarcastically as she slowly takes the gift from him and unrolls the fabric. Inside is a pair of four-inch black heels for her to wear when she dances. Looking at the shoes, she sees that they're made from black satin with an opening so that the first two toes are exposed. Then there's a small strap that ties up around each ankle for support.

He watches her expression as she looks at the shoes and says, "Try them on. I want to see how they look on you." Even though he knows about her and Liam, he's not going to let that get in the way of having her first. He wants her and any time *he* wants something, he gets it no matter the cost.

Where the fuck did he get these shoes? she asks herself as she silently obeys the captain's request. She rolls up her sweatpants to reveal her ankles and can feel him watching her do it. Ignoring him, she slips the right shoe on, affixes the ankle strap, and then repeats that on her left foot. Her toes line up, one after the other, and are painted blood red. When she stands up, she can see how the captain's looking at her like he wants to fuck her right then and there. *Just ignore him and move around in the shoes so that he can leave already*, she thinks as she follows her own advice and quickly ignores him looking at her.

Watching her slowly move her legs he asks, "How do the shoes feel? Are they good enough to dance in?"

Now he's playing games with me. Why is he looking at me like that? she thinks, feeling pissed at the fact that he knows about her and Liam and pretending like he doesn't. *He's trying to get between us and ruin what Liam and I have*, she thinks and as she decides to play along with the captain's little game.

She slowly starts rolling her sweatpants down to her hips, looks at him, and softly says, "I don't know, let me try them." She then ties her shirt in a knot to reveal her stomach and can see his eyes leave hers and goes straight to her breasts.

Mess with his head the way he's messing with you, she thinks as she slowly walks over to the CD player and puts in 'Til Tuesday's 1984 album and plays "Voices Carry."

From the start of the song, Alex closes her eyes and slowly moves her hips from side to side. She's able to spin around a couple of times without falling on the hardwood floor and catches a glimpse of the captain looking at her through the reflection of the mirror. Then she lifts both her arms and reveals her abs as she arches her back in mid-spin.

Seeing her body move in sync with the rhythm of the music makes him want to instantly fuck her on the hardwood floor. *I want her and I don't care what I have to do to get her because she's mine*, he thinks as Alex reveals her legs and stomach in front of him in mid-spin.

With her eyes closed, Alex slowly moves her hands over her sweaty body and caresses her neck down to her breasts and then down to her stomach. She knows he's watching and decides to play with his emotions even further by slowly walking over to him. "Thank you for the heels," she says softly in his ear, then leaves him there as she continues to dance.

He's watched her become more determined and confident with herself each month that goes by. He needs her to be focused on the mission and doesn't want her to be distracted by any other man, except for him, of course. *This mission is too important, and I can't fail again*, he thinks as he turns and walks toward the door.

Taking one more look back at her, he watches her long curvy hair flow and her neck arch back in perfect harmony with the music. With a slight grin, he realizes how much he wants her to himself and in that moment, he only has one thought on his mind. *Soon.*

Chapter 10
The Hard Truth

After her awkward dance session with the captain, Alex heads back to her room and starts getting ready for tonight. As she's taking a long hot shower, she goes over in her mind how tonight with Liam is going to be when he makes love to her for the first time. She closes her eyes as the hot water caresses her skin and slowly touches her naked body starting from her long neck down to her breasts. She imagines Liam's hard body on top of hers and pictures his warm, wet kisses on her mouth.

The thought of this makes her nipples hard as she starts to throb between her legs. Alex begins running her fingers down her wet body, between her thighs, and then slowly into her. As she leans her back against the wall, the hot water enters inside her with each stroke of her fingers. She pictures her and Liam's naked bodies holding each other as they kiss and make love.

As she continues pleasuring herself, her mind imagines straddling him and moving her hips back and forth. She can feel herself start to climax as she thinks about Liam's mouth and tongue caressing her nipple while thrusting himself inside her. With this final thought, she tilts her head back and lets out a slight moan before she orgasms.

As Alex walks back to her room, she can feel her body buzz with excitement. Slowly combing her hair, she looks at her wet naked body in the mirror and notices her abs are more defined from six months of training. Her arms and legs are nicely toned, along with the rest of her body. Before this deployment, she'd never looked at herself like this. She suddenly realizes how much she likes the confidence she has in herself and with that thought, she smiles at her reflection.

The sun is just starting to set, and Alex can hear the call to prayer outside her window. She can't decide if she should stay wet and naked when he comes into her room or should she have him take off her clothes one piece at a time. She thinks about it for a moment and decides to put on a black, lacy thong and a tight black t-shirt that reveals her perky nipples through it.

She waits for what seems like a long time, but he doesn't show. The sun is now completely down, and he still isn't there. Then another hour goes by and no sign of Liam. *What the fuck*, she thinks as she starts to panic, wondering where he is or if he's hurt. She paces the room back and forth in nothing but her thong and t-shirt before deciding to go see if Thompson and Cast have heard from him. She puts on a pair of sweatpants, a bra under her t-shirt, and sneakers. She then goes outside over to the next building and knocks on Thompson's door first.

Come on, Thompson. Answer, she thinks in a panic as she hears him come to the door.

"Thompson, It's me, Alex," she says slightly out of breath.

He answers the door, and it looks like he just got into bed for the night.

"Hey, man, where's Liam?" she asks.

Looking at her confused he asks, "Why? He didn't come back?"

"No! That's why I'm asking you!" she says loudly and then feels bad for yelling at him like that. She takes a deep breath before continuing and says, "I'm sorry. I'm just worried because he said he'd be back before the sun went down."

"He left on his mission this morning to drop off some personal locator beacons and was supposed to be back by now," Thompson says with concern.

"Who sent him and who did he go with?" she asks.

"Captain Marcs ordered him to go at the last minute and told Liam that he had to travel from one compound to the other to drop those PLBs off," Thompson says.

"What! Why would the captain make him do multiple missions like that? It's too dangerous," she says a little too loudly.

Many of the doors in the hallway start opening as people are come out of their rooms to see what is going on.

"Alex, I thought he told you he was going on a separate mission? Look, I'm sure he's fine. Just go back to your room, okay? He'll be back soon," Thompson says reassuringly.

Frustrated and angry, she turns and leaves down the hallway when suddenly, Captain Marcs comes in the entrance door of the building.

"What's going on? Who's yelling like that?" he asks sternly before seeing Alex coming toward him with her head down, trying to get past him through the door.

She doesn't expect to see him, so she quickly runs into her building and reaches her door. She isn't quick enough because he follows her into her room and slams the door shut.

Alex turns to see the captain standing there grinning at her as if to tell her that he sent Liam outside the wire this morning without his team.

Not thinking twice, Alex lunges at him and yells, "Where the hell is he?" at the top of her lungs.

The captain suddenly grabs both her wrists and slams her against the wall. He pins both her arms above her head and can feel how close their bodies are. The smell of her hair and the vanilla perfume on her skin makes him want her more than ever. He can feel her struggle to get out of his grip as he calmly whispers in her ear, "Shhh, it's okay, Foster." *Oh my God, she smells so good*, he thinks as he desperately wants to kiss her.

Alex can feel his mouth lightly kiss her neck and jawline and she can sense how bad he wants her from the way he's moving his body up against hers. *I can't take this, I need to get him off me*, she thinks as she continues to feel his hot breath on her neck and his attempt to kiss her on the mouth. She realizes that the only way to get him to loosen his grip on her wrists is to appease him and play his little game. She gives in and starts to lightly exhale and moan with pleasure in his ear.

Hearing her moan makes the captain move in closer to her mouth as he starts to relax his grip from her wrists.

Alex feels his grip loosen and suddenly uses the move Brock taught her in training. In one fluid motion, she releases her wrists in a quick downward movement then grabs his wrists while headbutting him on the bridge of his nose. She watches as the captain instantly falls to the floor as she quickly lands on top of him. She pins his wrists to the ground and plants her hips and legs wide so that he doesn't have room to move.

As her eyes widen in anger she yells, "Who the FUCK do you think you are coming into MY room and attacking me!"

He doesn't answer, he just stares at her, red-faced with blood running out of his nose.

She gets inches from his face and yells again, "WHERE'S LIAM!" while still pinning him to the ground.

He tries to speak but his mouth is now full of blood as he says, "Sergeant Anderson went to drop off..."

"I KNOW THAT ALREADY!" she screams. "Where...is...he... now?" she says through gritted teeth as she tightens her grip on his wrists.

"I DON'T KNOW!" he yells back with frustration. It doesn't occur to him until now how a woman her size can pin him on the ground and keep him there. Even after all her combat training, he never would've imagined being bested by her in this way. It makes no difference in his mind because he still wants her, even after this incident. *She will want me back*, he thinks as he continues to look up at her as she holds her grip.

Alex observes his expression and realizes that the captain has no idea where Liam is. She leans in, looks him in the eyes, and calmly says, "Tomorrow, I'm taking the team and we're going to all the compounds you sent Liam to. If he isn't found or if he's been hurt in any way, then you can find someone else to KILL the Shadow." She quickly gets off him, stands up, and opens the door letting him know to get the hell out of her room.

Captain Marcs lays there feeling defeated before he slowly gets up off the floor. He brushes off his clothes as he stares at her standing there by the door. *I should tell her how I feel about her*, he thinks as he confidently walks up to her and says, "You know I want you right? I think about you all the time and I can't stand the fact that you chose to be with him and not me. I've seen how far you've come in training, and I've also seen your confidence improve in your dancing. I want you, Alex, and I want you to want me back."

Jesus, is he fucking kidding me with this shit? Don't react, that's what he wants, she thinks as she doesn't react to his comments.

He tries to get her to look at him with her bright green eyes, but she doesn't say a word or look at him as she continues to wait for him to leave her room. After a few moments, he realizes that she'll not budge and scoffs at her as he wipes the blood off his nose and mouth. As he goes to leave, he leans over and whispers to her, "I hope you find him."

He hates admitting that he's jealous of Liam and hopes that she can see that he's only trying to get closer to her. In his mind, yelling at her and using reverse psychology by giving her things is his way of trying to bring her closer to him. After tonight's fight, Captain Marcs realizes that she prefers the nice guy. However, he wants her so badly he refuses to quit. He will find a way to make her truly his.

Alex slams the door behind him and lets out a gasp of air. She lays her back against the door and slides down to the floor as her elbows rest on her knees and her hands cradle her head. Realizing now that the captain is going to make her and Liam's life a living hell, she screams in frustration, "FUCK!" *He's never going to give up and take no for an answer, no matter how many times I make him bleed,* she thinks as she replays the fight in her head. Alex meant it; if Liam is hurt or not found, she isn't going to kill anyone for the captain. As far as she's concerned, Captain Marcs can go fuck himself.

After tonight, Alex has doubts about continuing her training. From the floor, she glances up at the red folder the captain had given her of the Shadow after their first meeting together. The Shadow isn't going to stop terrorizing little girls and women and she knows that it must be her that puts an end to him no matter what the captain does to her. However, she first needs to find out where Liam is.

Alex gets up, opens the door to her room, and looks out into the hallway to make sure the captain is gone. Then she walks over to Liam's door, slowly opens it, and steps inside. His room is dark and for some reason she imagines him lying on his bed waiting for her. She goes over and sits down on his empty bed and lays her head down on his pillow. She can faintly smell his scent on his pillowcase and closes her eyes, wishing he was there with her. As she lays in the dark, Alex lightly taps three times on the wall above the pillow and says, "Please come back to me." Laying in the fetal position with her arms around her knees, Alex falls asleep there, hoping that when she wakes up, Liam will be there to let her know he's okay and back with her safe and sound.

The morning call to prayer wakes her up in his bed alone. She sits up and stares at the door, hoping it was a dream and realizing that it wasn't. The early light of the sun is just coming through his window blinds, and she realizes that he didn't come back last night. Feeling frustrated, she takes in a deep breath, knowing that today is going to be long and intense.

"Come on Tate. Hurry up and get your gear on!" Alex yells because Tate is taking too long. In the meantime, Thompson is checking Cast's gear to make sure he has everything with him like his body armor, ammo for both his M9 pistol and M4 rifle, knife, gloves, helmet, sunglasses, a full canteen, MRE, or meal ready to eat, and a handheld radio that's fully charged.

"Okay, check me," Thompson says to Cast.

As the guys are getting their gear together, Alex heads into the Intel office and grabs a map to all three locations Liam went to. If they're going to find him, she has to make sure they take specific routes instead of side-tracking. Getting stuck outside the wire isn't a good thing, so Alex needs to make sure she has all the intel available.

Now that Alex has the maps and intel, she heads to the J1 office to speak with Captain Goodfellow. She lets her know that Sergeants Castillo, Tate, Thompson, and herself are leaving the compound to find Sergeant Anderson and will return before sundown.

Looking concerned, Captain Goodfellow asks, "Does Captain Marcs know of your departure?"

Smiling slightly at her while hoping she doesn't ask any more questions, Alex replies, "Yes ma'am, he's aware."

Goodfellow studies her for a moment then finally says, "Be careful out there in the shit, Sergeant. And come and see me when you return, okay?" She watches Alex walk out of the J1 office.

Alex quickly meets back up with Tate, Thompson, and Cast, who are waiting for her by the SUV.

"You guys got everything?"

"Yeah, let me check your gear while you check the radio?" Thompsons says to her.

He double-checks all her ammunition for her M9 and M4 that's strapped to her body armor. Then he makes sure her six-inch blade is sheathed to her right leg brace, her canteen is full of water, and her helmet is on her head.

"Alright, we're good to head out," Alex says as they all get into the SUV and leave the front gate.

As she gets in the front seat, she lays her M4 rifle against her right leg with the muzzle facing downward, then straps her M9 pistol on her body armor above her left breast. The fact that Alex's left eye is dominant, she fires her M9 with her left hand even though she's right-handed. By strapping her M9 to her armor, it gives her easier access to it while in the vehicle.

"Okay, first let's head to Delta compound," she says to Tate as he drives outside the wire and onto the main highway.

She notices that Tate doesn't need to look at the map since he's already familiar with every road in the city and beyond the city as well.

Alex trusts his judgment when it comes to driving in this country. If Tate says, "No, we shouldn't go this way," then we're not going that way.

"Sounds good. I can get us there in no time," Tate says with confidence.

"You guys back there keep your eyes peeled. If you see anything suspicious let me know. Oh, and everyone lock your doors," she says to them all.

It's nine in the morning and there are people and cars everywhere. The two-lane highway is covered in five lanes of cars and there are people walking alongside the road. Tate honks the horn to let the cars know to get out of the way. The last thing they need is to get ambushed in the middle of traffic.

Alex's job is to watch out for people walking beside the SUV while it's at a standstill. If Tate drives closer to the side of the road, then her job is to look out for any unusual items like trash or dead animals. During her time in combat skills training, she was taught that even a small piece of trash could be considered a bomb. On their trip to Delta compound, Alex can see trash everywhere, so she mainly focuses on bigger things like dead animals or boxes. She also looks out for potholes in the road because they can also be considered bombs. There's not a road in Afghanistan that doesn't have potholes, so she tells Tate to just look out for the bigger ones.

They finally reach Delta compound after two hours of being stuck on the highway. Tate pulls out his access badge for the guard and then parks the vehicle inside the gate.

Delta is a small compound that consists of a two-story dorm building for the contractors and military guards, a chow hall, and three buildings that hold most of the supplies for the other surrounding compounds. It has a small airfield where military planes land, drop off supplies, and then take off again. Tate and Cast usually make a run here once a month to pick up supplies that are needed for Alpha compound.

"Tate, stay with the vehicle. If you see Liam walking around, call me on the radio," Alex says. "You two head to the chow hall and see if he's in there. I'll head to the J1 office to ask if they accounted for anyone new that came onto the compound yesterday."

"Don't worry Alex. We'll find him," Tate says.

Alex branches off from Thompson and Cast and heads to the J1 office. She enters the small personnel office and asks the first sergeant if he'd seen Sergeant Liam Anderson come in yesterday to drop off some personal locator beacons.

"Yeah, he dropped them off yesterday morning and headed straight out," the first sergeant says.

Damn it, she thinks then says out loud, "Oh, okay. Thank you so much sir." Alex then heads out the door and calls Thompson and Cast on the radio.

"Head back to the vehicle and let's get over to Charlie compound," she says to them.

"Already heading back there now," Cast replies.

As she rounds the corner of the J1 office, she can see Tate, Cast, and Thompson already waiting by the SUV.

They all get back into the vehicle and head fifteen miles to Charlie compound. Alex shows Tate which route to take on the map, and he agrees that for this time of day, that route is the best way to go.

The road getting there is extremely bumpy, and from the way the noon sun hits the light they can see the smoke-filled air and pollution for miles. Alex suddenly feels nervous, like something bad may have happened to Liam. She slowly touches her lips to remember the feel of his when they kissed hers. She then closes her eyes and thinks about what she felt in the shower yesterday when he was supposed to come to her room. *Please Liam, where are you?* she thinks with concern.

"Guys, what's that?" Tate asks as he points toward the right side of the road.

Alex quickly opens her eyes and tries to focus on the spot where Tate pointed. The smoke in the air is thick and there's a slight glare on the windshield from the sun. She starts to see a large pile of garbage and something at the bottom of it that has black smoke emanating from it like it was recently burned.

As Tate slows down the SUV, Alex can see what it is and instantly puts her hand over her mouth in shock.

"Oh no," Tate says as he also notices what is burning on the side of the road.

"Keep going Tate. Don't stop. There could be a bomb inside," Alex says as she puts her hand over her nose and mouth.

"What is it?" Thompson asks while trying to catch a glimpse as Tate quickly drives past.

Alex tries to compose herself, but the image is too much. Finally, she answers Thompson and says, "It's a dead body. Someone burned what appears to be a small woman and left her on the side of the road with the trash." Alex did her best not to cry or vomit in front of the guys.

Liam where are you?

Chapter 11
Reality Check

They finally reach Charlie compound and follow the same procedure as before. Tate waits by the vehicle and makes sure the engine and tires are good to go. Thompson and Cast head to the chow hall to look for Liam, and Alex goes to the J1 office to talk to the officer in charge.

She doesn't want the guys to see her get sick from seeing the dead body, so she quickly instructs them to follow the same procedures as before and quickly leaves them. When Alex reaches the J1 office, she immediately asks where the bathroom is, finds it, and vomits. Not much comes up because she skipped breakfast that morning. However, she did let out some tears. She never thought she'd ever see anything like that in her lifetime. The image of the burned body will stick with her for the rest of her life. *I can't do this right now. I have to find him*, she thinks as she washes her face and rinses her mouth out with water.

After a few minutes composing herself, Alex goes back to the J1 office and finds where the desk clerk is sitting. She sees the sergeant reading a magazine with a bored look on his face. He doesn't even look up at her when she walks in to see what she needs. He just continues to read his magazine not caring that she's standing there, waiting for him to acknowledge her.

She patiently waits there in front of him then finally, she says, "Excuse me sir, can you tell me if a Sergeant Anderson came in here yesterday to drop off some equipment?"

After a few very long moments goes by, in a bored tone he replies, "Yeah, he dropped off the equipment and then went back to his vehicle to find out that he had a flat tire." He continues to look at the magazine and not at her. "He didn't have a spare, so *we* had to provide him one of *our* tires," he says sarcastically while still looking at the magazine.

Wow, what a little asshole, she thinks as she stares down at the sergeant.

Taking a deep breath, Alex does her best to be polite and asks, "Did he try to call anyone from his compound to let them know about this?"

Still not looking at her, he scoffs and says, "Yeah, his radio battery died too. What a fuck up."

A fuck up.... Does he think this is a joke? she thinks as she watches him casually read his magazine and not giving a care in the world about her issues. After traveling from compound to compound, seeing a dead body, and vomiting, she is not in the mood for this sergeant's attitude.

Alex reaches over, snatches the magazine out of his hand and flings it across the room. "So why didn't YOU call his compound to let them know he wasn't going to make it back in time?"

"Whoa, *Sergeant*, that's not my job! His ass got stuck here so as far as I'm concerned that's *not* my problem," the desk clerk says as he finally rises from his chair.

Quickly walking over to his side of the desk, she fiercely asks, "What the fuck did you just say to me?"

The lieutenant that's been listening to the entire conversation finally comes into the room and yells, "What's going on!" He can hear Alex yelling at his desk clerk from inside his office.

Alex composes herself and says, "Sir, I'm Sergeant Foster with the..."

"I know who you are, Sergeant Foster, and I would appreciate it if you wouldn't yell at my subordinate like that," he says as he looks at her sternly with a cup of coffee in his hand and while waiting for her to apologize.

Are you fucking kidding me right now? she thinks as she looks at the lieutenant in shock. *How does he know who I am?*

The lieutenant can see the confused look on her face and answers that look with a sarcastic reply.

"Captain Marcs called me and said that you and a few other individuals would be arriving at this compound asking about Sergeant Anderson. He also informed me to let YOU know that he expects you back RIGHT NOW or you and your team WILL be considered AWOL, that's absent without leave, in case you didn't know," he says dismissively as he nonchalantly takes a sip of coffee.

Alex's face is red from anger and embarrassment, but she knows better than to make this lieutenant angry. *Calm down. Don't show him how pissed you are*, she thinks. She takes a small breath and calmly replies, "Yes sir. My apologies for my behavior."

Studying her for a moment, the lieutenant gives her a cocky smirk then turns around and casually goes back into his office.

As Alex leaves, she turns around and flips off the desk clerk and then silently mouths the word *asshole* toward him. She can see the stupid look on his face as she closes the door behind her. *Fucking prick*, she thinks as she heads back to the SUV.

Still pissed by the way the lieutenant and his little lackey treated her, she sees Tate and the guys waiting for her there. They can see how mad she looks, and she tells them what the lieutenant said about Captain Marcs.

“What a fucking asshole,” Cast says regarding the captain’s threatening remarks.

“Seriously? He’s going to mark us AWOL because we’re looking for Liam.... What a dick,” Tate says.

“Well, that’s not the only reason,” she says as she remembers the night before when she made the captain bleed. Looking at Thompson she says, “You know Captain Marcs followed me into my room last night after I spoke with you in the hallway?”

“What the fuck! What did he do?” Cast asks out of concern.

“He fucking tried to kiss me and then told me he wanted me. I wouldn’t let him, and now he’s going to make my life a living hell.”

“Oh shit! Is that why he had a bandage over his nose this morning?” Thompson asks.

“Yeah, because I head-butted his ass for even trying that shit with me!”

“Well, damn girl,” Cast says impressed.

“Yeah, that’s what he gets. Jesus Alex, why didn’t you say anything to us about it this morning?” Tate asks.

“I was focused on finding Liam,” she says.

“Okay. We should head back before the captain sends out a search party and we all go to prison,” Cast says.

They get in their usual positions inside the SUV and head out the gate back to Alpha compound. Tate decides to take a different route so that Alex doesn’t have to see the dead body by the trash again.

“Tate, be careful and you two, keep an eye out for anything suspicious,” Alex says to Cast and Thompson sitting in the back seat.

She’s still upset about not finding Liam, but at least they know his tire had to be changed and that he had to stay the night at Charlie.

We probably passed him on the road, she thinks as she watches the cars go by on the other side.

As Tate makes his way on the outskirts of the city, he notices a few people standing in the middle of the road with a gate set up.

"Wait, there shouldn't be a guard posting here," Tate says as he looks at the three guards standing in the middle of the deserted road.

"What are you talking about?" Alex asks in a sudden panic. She can see the three Afghan guards posted at a small makeshift gate blocking the road.

The guards can see her sitting in the front seat and can tell right away that she's a woman.

"Those aren't guards," Tate says as he starts to slow down the SUV.

Alex takes a closer look at their weapons and uniforms. She remembers when she first arrived on the compound, over six months ago, and that Captain Goodfellow told her of one of the convoys that left Alpha compound and didn't come back because of men like this.

Those men would wait for single vehicles to approach and stop them at gunpoint. They would open the doors and take everything from them and leave them on the side of the road stranded. Later, Alex confirmed with Captain Marcs that those men belonged to the Shadow. Since then, she reminds herself to always lock the vehicle doors on every convoy she goes on.

"Check your doors and lock them NOW!" Alex says in a panic. She watches three guards look at the vehicle with curiosity.

Two of the guards remain standing on either side of the small gate, each holding AK-47s. Looking at the gate closing it looks like it was built out of scraps. The other guard walks over to the passenger side of the vehicle where Alex is and tries to open the door.

Alex quietly watches him with intent, not moving a muscle. She notices the dead look in his eyes that instantly gives her chills up and down her spine. Alex looks at the right side of his face, which has a long, deep scar that starts from his forehead, down the side of his right eye, and down to his cheek. Without looking away, she calmly says, "Tate, show him your badge."

Tate does as she says and slowly lifts his access badge and slightly waves it at him and the two men by the gate.

"Let us through," Tate says as he continues to wave his badge at them.

The two men don't move, while the man by Alex's window ignores Tate and stares directly at Alex with a lifeless expression in his eyes.

Fuck, she thinks as she stares back at him, trying to figure out how to get out of this situation.

The man with the scar continues to aggressively attempt to open the door while looking at her. He can't see her eyes since Alex is wearing her military-grade, polarized sunglasses, and helmet. The only things he can see are her lips and cheekbones. His eyes avert from her to the M4 that's laying on her right leg then he continues to intimidate her by trying to open the door again.

"What the fuck does he want?" Cast asks out of frustration.

"He wants my weapon and isn't going to stop until he gets what he wants. These men belong to the Shadow," Alex says calmly as she continues to stare at the man then looks him dead in the eyes.

"This motherfucker better stop or I'm going to get out of the car and fuck him up!" Cast says, pissed off and ready to go.

"NO, Cast! That's what he wants you to do, so don't do anything!" she says.

As the man continues banging on her window, Alex decides she's had enough and places her hand on her M9 and slowly removes it from the holster. Then she takes the barrel and taps the window and says, "Back the fuck off," loud enough for the man with the scar to understand.

He can't see the expression in her eyes. However, her tone makes him back away. He then motions the other two men to let them pass.

Slightly out of breath, Alex says, "Go Tate, before they change their minds." She continues to hold the M9 upright in her hand so that the men in the front of the vehicle can see it.

Tate quickly gets through the gate and hightails it out of there and back on the highway toward the compound. The vehicle swerves from side to side, kicking up dirt and rocks, leaving the three men standing there in the dust.

"Jesus Christ!" Cast says. "Alex you're one badass chick, let me tell you...Fuck!" he says again in relief.

"We're not home yet guys, so don't jinx it," she says as she closes her eyes and instantly thinks of Liam.

"Liam, please be home, please...or this was all for nothing," she says under her breath as Tate drives them back to the compound safe and sound.

Chapter 12
The Release

Tate does what he always does and drives like a maniac back to the green zone and through the front gate of Alpha compound. As Tate shows the gate guard his badge, they drive through, and Alex looks around to see if Liam is there waiting for her. Instead, she sees Captain Marcs standing there with his arms folded and glaring at the SUV with a stern look on his face.

Alex can see the captain staring at her and says, "Shit," under her breath. She's already in a bad mood from seeing the dead body, dealing with those assholes on Charlie compound, and to top it off, the fucking Shadow's men trying to ambush her team on the road. *Now I have to deal with this asshole and his bad attitude toward me and Liam*, she thinks as she gets out of the vehicle and slams the door.

As they leave the SUV and head over to the clearing barrel, she can see the captain approach her from the corner of her eye.

"So, you made it back in one piece…Good for you," the captain says sarcastically to her. He slowly walks up to her, leans in, and says in a whisper, "In my office Sergeant Foster. Now."

Feeling the pit of her stomach drop and not looking at him, she quietly responds, "Yes sir." Without looking back at the guys, she follows the captain back to his office in silence.

They both reach his office door, and the captain enters first then calmly says, "Close the door behind you." His back is turned away from her.

Shit, I don't want to deal with him right now, she thinks as she slowly closes the door. She then walks over to sit in the same chair she sat in the day he asked her to kill the Shadow.

With his back still turned he says, "No, you don't sit. You stand at attention."

Alex reluctantly does what she's told and stands at attention behind him. She doesn't say anything. She just waits for the inevitable tongue lashing he's about to give her for going to look for Liam.

Instead, the captain quickly turns and slaps Alex so hard in the face that it knocks her off balance and she falls into the chair.

"Don't EVER do that again! Do you understand me?" he says while pointing his finger at her face.

In shock with angry tears flooding her eyes, Alex sits there holding the side of her face. She can see that he also has tears in his eyes and doesn't understand why. She doesn't ask because she doesn't care about his fucking feelings. All she cares about right now is finding Liam and completing her mission with the Shadow.

Fuck, I shouldn't have slapped her like that. Just pull yourself together and fix this, he thinks as he slowly places both hands on the armrests of her chair. As he leans in closer, he can't help but want to kiss her to make up for everything he's done to her. Instead, he calmly says, "Sergeant, I can't afford to lose you after all you've done these past six months. We're so close to getting our opportunity to kill the Shadow, remember?" he says. He looks into her eyes as if to say sorry I hit you.

Just play along for now. You'll get him back later, she thinks as she slowly takes her hand away from her face where he slapped it. She looks at him and calmly says, "I understand you've invested a lot of time in training me and I know you're upset. That doesn't give you the right to hit me or stalk me or come into my room and attack me whenever you feel like it. Just because I agreed to kill the Shadow, doesn't mean you own me. I can stop now, and you would've wasted six months on me. I just have to find Liam and make sure he's okay.... He's part of this team, *your* team. I know what I need to do, and I still want to kill the Shadow, but Liam is helping me get through this and I need his support," she says as she looks at the captain intently.

Captain Marcs looks back at her for what seems like a very long time. He processes everything she said and feels bad for slapping her, but at the same time, likes how good it felt. The power he feels when he hits a woman is like nothing he's ever felt before.

She's trying to deflect the fact that I told her I wanted her last night... What is she trying to pull? he thinks as he continues to look into her eyes, studying her. All he can see now is the look of hatred she has for him for hitting her. *She'll come around. Just give her some time*, he thinks as he lets go of both armrests, stands up, and takes a deep breath.

"Sergeant Anderson came back an hour ago," he says as he looks away from her. He doesn't want her to see how jealous he is of her and Liam's relationship.

What the fuck! Liam's been back this whole time and he's just now telling me! she thinks as she leaps out of the chair and quickly runs out of his office. She runs across the compound and hurries to his room. "Liam!" she says as she slams his door open and notices his uniform on the floor, but he isn't there. She quickly goes into her room and doesn't see him in there either. *The shower!* she thinks as she runs toward the bathroom at the end of the hall and can hear one of the showers going.

Alex slowly opens the door and can see Liam in the shower, facing away from her. She takes a breath of relief, enters the steam-filled bathroom, and shuts the door.

"Hey, you," she says softly to him as she watches him turn to look at her.

Alex doesn't look at his body, just his eyes, letting him know that she's the happiest woman to see him alive. Without thinking about it, she starts to slowly take off her uniform.

Liam watches her slowly undress and enter the shower with him. He fixates on the hot water as it cascades down her face, neck, and down to her breasts. He then slowly reaches toward her and kisses her passionately as his hands caress her hard nipples. He moves his mouth from her neck, down to her clavicle, and then to her nipple. It's firm in his mouth as his tongue wraps around it with delight.

Alex closes her eyes, tilts her head back, and lets out a long breath. She slowly reaches down to feel his erection as the hot water runs through her fingers. She gently strokes him over and over as he tenderly sucks her hard, pink nipple. Her heart beats faster with every caress of his tongue and she can't wait any longer. Out of breath, she whispers, "I want you inside me."

Without saying a word, Liam slowly lifts her with his arms and places her up against the shower wall as he softly kisses her mouth again. The hot water continues to run down their bodies as he begins to slowly slip himself inside her.

Immersed in complete ecstasy, Alex tilts her head back and lets out a delightful moan as the hard pressure of him enters her again and again. Her arms and legs wrap around his body and while the water hits his back, she can feel his thrusts get harder. She reaches over and kisses him deeply as the steam envelopes their bodies.

Liam doesn't want to finish in the shower because he wants her laying on a soft bed as he pleasures her all night. "Let's go back to your room," he says out of breath, before turning off the shower. He gives her a towel and wraps himself in one as well. He swiftly picks her up in his arms, carries her into her bedroom, and then shuts the door. Liam takes her chair and props it under her doorknob so no one can disturb them.

By the time he puts her down, Alex is already naked and laying on the edge of her bed, waiting for him to make love to her again. Her hair is wet, and she still has droplets of water resting on her naked breasts. Patiently laying there, she watches him slowly take off his towel as she gazes at his muscular body then into his eyes. *He's perfect*, she thinks as he stands in front of her naked and wet.

Liam takes his time and slowly walks toward her before kneeling and whispers, "Lay back, beautiful."

Alex does what he asks and lays down on her back with her legs wide open fully revealing herself to him.

He gently places his hands on her hips and pulls her toward him then puts his lips on her inner thigh and lightly kisses her there. Droplets of water from her thigh enter his mouth as he kisses her further down, reaching between her legs. His lips and tongue begin to slip inside her, which makes Alex arch her back and moan with pleasure. He can feel how soft and wet she is as his tongue continues to caress her down there.

Alex continues to breathe hard and is on the verge of coming and with every stroke of his tongue, she feels small, delightful explosions going off inside her. Her body tingles and she can feel herself throbbing where his lips and tongue are working her. Gently caressing his hair, she lightly arches her back again as she bites the bottom of her lip. Trying her hardest not to come, she begs him to enter her again. "Liam… please," She says out of breath.

Liam complies with her plea and slowly kisses her stomach then to her breast and into her mouth. Slipping back into her, he can feel his wet body move in rhythm with hers as she wraps her legs and arms around him. Hearing her moan with satisfaction with each thrust makes him kiss her harder on the mouth. The soft and wet tightness of her below makes his hips move faster as he's on the verge of coming.

Their bodies and breath are in sync with one another, and they finally reach their inevitable climax as the large explosion of ecstasy fills within them. Out of breath and satisfied, Liam remains on top of Alex watching her as she closes her eyes and smiles lightly from what they finally did together.

He doesn't want to hold back the feelings he has for her anymore, so he says those three little words that can either make or break a relationship.

Looking into her green eyes, he says, "I love you."

Alex looks back into his eyes as she smiles up at him. *He loves me*, she thinks happily as she brings him closer to her and kisses him long and deep. She never thought she'd say those words because of how Jacob treated her and how Kyle left and moved on. Liam is different though, and she doesn't want to lose him.

"I love you more," she replies as she rolls him over onto his back and straddles him.

He watches her on top of him as her long, dark wavy hair cascades down to her bare breasts. *Don't ever let her go*, he thinks as his eyes move over her body as she moves her hair behind her to reveal her long, sensual neck. Her skin is smooth like silk and her breasts are supple and firm to his touch.

Wanting to make love to her again he whispers, "You're so beautiful."

She smiles down at him as she takes his hand and places it on the side of her face. Letting his thumb caress her bottom lip, she lets it enter her mouth as she kisses it while slowly rotating her hips. This makes him get hard again, so she slowly places him inside her while straddling him from on top. The combination of her being soft and wet with his deep and hard thrusts makes every part of her body hum with pleasure. She takes her time and arches her back while slowly rolling her hips around, then forward, and then back.

Looking up at her with passionate eyes, he gently reaches up and places his hands on her breasts and gently caresses them. He watches the dim light caress her long, slender body as she seductively moves her hips back and forth. His hands then move down to her hips as he gently moves them faster and harder. With every stroke, her moans get louder, and their breaths quicken. The sweat forms on his body as he arches his neck and lets out a moan of pleasure. He can hear her finish as well as she lays on top of him, breathless and satisfied.

"I love you so fucking much," he whispers in her ear as he holds her tight, not letting go.

All the while, on the other side of her door, is Captain Marcs. He's standing there in complete silence, listening to them make love for the second time. The reason for his visit is to apologize to Alex for slapping her. As he leans against her door, he suddenly realizes how he blew his chance with her.

Hearing them profess their love for one another makes him jealous and angry. *That's supposed to be me in there, not him*, he thinks as he slowly moves away from her door. He's never been betrayed like this by a girl, and this feeling of not getting what he wants is not what he's used to. In the past, he's had every girl obey him and finally bend at his will. *What makes her different than the rest of them? I gave her things, I trained her to fight, and this is what I get in return?* he asks himself as he slowly walks down the hall feeling angry, defeated, and alone.

Chapter 13
The Officer

Captain Tyler Marcs comes from a long generation of soldiers. His great-grandfather, grandfather, father, and older brother all served honorably in the United States Army. His older brother, Michael, a sergeant in the infantry, died in Iraq when Tyler was still in high school. His father was so proud of Michael because he continued the military line.

Tyler knew at the time the only way he could ever measure up and be better than his dead brother was to join the Army as an officer. Right after high school, Tyler got into West Point, the oldest and most prestigious academy in the U.S. Army.

All these years he suspected that he got his talents from his father. Tyler was, after all, the first generation of being an officer in the Army, and his father was incredibly pleased by this.

Tyler's mother, however, never got over Michael dying in combat in a foreign country. He remembers her sitting in her room for a month and not talking or eating. One day his father kicked the door down and slapped her repeatedly and kept screaming at her to accept the fact that their son died with honor.

That wasn't the first time his mother was beaten by his father like that. Throughout Tyler's entire childhood, when his mother wasn't obedient, his father would backhand her until her lip would bleed. Sometimes, she'd have a bruise on her eye the next day. Nevertheless, his mother always complied after her beatings and Tyler grew up thinking that's the way it was in every household. The man punished and the woman complied. This made him realize that by treating women this way, they'd have to comply with him just as his mother did with his father.

When Tyler reached high school, he fell for a girl in his class and constantly asked her to go out with him. She was reluctant, but Tyler Marcs was the star quarterback and was particularly good-looking. After a couple of dates, he tried to have sex with her, but she told him she wasn't ready. But in Tyler's mind, she was supposed to comply with anything he asked of her since that's how it's supposed to be between couples.

He didn't take no for an answer and continued to pester her, so she finally gave in with the hopes that he would leave her alone. He took her behind the school bleachers and fucked her there. Afterward, she tried to break up with him. She didn't realize how violent he was going to be with her during sex. She didn't like the things he said to her during the act either. For instance, "You like it rough, don't you?" and "From now on you belong to me." She continued to try and break it off with him, but he wouldn't let her.

Tyler constantly stalked her after school and told her, "You're mine now, so obey." It got so bad that the girl suddenly changed schools and Tyler never saw her again. He gained a reputation that superseded Michael's. Tyler was known for getting what he wanted and when he wanted it. He took after his father, and according to the guy that was supposed to become the star quarterback, Tyler caught him smoking weed behind the bleachers and ratted him out to the coach and principal. The guy was expelled, and the position of quarterback was given to Tyler.

Throughout the remainder of his high school days, Tyler was also known for taking pretty girls away from their boyfriends. He would seduce them by giving them gifts and then persuade them to have sex with him. The girls never stayed with him long because when they had sex, he would sometimes slap them as they fucked and say things like, "You're my dirty, little secret."

There were also rumors that he would choke them while he was on top and then tell them, "If you say anything to anyone about this, I'll tell them you're lying. Nobody will believe you anyway." This behavior was as normal to him as putting on his shoes in the morning.

Tyler was not a team player either but still managed to get on the principal and coach's good side. He was the type of guy who would play hard and get wins for the school record. This made him unstoppable but also hated by the rest of the team. His grades were phenomenal as well since his goal was to become an officer who graduated from West Point. To do that he had to get top grades and be part of any type of sports or school activity to show that he was a well-rounded guy.

When he graduated from high school with full honors, his father was so proud. It didn't take long for Tyler to get accepted to West Point and he was off to start the next chapter of his life.

His time at West Point flew by. Tyler never received any type of punishment for being late like many of his classmates, and he didn't waste time making friends either. According to him, everyone there was competition, and he wasn't going to let any of them get in his way.

Tyler kept himself busy not only with his academics but also with playing sports. He was part of the soccer and lacrosse teams and was a natural-born leader. The only thing he missed during his time at West Point was fucking girls. There weren't any girls there, which to him, may have been a good thing since girls were a distraction. *Plenty of time to fuck girls when you're an officer*, he thought as he graduated from West Point.

He was then sent to infantry school to learn how to be an infantry platoon leader. Tyler excelled in every category, and when he completed his training at Fort Benning in Georgia, he received his first tour to Afghanistan as a lieutenant.

His leadership allowed him to lead a small tactical unit that consisted of a communications specialist, a medical specialist, and two demolition and weapons specialists. The team's objective was mainly focused on the drug problem that plagued the country. Close to two hundred thousand Afghan women and children were addicted to drugs in the year 2005 alone.

It was Lieutenant Marcs' job to get his team to infiltrate the coca and opium farmers to get information on who was distributing the drugs to the United States and the rest of the world. They would leave the compound in the middle of the night, dressed in black, and drive to the villages that produced these drugs. Their missions were top secret and were not to be discussed with anyone outside the need-to-know basis.

On one of the missions, Lieutenant Marcs positioned each member of his team on the four corners of one of the poppy fields. They were to signal to each other when the area was clear and listen to the guards talk about timelines and drop points. The lieutenant didn't recognize those particular guards that night because they wore different uniforms and carried AK-47s. *Where did they get those weapons?* he thought as he watched one of the guards smoke a cigarette.

When it was time to quietly head out, Lieutenant Marcs' team was short one person. His communications specialist, his only female soldier, was captured by one of the Afghan guards that patrolled the area. The team found her body three days later with a video recording taped to her bare chest. The lieutenant watched the tape of her being brutally raped, tortured, and then violently eaten by dogs. He had never seen such evil and to see his team member tortured in such a way changed his view on why he was there in Afghanistan.

Her name was Sergeant Julia Walker, and she had a husband and daughter back home in upstate New York. She wasn't very pretty and not the lieutenant's type. However, he trusted her enough to be part of his team. When Lieutenant Marcs personally cleaned out her room, he found a picture of her little girl on her nightstand. She may have been six or seven years old with long, curly blonde hair and little pink barrettes on each side. She was missing her front tooth as she smiled in the picture.

Those sons of bitches are going to pay, he thought as he stared at the picture for the longest time. He wondered how he was going to give his condolences to her family after what happened to her. Lieutenant Marcs put the picture of Walker's little girl in his pocket and continued to put all her possessions in a small box to be sent home to her family. He always carried the little girl's picture as a reminder of the evil in the world, and he wanted nothing more than to find the men who did this and make them suffer.

Lieutenant Marcs asked the locals around the compound who would rape and torture women this way. They were reluctant to tell him what they knew, but as soon as he mentioned the dogs, they told him of a man named Asim Barzan Majid, the man also known as the Shadow. He was told of many accounts of what the Shadow was capable of and how nobody would dare challenge him for fear of their families being murdered.

Lieutenant Marcs asked his command to see if he could do another tour in the country. He wanted to catch the motherfucker who was responsible for the rape and murder of one of his team members. His tour was almost done there and since he'd lost one of his team members, they felt that it was time for him to return to the U.S. and continue to lead from home. This made him angry because he wanted to find out more about this Shadow who the locals spoke of. He wanted to make this man pay for what he did to Sergeant Walker, but it was mainly about the Shadow making him look like a failure.

His last couple of months there were spent gathering information on Asim and his dealings with the political climate, drug smuggling, and human trafficking. He wasn't going to stop until this mad man was found and paid for his crimes.

By the time he received enough information, his tour was over and no matter how much he pleaded with the higher-ups, they wouldn't listen to him. He felt defeated but knew that this was just the beginning. He knew that one day he would return with a new team, outsmart the Shadow, and finally give the mad man what he deserved.

Chapter 14
The Gift

Alex and Liam made love three more times that night. At early dawn, Liam wakes up and finds that he's never felt this happy in his life. He lays on his side as Alex faces him and watches her sleep. He watches her as she breathes in slowly then lightly exhales while making a cute grunting sound. Liam observes as the light from the dawn warmly caresses the curves of her hips and breasts.

He thought that his high school girlfriend, April, would be the only love of his life. That was a long time ago and she had her reasons for breaking up with him after he joined the Army. April was always in his thoughts as the years went by, but with time she faded away. When Liam met Alex for the first time at the airport, it was like he was hit with a bolt of lightning. He's seen how Alex is stronger-willed than April could ever be, and he loves the fact that she faces her fears and isn't afraid to open up to him.

Liam lightly reaches over and gently kisses her soft lips. As she continues to sleep, he starts to run his finger from her shoulder, down her arm, and toward her hip. Watching her move slightly he continues to run his finger down her thigh and then between her legs. He places his fingers between her thighs and slowly starts to gently move them inside of her. Massaging her over and over, she moans with pleasure in her sleep as he places his mouth on her exposed pink nipple as he continues to massage her below.

She gets wetter with every gentle stroke, and with her eyes still closed, she slowly arches her back and bites her lower lip. Breathing harder, Liam pleasures her out of her sleep and she can feel his lips move down her body to where his fingers are working her. She feels his warm, wet tongue enter her softly. Alex has never been woken up this way and the feeling she has is indescribable. She slowly moves her hips back and forth in unison with every stroke his tongue makes. She lightly caresses his hair as she tilts her head back moaning passionately. Feeling those little explosions within her she lets out a hushed moan and finally comes. In overwhelming ecstasy and complete bliss, she looks down and sees Liam look up at her from between her legs with smoldering eyes and a satisfied grin.

"Good morning, beautiful," he whispers.

With her body still tingling she replies, "Morning." She lays there smiling from having the best sex she's ever had in her life.

Kissing her lightly on the neck he says, "I brought you something. Wait here." He gets out of bed, puts the towel around his waist and heads to his room next door.

Slightly surprised, Alex lays up on her elbow while crossing her long legs and waits patiently for him to get back. When he does, she watches his strong, naked body from the reflection of the mirror on the wall. The reflection of the light softly hits his muscular arms and back which makes her want him again. *I'm so lucky he's in my life. Please don't ever leave me Liam*, she thinks as she sees him holding a small wooden box in his hand.

Holding his hand out for her to take, he says, "Come here, and stand in front of the mirror."

Smiling, she rushes out of bed and stands in front of the full-length mirror as he remains behind her.

Liam places his lips toward her ear and lightly whispers, "Lift up your hair," then softly kisses the side of her neck.

Alex complies and slowly gathers her hair and holds it up over her head with one hand.

He opens the box and places a long silver necklace with a round, six-carat ruby around her neck. He watches as it falls and hangs perfectly between her bare breasts. He then softly kisses her neck again as Alex caresses the ruby with her fingers in awe of how stunning it is. The red color is deep and looks splendid with her complexion. The facets of the stone make the light reflecting in the mirror sparkle and dance.

"Happy birthday, Alex," he whispers softly in her ear while caressing her body. "I love you so much," he says as she turns, places her hands on his face, and kisses him.

The ruby he gave her was the same one that Alex asked Jabar about the day before. Liam knew it was her birthday even though she didn't tell anyone, and he knew that she liked the ruby because he was there with her when she first saw it.

Alex continues to kiss him passionately as she wraps her arms around his shoulders.

Liam can feel her warm tongue wrap around his as he gently lifts her, places her against the wall, and makes love to her.

They can hear the man singing the call to prayer on the loudspeaker in the middle of the city, which means it's almost time to go to training and start the day.

During her training with Brock and Decker, Alex only thinks about the amazing night she had with Liam and the incredible way he woke her up that morning. She starts to blush at the thought of it and quickly runs to the bathroom to wash her face with cold water. She doesn't want Decker or Brock to see her like that because they will come up with a way to punish her for not paying attention.

Studying her demeanor, Brock circles around her on the mat and asks, "How are you feeling this morning, Foster?"

With a quick smirk, she answers, "Good…good," in a tone that suggests she isn't going to let him ruin her day.

He catches on and tries to distract her as he quickly lunges at her low and straight.

Alex sees him coming and moves so quickly that Brock fumbles a little due to his size. She scoffs at this as she moves from left to right, light-footed, and aware of his presence. She knows what he's trying to do and waits for the right moment. Alex also makes sure that Decker is in her peripheral vision because he too is a sneaky one.

Brock tries again to sweep her leg to make her fall, but Alex quickly jumps over his leg and elbows him in the back of the head. He falls to the ground onto his stomach and Alex jumps on his back and wraps her right arm around his neck. She then places her left arm under his left armpit and wraps it around to connect to her right arm.

Brock isn't getting out of this headlock because both of her arms are securely locked together. He foolishly rolls on his back thinking that his weight will crush her, and Alex counts on this mistake.

She knows that she only needs to stay in that position for a short time because he's already starting to run out of air. She also knows that his vision will start to close in, and panic will soon follow. All she needs to do is wait for either his arms to go limp from passing out or for him to tap out in defeat.

"Shhh, go to sleep Brock. You know you want to," she says, taunting him. "You're starting to panic about now, so just give up," she continues, speaking in his ear as calm as ever.

Brock holds on for as long as he can, and finally taps the floor.

Alex lets him go and gets up quickly. She looks down at him as he sits there catching his breath.

Red-faced and with beads of sweat rolling down his forehead, he says, "Fuck!" with exhaustion in his voice. He reluctantly looks up at her as she stands there, arms folded, while looking down at him in silence. He's been standing in her position for over six months and now it's *her* standing over *him*.

"Good job, Foster," he says with defeat, but he's also proud of how far she's come.

Alex spends the rest of the session practicing her moves on the mat when she sees Tate coming quickly into the room. It looks like he's just run over from across the compound.

"Hey Alex, the captain wants to see you in his office," he says out of breath.

"What for?"

"He didn't say. He just told me to come get you right away and report to his office."

What the fuck does he want now? she thinks as she looks at Decker and Brock. They both have a look like they don't know what is going on. She knows this isn't going to be a quick meeting, so she tells the guys that she'll see them tomorrow for training and leaves.

Alex is sweating and her hair is in a ponytail that hangs well below her bra strap. Her shirt is soaked with sweat, so she changes into a fresh shirt before going to his office. Dreading to go see him, she takes her time and walks slowly to his office.

She reaches his office door and reluctantly knocks two times. *He better make this quick*, she thinks to herself wondering if he just got new intel on the Shadow.

"Come in," he says in a tone he reserves only for her.

I don't want to be here right now, she thinks as she opens the door and sees Captain Marcs sitting behind his desk with a slight playful grin on his face. This makes her nervous because she remembers the conversation they had the day before in his office.

"Sit down, Alex. I want to talk to you," he says calmly with that grin still on his face. "So, how was your night? Did you sleep well?" he asks as he pauses to see her reaction. "I came to your door last night to apologize to you, but you were…let's just say you were preoccupied."

Oh my God, he heard us…shit! she thinks as she sits there frozen and afraid to say anything. She feels like the captain can read her thoughts because of his icy stare. Suddenly, flashes of Liam's face come over her and she can feel his tongue inside her mouth and his hands caress her body. Little did she know that the captain heard them make love last night from the other side of her door.

The captain looks at her with that playful grin and says, "I wanted to be the one to tell you that Sergeant Anderson is gone. He's been placed on another compound for the remainder of his time here in the country. When his time is up, he will be flown back to the States to rejoin his unit. I'm afraid you will have to continue to train without his presence," he says with great satisfaction in his voice. *Now she's mine*, he thinks as he watches her reaction to the news.

Alex sits there in silence as her eyes begin to fill with hot tears. She wants to scream out loud in frustration but refuses to give him the satisfaction. She doesn't let her tears fall either; she just continues to stare at him with a blank expression on her face. *Don't give him the satisfaction*, she thinks. The pit of her stomach suddenly feels like a brick is sitting in it. She doesn't want to believe this is happening but at the same time is not surprised by the captain's actions. It was only a matter of time before he decided to get rid of Liam.

Alex never had someone like Liam in her whole miserable life. He was everything to her and now he's been taken away by a jealous man she refused. *I'm going to make him pay.*

"I hope you understand that I'm only doing this because I need you to be focused on the mission. You're so close, Alex, to achieving the greatest accomplishment you may ever have in your life," he says in a fake, compassionate voice.

At this comment, she refuses to look at him. All she can think about is the fury and hate in her heart toward him. The captain managed to rip the only thing here that makes her feel safe. Alex quickly composes herself and looks at the captain, who's been watching her reaction the entire time. *I want to rip that fucking grin off his face*, she thinks.

Finally, she looks at him and calmly says, "I understand."

Alex leaves the captain's office and runs to Liam's room with tears falling down her face. She swings his door open and finds that all his things are gone. Breathing hard and crying, her body falls to the floor. Sitting there for what seems like the longest time, she thinks of how she can get in touch with him. *There has to be a way to find out where he is*, she thinks as she realizes that Afghanistan is a huge country with many compounds. She feels this will be an impossible task but needs to try. Somehow, she must find him.

After taking some time to calm down, she slowly gets up, leaves his room, and goes into hers. Alex slowly shuts her door and stands there in silence for a while looking over to the bed where they had an amazing night together. Then she looks over to the wall where he gently lifted her and made love to her there that morning.

Closing her eyes, she feels tired, frustrated, lonely, and broken—like a piece of her has suddenly disappeared. The room is quiet and still, and all she wants to do is fall asleep and not wake up until Liam is found and back in her arms.

She slowly walks over to her bed and sits on the floor with her back leaning against the metal frame. On the edge of her nightstand lays the red folder containing the gruesome photographs the captain had given her so many months ago.

Alex realizes that Liam is no longer going to be there for her on the bad days of training or when the captain gives her a hard time. She's no longer going to ride with him on those convoy missions to the other compounds where they'd spent time with the local vendors and each other.

I can't do this alone, she thinks as she grabs the red folder and opens it to see the dead girls once more and the Shadow's sick, determined face staring back at her. Her head begins to spin, and the voices whirl around and echo from within her mind.

As the echoes in her mind grow louder, she sees Liam's face as he says, "*You can do this Alex. I'll be with you every step of the way.*" Then the captain's face appears and says, "*Don't you want to kill the Shadow? I'm only doing this for your own good.*" Then her father's face as he screams to her, "*You worthless piece of shit!*"

Alex can't take it anymore and places her hands on either side of her head and screams, "STOP!" Her voice vibrates loudly off her walls as she suddenly feels helpless and alone. *I can't do this anymore*, she thinks. As she gets up, the photos of the dead girls and the Shadow scatter all over the floor.

She can see the mangled and distorted bodies of all the girls in the photos and starts to break down crying. She cries so hard that she loses her breath and slowly falls back down to the floor. She sits there near the edge of her bed for a few moments to compose herself.

Suddenly, the afternoon sun comes through her blinds and a beam of light catches her eye. It reflects off the ruby Liam gave her that morning. She watches as the sunlight penetrates the deep red stone.

It glares back, giving her a warm feeling and a sense of clarity, as if a blanket was placed on her. She instantly felt at ease and crawls over to the necklace, picks it up, and holds it in her hand.

Alex holds the ruby in front of her and lets it swing back and forth, watching as the light reflects through it. The stone is round and about the size of the nail on her pinky finger. It's a deep red color and she remembers how it looked between her bare breasts when Liam slipped it around her neck.

She closes her eyes and smiles lightly as she holds it to her heart. She can feel Liam caress her body even though he isn't there with her. At that moment, Alex decides that she needs to make the captain pay for the game he played with her and Liam. She may have started out as a quiet, mousy little girl when she arrived, but after being here and doing everything she's done, it has turned her into a confident, badass bitch. She is going to see Liam again, get revenge on the captain, and kill the Shadow. It's going to take everything in her to complete the task, but she is determined to do it all.

Alex holds the ruby up once more in front of her and looks at it with determination and confidence. This makes her smile because she's not going to let a man like Captain Marcs get under her skin ever again.

But how will I get back at him? she asks herself. Alex knows that the captain wants her, so she's going to have to use that knowledge to her advantage. She's going to make him feel like he has a chance to be with her and then take it all away, leaving him helpless and broken. She's going to seduce him so badly that he won't be able to contain himself around her. Alex wonders how she's going to pull this off without giving herself away. She knows he's a sneaky son of a bitch, so she needs to make sure to play this right.

Alex remembers when Captain Marcs watched her dance for the first time. *That was it. That was the moment,* she tells herself. Alex needs to make sure she continues to practice her dance moves but in her room this time. She plans to find a way to lure him to her room and dance for him where no one can see so that she can make her move.

First, she needs to find something seductive to wear, which is going to be hard to find in this country. She already has the shoes the captain gave her, and God only knows where he found them. But after only a few minutes, she knows exactly who to ask for something unique to wear for this dance: Farid.

Farid is a local who comes on the compound to help the team get intel on the Shadow. He too wants the Shadow killed for what had happened to his daughter, Afia. The Shadow kidnapped Farid's daughter along with many other little girls in the city. Afia was only twelve when she was taken and was never seen again. Farid vowed that he would do anything he could to bring the Shadow down, even if that meant getting killed for helping the Americans.

Alex is still sitting on the floor, resting against her bed frame, and thinking about her plan to seduce the captain. She finally gets up, cleans her face from when she was crying, and leaves her room to find Tate and the guys.

She finds Tate sitting alone at the picnic table, eating a sandwich before his next mission outside the wire.

"Tate!" she says as she runs up to him and sits down at the table.

"Hey Alex. Sorry to hear about Liam. That's so fucked up of the captain to pull that bullshit," Tate says with his mouth full of his turkey and swiss cheese sandwich.

"That's what I wanted to talk to you about. Do you know where Liam was sent to? Can you use your radio and call over to all the other compounds to see if anyone there had seen him?" she asks hoping that Tate can find out.

He nods his head as he eats the sandwich and replies, "Already on it, and so is Thompson and Cast. Don't worry. We'll find out where he is and find a way for the two of you to talk," he says as his dimples come out from smirking at her.

Alex closes her eyes and takes in a breath of relief. "You're the best Tate. And when you see the other two, tell them they're awesome for having my back."

"Yeah, the captain's an asshole for doing that to you guys," he says.

She smiles at him in a way that makes her feel like he's the younger brother she never had.

"Yeah, don't worry. The captain will get what he deserves," she says to him. "Speaking of which, have you seen Farid around the compound? I need him to get something for me."

"The last time I saw him was just a few minutes ago briefing the captain on the new intel on the Shadow," Tate says.

"Good, I'll head up there now and thanks again for helping me find out where Liam is," she says and walks to the captain's office.

Alex doesn't care that she has to look at the captain's face again today after giving her the bad news about Liam. She approaches his office door and can hear him and Farid talking. She can't make out what they're saying however, she can pick out the words shadow and eclipse.

After waiting for a few moments, she knocks lightly on the door and hears someone approach. As the door opens slightly, she sees Farid's face through the crack.

"Hey, Farid! How are you?" Alex says in a cheerful tone. She's still hurting on the inside about Liam being gone, but she tells herself to put those feelings aside and deal with the captain. *Just act normal.*

Don't show the captain you're hurting, she thinks as she sees the captain standing behind his desk.

"Alexandra," Farid says in his thick accent. "How are you, my friend?"

"I'm wonderful, Farid," she says smiling while looking straight at the captain.

The captain can see that she isn't sulking or upset about the bad news he gave her earlier. *Good. She needs to get over him*, he thinks as he watches her smile at him and Farid.

It's working. Just keep smiling and get this meeting over with, she thinks as she tries her best to keep from reaching over the desk and throat punching the asshole.

"Farid and I were just going over the intel he found out about the Shadow," the captain says to her with optimism in his voice. He needs Alex to be on board with this and forget about Liam.

"Okay so, what do we got?" she asks with the same optimism in her voice as his.

"He will be having a lavish party on the day of the total solar eclipse, which is to happen a month from now," Farid says. "It is known that the Shadow has requested that an exotic dancer be present during the exact moment the eclipse happens," he says as he looks at her.

"That's where you come in Alex. Do you think you're ready for this?" the captain asks with a slight grin.

Did he just call me Alex? The nerve of this son of a bitch, she thinks as she looks at him and smiles. That makes her want to punch that grin off his face. "Oh, yes and I can't wait," she says as she gives him a grin back while thinking, *You poor bastard.*

Chapter 15
The Bazaar

After leaving the captain's office, Alex catches up with Farid outside.

"Hey, Farid, can I talk to you really quick?" she asks as he's about to head back out the gate to go home for the night. She pulls him away from prying eyes to the side of one of the buildings.

"I need something to wear for when I go to the palace on the day of the eclipse," she says.

"Yes, my friend. I am having something made special for you that would entice the devil himself," Farid says with enthusiasm in his voice. "I will bring it to the safe house along with jewels and makeup for your eyes as well. You *must* look perfect!" He says as he raises his chin and hands in the air.

Farid always brightens up her day when they talk, and he always talks about his wife, Fatemah, who's an artist. She paints and is going to help Alex get ready at the safe house on the day of the eclipse.

"Yes, thank you very much for helping me with this," she replies.

"No, no, no, my friend, please. I thank you very much for bringing justice to all the women who have suffered at the hands of that madman," Farid says. He gently lifts Alex's right hand and lightly kisses it, then places his right hand over his heart. "Salam Alaikum," he says.

"Walaikum Al-Salam," Alex responds, also placing her right hand over her heart. Liam taught her how to say that the day Hamid's wife gave Liam his patch.

Farid suddenly feels impressed by her response and smiles proudly at her as if she were his own daughter. "When I come back, I will bring my wife, Fatemah. She is an artist," he says with enthusiasm in his voice.

"I would love to meet her Farid. Thank you," she replies.

"Oh yes, Fatemah will make your eyes look more beautiful than the rising sun," he says as his hands reach toward the sky.

Alex watches him and wonders how he can be so positive with so much negativity around him. Farid risks his life every day to find information on the Shadow for her. He's a true hero in her eyes and she knows that he will stop at nothing to make sure the Shadow is brought to justice and in this country, justice means death.

The afternoon is gone, and everyone is getting ready for the bazaar. Thompson and Cast are going over the security for the vendors entering the compound. Their job is to make sure everything is checked on the vendor's person, their merchandise, and their vehicles.

Alex loves when the bazaar comes onto Alpha compound. Many of her favorite vendors come, including Jabar. Some vendors bring in Persian rugs and colorful blankets that have intricate stitching and others bring handmade trinkets. Alex mainly loves when Fin, the combat working dog, comes. She always gives Fin some beef jerky that she carries in her cargo pocket.

He's a short-haired German Shepard and wears a bulletproof vest with his unit patches and name tag. Fin's job is to sniff for bombs or other explosive devices. His handler, Sergeant Jackson, walks with Fin as he sniffs all the merchandise and the vehicles. Alex can only spend time with Fin after he is done working. When he comes onto the compound, Alex makes sure she's hidden from his sight so that he can do his job. She doesn't want him to break his focus because if Fin sees her, he knows it's beef jerky time.

Fin does his job and goes through and sniffs all the rugs, blankets, and boxes. There are boxes of bootleg DVDs and more boxes of small wooden figures that are hand-carved that he checks. Many of the vendors do their best to stay clear of Fin while he's working. It could be because they don't want to look suspicious in case they did have something hidden in their merchandise or it could be that they are afraid of dogs.

The bazaar turns out to be a success. There are many Afghan painters selling their artwork and are truly talented. The Persian rugs have elaborate designs and when Alex runs her hand across them, they are as smooth as silk.

She tries not to think about Liam while perusing all the items on display. They usually did that together and with him not being there, she starts to feel alone. She remembers how Liam would always mess around and wrap an Afghan scarf around his waist and model it for her to make her laugh.

Through the crowd, Jabar sees Alex and waves his hand for her to go to him.

"Hello Alexandra, my friend," Jabar says happily to her. "I have something for you."

Jabar reaches into his pocket and takes out an envelope with a handwritten note inside.

She takes out the note, unfolds it, and notices it's from Liam.

"Why is he not here with you?" Jabar asks.

"He was sent to another compound for the rest of his time in-country. How did he give this to you? Is he there on your compound?" she asks quickly.

"I do not know. He came into my shop and asked me to give this to you tonight," he says.

"Thank you so much Jabar," she says sadly while holding the note.

Jabar looks at her then smiles. "Do you like the ruby, Alexandra?"

Preoccupied with her thoughts of Liam and the note she says, "Oh, yes, of course I love it!"

Jabar can see the sadness in her eyes. "Do not worry my friend, you will see him again. I promise you," he says with complete surety in his voice.

Alex smiles at Jabar and quickly leaves him to go around the corner of the building so that no one can see her read Liam's note. She opens the note slowly and starts to read it as her eyes fill with tears.

"Alex, I know this sucks, and I wish the captain wasn't such an asshole, but at least I wasn't sent back home. I'm at Charlie compound, which means I can still see you when we're out doing missions. I got you something, so after you read this, go see Cast. If you get the feeling that you need me there with you, I want you to hold the ruby in your hand, close your eyes, and think about my hands caressing you, me kissing your lips, and most of all, the time we spent together in bed. I love you Alex, with all my heart, and soul and when we make it out of this country, we're going to have all the time in the world to be together."

She finishes reading the note and holds it in her hand as she leans her back against the building. The tears don't fall but she has a slight grin on her face from what she read. She pictures in her mind what Liam wrote in the letter, and it suddenly makes her blush. The note is short, but it lets her know that he's thinking of her and that he's going to be able to communicate with her daily. *I need to find Cast.*

The bazaar is quickly coming to an end and many of the vendors are starting to pack up the unsold merchandise and head back to their beat-up trucks and vehicles. Alex suddenly stops by to see Fin before he goes back to Echo compound and to his kennel with the other dogs. She talks with the dog handler first, who she thinks may like her since he always flirts with her a little every time he comes.

It's harmless flirting that he does with her, and she acts like she doesn't notice because she doesn't want to ruin not being able to see Fin again. Fin comes up and sniffs Alex's hand like always just waiting for that tasty treat.

She sits on the ground, cross-legged, and lets Fin lay his body on her legs while she pets him. The dog handler, Sergeant Jackson, says that Fin only does this with Alex, but she thinks the sergeant is just saying that.

Alex can see Cast watching her as he leans up against the building. He gives her the look that says he has something for her and puts his hand on his right-side cargo pocket to show her where it is.

"Okay, Fin. It's time for me to go," she says while getting up off the ground. "Is it snack time?" she asks as she reaches into her pocket.

Fin goes nuts because he knows what's in her pocket. He starts twirling around and panting as drool comes out the side of his mouth.

Alex holds out a long piece of beef jerky and Fin gently takes it out of her hand. Most dogs would snatch it, but Fin is well trained and knows how to be polite.

"Good boy, Fin," she says while petting him on his back as he eats the jerky.

"He likes you," Sergeant Jackson says, giving her that look he always gives her when he comes to each bazaar. It's a look that says, I like you and I want to get to know you.

"Thanks, I'll see you both at the next bazaar," she says to Sergeant Jackson, kindly dismissing his look as she walks off to see what Cast has for her.

"Yeah, see you later Foster," he says as he watches her walk away.

Alex approaches Cast with the note in her hand. He can see on her face that she read it and wants to know what he has for her.

"Not here. Let's head to the back building where no one can see us," he says to her quietly.

They both reach the back of the building where they usually play cards and watch movies and of course where Alex trains every day. It's dark back there and no one is around.

"Cast, please tell me you got what I think you got," she says hoping she's right.

Cast reaches into his side cargo pocket and pulls out a disposable cell phone with a card to load minutes on it. "Girl, I'm risking a lot to give this to you," he says. "You and Liam both owe me." He hands her the phone and card while rolling his eyes sarcastically with a grin on his face.

"Thank you so much, Cast!" she says like a schoolgirl.

"Here is his number. Now, don't run those minutes out because it's hard to get those cards too. This card has about sixty minutes on it, so don't waste them, okay?" he says.

"I'll do my best, man," she replies while reading the back of the card on how to put the minutes on the phone.

She goes to the side of the building where no one can see, types in the code to put the minutes on the phone, then dials Liam's number. Within the first couple of rings, he answers.

"Hey beautiful," Liam says, already knowing it's her on the other end.

"Hey baby," she replies, happy to hear his voice.

"I can't believe that asshole is doing this to us."

"Shhh, don't waste our minutes on talking about him okay. Besides, I want to talk about that note you wrote me," she says in a sexy voice.

"Oh, you liked that, didn't you," he says in a sexy voice back to her. "Well, when I see you again, I'll put those words to action."

Alex starts to remember the feeling she felt when Liam woke her up that day and when he gave her the ruby. "Baby, I would love nothing more," she says smiling.

"Alex, come on. Let's go before the chow hall closes," Cast says with frustration.

"Okay, just a minute," Alex yells back at Cast who's twenty feet away trying to give her some privacy.

"Baby, I'm going to say goodnight and talk with you tomorrow," she says.

"Okay. Sweet dreams and tell the guys I said hey. Talk to you tomorrow. I love you," he says.

"I love you more," she says and then hangs up the phone.

"Come on. Let's go get some food. Thompson and Tate should be done checking out all the vendors by now. Plus, I'm fucking starving," Cast says.

“You’re *always* hungry. How many times do you eat a day, man?” she asks laughing. The phone put her back in a good mood. She just needs to make sure the captain doesn’t see it, or he will get suspicious and take it away.

“Girl, you see these guns, right? I gotta keep eating to fuel these babies,” he says while flexing his big arms and chest.

“Oh my god, you’re crazy,” she says with a slight grin as they reach the chow hall.

When they walk in they can see that Tate and Thompson are already sitting at a table with their food.

“Well, shit. You guys couldn’t wait for us, huh?” Cast says annoyed.

“Don’t mind him. He’s just hungry from not being able to eat within the last hour,” Alex says, smiling as she tries to push Cast aside. She has a hard time moving him since the guy weighs a ton.

Alex doesn’t want to admit it, but she is hungry too. With training all morning and dealing with the bazaar all afternoon, she didn’t eat all day. Besides, she isn’t thinking about food. All she can think about is Liam and that note.

“Alex? Where are you right now,” Tate says, smiling at her. He knows exactly where her mind is as he laughs out loud. “Busted!” he says as he points at her face.

“Shut up, Tate,” Alex says as she throws a French fry from her plate at him.

“No seriously. We were talking earlier, and it’s fucked up that the captain would send one of our own to that shitty compound. Why would he do that?” Tate asks.

Alex looks at Tate with an are you serious? look on her face. “Come on man. You know why. The captain is jealous of me and Liam, and he's been trying so hard to come onto me the whole time I've been here," she says, annoyed at the whole situation. "Don't worry, like I told you earlier, he's going to get what he deserves."

"Be careful, Alex," Thompson says in his older brotherly tone he reserves only for her. "Don't mess too much with that one because you know the type. If they don't get what they want, they'll do whatever it takes to get it."

Alex watches Thompson for a minute while taking in the advice he gave her about the captain. Then she grins at him. "Thompson, you got my back, right?" she asks while leaning into the table toward him.

"Of course," he says slowly. "We all do." They all nod while looking at her in agreement.

She turns toward Cast and gives him that same grin as before and asks, "Where did you find the phone? The only reason I ask is because now I'm going to need something else…a video camera."

Chapter 16
The New Guy

Arriving at Charlie compound, Liam stands by as the driver opens the back of the SUV for him to grab his bags. Feeling pissed off and angry at the situation, Liam takes longer to get his bags out of the vehicle.

The driver suddenly gets impatient, reaches in, and starts grabbing and throwing Liam's stuff to the ground.

"I don't have all day to fucking wait for you to get your shit," the sergeant says as he gets back in the SUV and speeds off leaving Liam there in the dust.

As he stands there, speechless and looking around the compound, he thinks about the last time he was here the day he got the flat tire.

This fucking shitty ass place, he thinks as he slowly starts to pick up his bags and head to the J1 office to report in. As Liam walks into the office, he sees the same desk clerk who gave him a hard time the last time he was there.

The desk sergeant's feet are resting on his desk as he's leaning back in his chair, reading a magazine. He takes one look at Liam from the side of his magazine and rolls his eyes in disapproval. *This fucking guy again?* he thinks as he looks at Liam like he's wasting his time.

"Lieutenant…Sergeant Anderson is here to report," he says sarcastically while still looking at Liam with disdain. He remembers the day Alex came to his office and threw his magazine across the room because she was looking for Liam.

"Send him in," the lieutenant says with a stern but also with an *I don't give a fuck* tone in his voice.

What the fuck am I doing here? Liam thinks as he passes by the rude desk clerk and stands in front of the lieutenant's open door. Even though Liam can see the lieutenant sitting there, he still knocks once to announce his presence.

The lieutenant looks up from behind his desk with annoyance written all over his face but doesn't say anything. He just motions his head toward the front of his desk where he wants Liam to stand and report.

Liam quietly obeys and walks up to the front of the lieutenant's desk and starts the mandatory reporting statement the enlisted are supposed to say to the officer who summons them.

"Sir, Sergeant Anderson reports as…"

"Yes, I know, at ease Sergeant Anderson," he says once again with that *I don't give a fuck* tone in his voice.

After a few seconds of silence between them, the lieutenant looks maliciously at Liam then finally says, "Here's what's going to happen. Since I'm *stuck* with you for the next few months until your tour in this *lovely* country ends, *you* are going to be my delivery boy."

What the fuck? A delivery boy? What kind of shit is this? Liam thinks as he looks at the lieutenant with confusion, one for being sent here and two for being called a delivery boy.

The lieutenant doesn't like the look Liam is giving him. "Why are you looking at me like that? You know why you're here right?" the lieutenant asks with a cocky smirk on his face. "Well, according to Captain Marcs, *you're* here because you're too much of a distraction. So now you're my fucking responsibility!"

Liam stands there helpless and frustrated. He just wants to get far away from this asshole of an officer. *Fucking Captain Marcs*, he thinks. He can see the lieutenant studying him with his piercing eyes. Liam can only think about Alex at that moment and realizes that he's not the distraction. It's Captain Marcs who's distracting Alex. Finally, he tries to answer the lieutenant back by saying, "I'm not a dis…"

"Did I say you could speak, Sergeant?" the lieutenant asks with wide eyes and a pissed-off look on his face. "Like I stated earlier, *you* are going to run my errands from compound to compound until you leave here. You will be on the road all day, every day, so you may want to keep your eyes open while on the road, understood?"

Liam tries his best not to react even though he wants to jump across that desk and punch the lieutenant in the face. Instead, Liam calmly says, "Yes, sir."

The lieutenant looks at him for a few moments and finally says, "You will report here tomorrow morning at 0600 hours, understood? Now get out!"

Liam does an about-face and leaves the lieutenant's office.

The desk clerk, still reading his magazine also has the same cocky grin on his face just like the lieutenants. He apparently could hear everything that was said in the office and scoffs loudly as Liam walks past him.

Ignoring the asshole behind the desk, Liam walks past him and leaves the main office. He reaches the outside of the building and in a pissed-off rage, he kicks the nearby trash can. It goes flying toward the five-ton truck that's parked there and suddenly the driver gets out and yells, "What the fuck man!"

"Sorry," Liam says as he slowly walks off to calm himself down while heading to his new room. He opens the door, and the room is the same size as his last room on Alpha compound. The only difference is the bunk bed, which means he has a roommate, and that Alex isn't next to him on the other side of the wall.

Sitting on the bare mattress, he thinks of a way to get in touch with Alex to let her know where he is. *Fuck, I miss her already and she's probably freaking out by now wondering where I am*, he thinks as he closes his eyes and pictures her face. His mind starts to wander about and the time they made love in the shower for the first time. Suddenly, he remembers the smell of her vanilla perfume and the feel of her soft, silky skin.

Liam hates the fact that Captain Marcs is punishing him because he can't control himself around Alex. Now he's forced to spend the remainder of his time on Charlie compound, away from Alex and his team. He suspects that when he reports tomorrow morning at 0600 hours that he will be meeting his new convoy team.

There's nothing worse than being part of a new crew you don't know when leaving the compound and heading out into the shit. Every time he left Alpha compound with Tate, Cast, Thompson, and Alex, he knew he would be safe because everyone had their job and did it right. With a new crew, Liam has no idea who they are and what they are capable of. Now he's stuck on this shitty compound with an asshole in charge and without his friends, and worst of all, without Alex.

After dealing with this new lieutenant, Liam doesn't know who's worse, Captain Marcs or Lieutenant Jones. At that point he doesn't care. All he knows is that the next few months are going to be hell.

Liam slowly walks around the compound to help get his mind off her. He can see some vendors cleaning up for the night to head home. As he walks up to see the merchandise, he notices that one of the vendors has some old electronics and those disposable phones people use in-country. Liam quickly askes the vendor if he can buy two of the phones.

The vendor starts bargaining with him and says, "You buy two phones, I take half off minute cards."

Liam realizes that with this type of phone, you need to put minutes on it to use it. Once the minutes run out, then the phone doesn't work until you load more minutes onto it. He knows that Cast and Tate are heading this way for one of their missions, so he buys the two phones with two sixty-minute cards and patiently waits for them to arrive. As soon as he sees Cast and Tate get out of the SUV, he quickly runs up, and body slams Tate into the side of the vehicle.

"Get off me, loser," Tate says, feeling the size of Liam's body hit his.

"Oh man. Can you believe this fucking shit?" Liam asks.

"Yeah, this sucks that we're only going to see you when we come this way for missions," says Cast.

"No, get this. So that asshole lieutenant in J1 is having me be his fucking errand boy for the rest of my time here. He doesn't realize it, but that means I get to go off the compound and meet up with you guys whenever I want." Liam scoffs at how stupid the whole situation is.

"You mean to meet up with Alex…not us!" Cast says, shaking his head and laughing at Liam.

"Yeah, we're not stupid man. She misses you just as much!" Tate says as he scoffs at Liam.

"That's why I bought these so that her and I can talk. Cast, can you give her one and tell her she has to add minutes to the phone?" he asks as he hands him the phone and a sixty-minute card.

"Oh, Jesus, bro. You trying to get me in trouble? What if the captain finds out?" Cast says.

Liam gives him a look suggesting that a friend would help another friend in this situation. Finally, Cast gives in. "Fine, give me the damn phone." He snatches it out of Liam's hand turns toward Tate and Thompson and says, "These fucking love birds, Jesus."

Ignoring that remark, Liam slaps Cast on the arm and says with a slight grin, "Thanks bro. I owe you one!"

"Yeah, damn right you owe me," Cast says sarcastically, but also with a slight grin.

"So, how's my girl doing?" Liam asks them.

"How the fuck do you think she's doing? Dude, she's a mess. First of all, that asshole captain puts her through hell with all that training. Second, he punishes her for being with you.... How does that shit make any sense," Cast says.

"I know. I can't stand being away from her, especially with the captain there," Liam replies.

"Look, me, Tate and Thompson are going to do our best to keep an eye on her and make sure that asshole doesn't try anything, okay? Don't worry," Cast says reassuringly.

"Thanks, man, and thank you for getting her the phone. Just hearing her voice every day won't make it so hard being away from her," Liam says.

"Man, you both have it bad for each other but hey, if that was my wife, then fuck yeah I would feel the same way," Cast says shaking his head and laughing.

"I tell you what, man, Alex is coming along with her training. I wouldn't even mess with her," Thompson says.

"I know, I'm so proud of her, but I'm nervous about her going up against a man like the Shadow. I think I'm going to try and talk her out of doing it," Liam says with concern.

Cast suddenly looks at Liam in disbelief. "You can try bro, but I think she made her mind up a long time ago. When I see her after training with Brock and Decker, she has this look about her that shows that she can't wait to face that son of a bitch. But yeah man, if you really love her then you should try and stop her from going on that suicide mission," Cast says.

Liam leans against the SUV, thinking about what Cast said and has a sudden feeling of panic in the pit of his stomach. *What if the captain sends her too early to face the Shadow? What if she's not ready and I'm not there in time to talk her out of it?*

"Yeah, I get that. But how do I stop her from doing something she's been training for since the moment she arrived in-country? How do I explain to her that I'm afraid of losing her to that psychopath, but at the same time I don't want to let that man continue to rape and murder innocent women and children?" Liam says with concern while the guys stand beside him in silence, unable to answer his questions.

Chapter 17
The Temptation

It's midmorning, and Alex spent the whole time during her hour-long run and shower thinking about Liam and how she's going to get back at the captain for what he did. Heading to combat training with Brock and Decker, she suddenly sees Captain Marcs come up and pull her to the side. *There he is*, she thinks cleverly as she moves her arm slowly from his grasp.

She knew he'd been watching her all morning. From the time she woke up, during her morning run, and then after she finished getting ready. She knew because she could feel his shadow follow her around ever since he made Liam go to Charlie compound.

"Hey Alex. After training today, come to my office so that I can go over with you what Farid found out about the Shadow," Captain Marcs says in an unusually kind tone.

She can't believe the audacity the captain has as he calls her by her first name. *Who the fuck does he think he is? We're not friends, and yet he calls me Alex,* she thinks as she tries her best to just smile at him and pretend she enjoys his company.

"I will. No problem, sir," she says with a slight grin on her face and turns to open the door to the back building.

"Wait," he says as he lightly grabs her arm again to turn her around toward him. "You don't have to call me sir when no one is around you know," he says softly while continuing to hold her arm.

"You can call me Tyler if you want." He talks to her in almost a whisper while looking at her lips and then back to her eyes.

Alex, keep your cool. Don't let him see your anger right now, she thinks as she gazes into the captain's eyes and nods her head in agreement. She makes sure to also look at his lips and then back into his eyes. *Play with his mind, make him suffer*, she thinks as a slight, devious grin appears on her face.

The captain sees her gaze and inviting grin and instantly wants to kiss her. *I want her and I want to taste her*, he thinks while feeling relieved that Liam is out of the picture.

"Yes, I'll meet you after training…Tyler," she says as she opens the door to the back building and leaves him there with his thoughts.

Rolling her eyes at how gullible the captain is, she walks in and sees Decker waiting for her on the other side of the room. Not watching her surroundings, Alex suddenly feels someone come up from behind her. She quickly moves out of the way and gets in the middle of the floor mat.

It was Brock who tried to take her down while she wasn't looking. He stares at her but doesn't come closer, which is odd because he's always the one who starts the training. They both stand there looking at each other when suddenly, Decker whistles.

Alex looks over toward the back room and five other guys come out. They're the same build as Brock and wearing the same black sweatpants, black tank tops, and black sneakers as well. Remaining where she is in the middle of the room, none of them say a word as they start surrounding her.

What the fuck, she thinks as she looks at Brock in a panic.

Brock looks at her and answers, "You wanted this Alex, so now you're going to *try* and get out of this situation."

Alex suddenly realizes that these men are here to beat the hell out of her and not hold back.

Breathing hard and feeling nauseous, she sees one of them charging from her right side and instantly uses her back fist and forearm to hit him in the face. Another comes at her from behind and puts her in a chokehold as another comes at her from the front. She quickly uses her right heel and kicks the guy from the front in the balls. For the guy who is holding her, she grabs his wrist, steps to the side, and grabs then twists his balls. When he screams in agonizing pain, she uses her other hand and strikes him hard in the nose, breaking it.

The last two guys also decide to take her on at the same time. One of them comes at her full force and kicks her right on the side of her face. Losing hearing in that ear, her body collides with the fifth guy and they both hit the ground. The guy who kicked her grabs her by the hair and wrist, lifts her, and swings her to the wall, dislocating her shoulder. But she barely realizes it since so much adrenaline is coursing through her veins.

He comes at her again and this time as he goes to grab her by the throat, she takes hold of his fingers and bends them backward until she hears that awful popping sound of dislocating them. The last guy who fell on the ground with her earlier is already coming at her full force when she quickly throat-punches him.

Finally, Decker yells, "STOP!"

Many of the men are on the ground writhing in pain from where Alex hit some of them in the testicles. Another guy has a broken nose, another with dislocated fingers, and another is cradling his neck from where she throat-punched him.

Alex didn't come out unscathed. She has a dislocated shoulder, her ear is still ringing from being punched there and her tongue is bleeding from when one of the guys kicked her on the side of her head.

She can feel the blood in her mouth and her lip starting to swell. She's pissed off and angry until she turns around and can see that all her training paid off.

She watches all those guys on the ground in pain. Alex now knows she's capable of anything, especially watching Brock set the guy's broken nose back in place and the other guy's fingers. She doesn't regret doing any of the training and is no longer pissed at Brock and Decker for pulling this on her without her knowing. It's better this way because the Shadow's men are not going to be as forthcoming, and they'll also be armed.

"Excellent job, Alex. How do you feel?" Decker asks with a proud look on his face.

"Like fucking shit," she says annoyed as she caresses her shoulder, and touches her lip, which feels like there's a house sitting on her face.

"Go to the chow hall and ask for some ice for that lip okay and oh… Wait a second," he says as he quickly grabs her arm and lifts it upward so that her shoulder can go back into place.

Not expecting that, Alex makes a high-pitched scream but instantly feels better.

"Fuck, Decker!" she says loudly, before taking a deep breath and continuing with, "Thank you." She wants to let him know that she's grateful for his time and patience. Training her for the whole year and preparing her for what's to come has been a challenge.

She slowly gets up and leaves to go to the chow hall to get some ice for her face. Surprisingly, the guys she just fought follow her to get ice as well. When they all enter the chow hall, everyone turns and stares as they all walk in and wonder what the hell happened to them. They look beaten like they just fought fifty men.

Alex gets the ice, and as she starts to walk back outside, the guys slightly move away from her. She sits at the picnic table and places the ice on the side of her face. The feeling is soothing as the condensation runs down her face and onto her swollen lip.

I wish you were here, she thinks as she pictures Liam's face. He would always be there for her after a hard day of training and right now he's the only person who can comfort her. She wants to call him and talk but she knows the captain is waiting for her. She gets the bag of ice, heads to the captain's office, and knocks slowly on his door. By this time, her body is starting to feel the effects of the fight.

The captain opens the door, takes one look at her battered face, and quickly pulls her inside. He shuts the door behind her and slowly leans her up against the wall to see her more closely.

Let him. Let him move in closer to you, she thinks as she watches him inspect her with his eyes.

"What happened? Are you okay?" he asks with concern as he lightly touches her swollen lip.

"It's okay, sir," she says as she winces with pain from his touch.

"Tyler," he reminds her softly.

She hesitates for a moment then replies, "It's okay…Tyler. It was part of my training today that's all." She watches him slowly reach out and touch her swollen lip again.

Kiss her, he thinks as he gently takes the bag of ice out of her hand and places it lightly on her soft, swollen lip. *Do it*, he thinks as he leans in closer. The captain takes his finger and moves a strand of her hair away from her face as he kisses her lightly on her mouth.

Not yet. It's not time yet, she thinks as she lets him kiss her.

"Does that feel better?" he whispers.

She plays along. “Yes,” she says lightly as she holds his hand. She knows she’s playing with fire but at that point, she must let this happen.

I need her so bad, he thinks as he looks straight into her bright green eyes. He then takes her other hand and places it on his hard-on to stroke as the bag of ice drops to the floor.

Alex doesn’t expect that and can’t believe this is happening to her right now. She watches him as his eyes close and his head tilts back in pleasure. She continues to let him force her hand up and down as he forces her to stroke him. Her heart is beating with rage, but she doesn’t want to push him away in fear that her plan will be ruined. *Just let him*, she tells herself.

Do it to her now, he thinks as he can’t stand it any longer. He quickly turns her around and slams her against the wall face first. Then he starts unbuckling his belt so that he can take his pants off and fuck her right there in his office.

No, no. Please stop, she thinks. She starts to panic, then says, “Wait, not here!” She slowly turns and says out of breath and in a whisper, “Meet me in my room…tonight. It’ll be better there, I promise,” she says hoping he doesn’t see right through her.

The captain looks at her suspiciously but agrees that fucking her in her bedroom all night would be better than fucking her quickly in his office against the wall.

“Make sure you clean yourself up and wear that vanilla perfume as well,” he demands as he buckles his belt back up.

You son of a bitch, she thinks as she tries her best to sound normal. “See you tonight,” she says softly as she leaves his office. Out of breath and pissed off, Alex runs back to her room and slams the door shut. Her whole body is shaking from anger, so she picks up the chair and throws it violently against the wall. Standing in the middle of her room, she feels ashamed of herself but quickly puts those feelings aside. *That son of a bitch is coming here to fuck you in less than two hours, so pull your shit together!* she tells herself. She needs to do her best to make sure it doesn't get that far.

Alex cleans up her room, takes a shower, and makes sure to wear the vanilla perfume as instructed. She decides to put on tight, boy shorts and a tight, black t-shirt with no bra. Alex can see the sun is setting and hears the call to prayer. *He's coming*, she thinks as she swiftly gets the room ready. As planned, she gets the disposable phone and calls Liam. After two rings, he picks up knowing it's her on the other end.

"Hey beautiful, you miss me?" Liam asks.

"Hey baby. I miss you so much," she says loud enough so that anyone on the other side of her door can hear.

He can hear the panic in her voice. "Is tonight the night?" he asks.

"Yes, so listen. Whatever you hear please don't freak out, okay?" she whispers to Liam.

"Fuck, Alex. I don't like this," he says with concern.

"Just stay on the other end and keep talking with me until he comes," she says.

"Okay. You're going to be okay. Please be careful and remember your training."

At that moment Alex can see a shadow under her door as if someone is standing there listening. Suddenly the door flies open, and the captain comes slowly into her room glaring at her.

"Who are you talking to?" he asks as he slams her door shut.

Alex stands there frozen with the phone in her hand and with a look of shock on her face.

"No one," she says, trying to move away from him.

"Bullshit!" He lunges toward her and punches her hard in the eye.

She falls on the bed as the phone drops to the floor.

The captain quickly climbs on top of her in a fit of rage. He can hear Liam screaming on the other end of the phone, "STOP! DON'T YOU FUCKING TOUCH HER!"

"You're a lying CUNT!" the captain says as he rips her boy shorts off and punches her again. This time in her swollen lip, which breaks open and starts to bleed.

"Please stop! Captain Marcs, please!" she screams as he begins to rip her shirt off revealing her breasts.

Hearing her plead for him to stop, he gets a sudden rush and decides to put one hand on her throat while the other hand is holding her down on the bed.

"Stop fighting Alex. It's your word against mine and besides, everyone will assume you got these bruises on your face and neck from training, so fight all you want! I like it rough anyway," he says to her as he watches her struggle to breathe.

Alex is furious with anger, but she holds on longer than expected. She can feel the blood from her cut lip run down the side of her face as he starts to kiss her.

"You smell so good," he says softly in her ear. He wants to taste her between her legs, so he lets his hand go from around her throat and starts moving down, kissing her body along the way.

Do it, NOW! she thinks as she punches him in the face and then takes the heel of her foot and kicks him in the chest. She watches as he falls off the bed and onto the floor. She then quickly gets off the bed and repeatedly kicks him in the stomach.

He rolls to his side to avoid her kicking him, so she continues striking him in the back. When she finally finishes, Alex looks down at him with disgust and says, "I never wanted this or you. The only thing between us is the mission you set me to do and that's it, Captain Marcs."

While coughing and laying in the fetal position, he looks up at her busted lip and swollen eye. "Alex, please don't turn your back on your mission with the Shadow because of this," he says out of breath as he starts to slowly get up.

"Oh, don't worry about that Captain. My mission stands and if I catch you anywhere near this building, you'll get more than what I just did to you. Now GET THE FUCK OUT!" she says as she walks over to her door to open it.

The captain is disoriented and in pain as he slowly walks toward the door far enough away from Alex so that she can't hit him again.

She watches him intently and makes sure he isn't going to try and attack her again. After she slams the door in his face, she picks up the phone off the floor to see if Liam is still there.

"Liam?" she says, shaking from the aftermath of the fight.

"Hey, I'm here. Jesus, Alex. That sounded bad. Are you okay?" he asks with worry for her.

"You should ask him that," she says as she takes the video camera Cast got for her out of its hiding place and presses the stop button. She grins and says, "Yes, I'm just fine."

"Did your plan work?" Liam asks, hoping that she didn't do all that for nothing.

"I hope so. Let me see," she says as she hits the rewind button and then hits play on the video camera. She can see that she put the camera in the perfect spot. It was placed in the corner of her room, facing her bed and the door. She watches as the captain comes into her room violently and then punches her in the face. She then watches how he climbs on top of her and hits her again in the mouth and then rip her clothes off. She also makes sure she can hear herself say his name out loud so that anyone who sees this knows it's him.

Alex isn't happy that she had to go through such a thing, but men like the captain are never going to stop. If she didn't do something about it, that kind of abuse would continue.

"Liam, I'm sorry you had to hear all of that on the other end. I just reviewed the tape, and everything is good. I'm going to erase the conversation toward the end about the Shadow and then make a copy. I'm going to send this off to his company command anonymously."

"Do you think it's going to work?" Liam asks.

"I hope so, because if it doesn't then this was all for nothing."

As she said good night to Liam, she lays down on her bed and watches the video over and over. Alex realizes how just one man can be so destructive. She knows she'll be facing not only the Shadow in a week but all his armed men as well.

She tries to put it out of her mind, but her body and face are in pain and her clothes are ripped to shreds. Alex slowly gets off the bed to change her clothes. She walks over to the full-length mirror and looks at her battered face. *Jesus*, she says under her breath as she moves in to take a closer look.

The pain is getting worse, and she can't take it anymore. Alex remembers that Cast was able to sneak in a bottle of vodka a few days ago on one of his missions. *Time for a drink*, she thinks as she leaves her room, walks over to his building, and knocks on his door.

When Cast answers, he takes one look at her face and is in shock.

Without saying a word to him, she moves past him and starts going through his things. She accidentally let the picture of his wife and two kids fall on the nightstand as she rummages through it.

"Hey, watch it! What are you looking for?" Cast asks, annoyed as he picks up the picture and puts it back upright on the nightstand.

"Where is it?" she asks in frustration while opening his drawers and goes through his things.

"Alex, what the hell happened to your face? What are you looking for?"

She slams the drawer shut with aggravation and says loudly, "The fucking vodka Cast. Where is it? I need it now!"

He can see that she isn't joking around and that she probably wants the vodka to numb the pain. He looks at her eye, which is completely swollen, and her mouth has dried blood from the massive cut on her lip. Cast doesn't say a word. He just climbs on top of his bed, lifts the ceiling tile, and pulls out the unopened bottle of vodka.

Alex can see some other hidden items up there and notices a pack of cigarettes.

"I want those too," she demands as she points to the unopened pack of Marlboro cigarettes.

"Damn, Alex. Fine. Just don't tell the guys, okay?" he says in frustration.

Alex ignores him, grabs the lighter he left on his nightstand, and one of his T-shirts he left on his bed to wrap up the unauthorized items.

Cast looks at her face again and bruised body with worry and says, "Please Alex. Tell me what the fuck happened?"

Feeling the lump in her throat and her eyes start to water she says, "Cast, I'm really tired and just want to drink this and smoke these."

She lifts the bottle and cigarettes that are rolled up inside his T-shirt. "I'll explain tomorrow. I promise," she says with exhaustion in her voice.

"Yeah, tomorrow. You're going to tell us who did that to your face because I know it's not from training with Brock and Decker," he says patiently.

Alex waves her hand dismissively at him as she leaves his room. As she walks outside back to her building, she can see the captain watching her from the picnic table.

The sky is dark and nobody's outside except for the two of them. There's just one light that shines down from where he's sitting, and it makes his dark silhouette look bigger than normal.

She stops to look directly at him, letting him know she's not afraid of him and that he better stay on that side of the compound, far away from her.

The captain looks back at her for what seems like a long time. He thinks back to when he first saw her up until now. Her demeanor has changed drastically from a mousy and insecure girl to a dominant and capable woman.

Alex keeps her eyes on him as she slowly starts to walk back to her building. Feeling the pain in her mouth, her eye, and the rest of her body, she clutches the T-shirt with the hidden items away from his line of sight.

He doesn't seem to notice because he too is feeling the pain in his face and the rest of his body. *This is not over, not by a long shot. Besides, she never would have made it this far without me.*

Chapter 18
The Long Kiss Goodbye

Hungover and sore from yesterday's fight, Alex can feel her head pounding and her body ache as a reminder of the gang fight with Decker's guys. The fight she had with the captain last night doesn't help either.

She's in her room and still slightly drunk as she slowly dances to her favorite rock star's voice. With her eyes closed, she listens to him sing because it helps her forget about all the shit that happened the night before.

Walking over to the mirror on the wall, she can see her beaten and battered face and instantly gets upset again. *The captain didn't hold back*, she tells herself as she touches her bruised eye and cut lip. Alex remembers watching the video over and over last night and how she now has leverage against the son of a bitch.

But how am I going to bring him down? Who the fuck is going to believe me? she asks herself as the music continues to deafen her ears. She likes to play it that loud because it helps her cope with the pain.

Alex feels bad and has a lot of explaining to do. The way she treated Cast last night was unacceptable. Barging into his room, going through his things, and not letting him help her. *Yeah, what a great friend you are...Jesus*, she thinks sarcastically about herself as she takes another drag from her cigarette.

It's been a very long time since she smoked and as she inhales it reminds her of her high school days when she smoked with her friends behind the gymnasium.

Alex walks over to look at the photos of the dead girls on her wall and then over to the Shadow's photo. His dead eyes stare back at her as if they're following her around the room, judging her and making her feel uneasy.

I can't wait to see your blood hit the floor, she thinks as she takes another long drag and blows the cigarette smoke in his face.

It's already after dawn, and she isn't in the mood to train today. Instead, she lays on her bed, smoking and dizzy from drinking Cast's vodka. The rock star's voice continues to blare in her ears, and she can feel the vibration of the loud music on her skin.

Someone starts banging on her door as she lays on her bed, buzzing from the vodka. Even through the loud music, Alex feels as if it's about to come off the hinges. After a few minutes, a pissed-off Alex gets up, puts on a T-shirt and sweatpants then violently opens the door.

"WHAT!" she yells as Cast, Tate, and Thompson stand there staring at her beaten face.

Without saying a word, Cast slowly walks up to her, gently moves her aside, and goes into her room followed by Tate and Thompson.

She watches as they look around the room to find the half-empty bottle of vodka, cigarette butts on the floor, photos of dead girls, the Shadow's face pinned to her wall, and a stale smell of sweat and cigarette smoke in the air.

Tate and Thompson follow Cast as he goes over to the CD player to turn off the loud music. They all simultaneously turn and look at her with worry, mainly because they want to help her get through whatever happened to her the day before.

She doesn't like their judgmental eyes and with frustration, she puts the cigarette out and folds her arms at them.

"What are you guys doing here?" she asks with irritation in her voice.

"We're worried Alex. Who did that to your face?" Cast asks with concern.

Tate slowly starts to clean up her room and opens her window to let fresh air in.

Thompson moves closer to her and gently lifts her chin to inspect her eye and cut lip.

"Here, sit down so that I can clean this up," Thompson says while dabbing a swab at her lip.

Cast told Thompson the night before how Alex showed up to his room with a beaten face, so he came prepared and brought his medical kit with him.

As Tate straightens up and Thompson cleans her wounds, Cast stands in front of her with his arms folded and looks at her for answers.

"Alex, tell us what happened last night and don't leave anything out," he says demandingly to her.

She huffs in derision as Thompson continues to dab a cotton ball with peroxide onto her busted lip. She winces at the pain as she starts to answer Cast's question.

"Remember that video camera I asked you to get for me?" she asks.

"Yes.... Why...?" Cast replies with worry. He can already see where this is going.

"Well, it's better if I just showed you instead of explaining it. Tate get the camera on top of my closet and hand it to Cast," she says.

Tate sees the camera, reaches for it, then hands it over to Cast.

"Press play," Alex says as she winces again at the pain Thompson is causing her.

As Cast is watching the video, Alex can see the look on his face change from curiosity to anger. Thompson and Tate stop what they're doing and stand behind Cast to watch as well. As she sits from her bed, she can hear when the captain punches her and the sounds of a struggle. She can also hear herself say the captain's name and for him to stop.

When the video ends, Alex can see the anger in their faces. Tate puts his hand on his forehead in shock. Thompson slowly shakes his head and looks disgusted. Cast hands Thompson the camera, turns around and punches the wall behind him leaving an imprint of his fist on Alex's wall.

"That motherfucker!" Cast says, angry and out of breath.

"Cast, I'm okay. I promise. I got him, don't you see that? I'm going to mail a copy of this to his company command, so he's finished," Alex says with a sense of finality in her voice.

"Yeah, but what about the day of the eclipse. Is that still happening?" Thompson asks.

"No. No way. You're not doing that anymore, Alex. No," Cast says as he waves his hands back and forth.

"Oh yes I am. I've trained for that all year and now that I'm a week away you want me to quit? No, absolutely not!" she says in anger.

"Does Liam know about this?" Thompson asks as he holds the camera up.

"Of course, he knows. He was on the other end of the phone when the captain came into my room. Why do you think the captain was so angry?" she asks.

"Are you fucking kidding me, Alex? Do you know how dangerous that was? He could've gone even farther than that and Liam knew this whole time? I don't understand how he could allow that," Cast says, clearly upset.

"But he didn't, Cast. I made sure of that. I could've kicked his ass all around my room if I wanted to, but I didn't because I needed him to hit me and tear my clothes off. Those actions alone will put him away so that he can't do this shit to anyone else anymore. The same thing goes for the Shadow. I *will* continue my mission without the captain and *kill* the Shadow once and for all. Are you guys still with me or not?" she asks in frustration and looks at all of them for an answer.

Thompson looks away from her and sees the photos of the dead girls on her wall. He instantly thinks about his wife and daughter back home. If someone ever did this to his family, he would want that person to suffer. He would want someone to kill the monster that was responsible.

"Of course, we're with you. How could you even ask us that?" Thompson says as he looks away from the horror on her wall and places his hand on her shoulder.

"Oh shit. Thompson not so tight. My shoulder was dislocated yesterday," she says while wincing in pain.

"Yeah, I've been meaning to ask you about that," Cast says. "Someone told me that you and five other guys came into the chow hall yesterday looking all shot to shit. What the fuck happened?"

"Well, you know there's only a week left until I face the Shadow and his men, right? Well, Brock and Decker decided to throw a curveball and have me fight five of their well-trained guys all at once. I didn't even know about it until they all surrounded me, and I had to defend myself," she says.

"Jesus, they dislocated your shoulder and what else?" Thompson asks as he grabs his medical kit.

"One guy kicked me on the side of my head, but it feels okay today. Another guy kicked me in the face, and that's when I cut my tongue and my lip swelled up. Another guy dislocated my shoulder and Decker had to fix it," she says. "Then you all saw what the captain did that night, so I'm feeling a bit sore this morning," she says while touching her lip where the swelling is already going down.

"Fuck. It sounds like I missed a good fight," Cast says as he stands in front of her with his arms folded and a grin on his face. He shakes his head in awe of her and can't believe that a girl like her can take such a beating and still have the determination to face a man like the Shadow on her own.

"If I haven't said it before, I'll say it now. Girl, you got some massive balls on you, I tell you what," Cast says, still grinning from ear to ear as he unfolds his arms and sits on the other side of her.

Feeling awkward at his comment, she says with a slight grin, "Oh, thanks, Cast. I really appreciate it."

Tate laughs at this as he's looking over Alex's things.

"Why is the CD player in your room and not in the back building?" Tate asks as he flips through all the CDs people have left behind over the years. Some of the new ones he hasn't seen before, like The Raconteurs 2008 album *Consolers of the Lonely*. Curious, he takes the CD out, places it inside the player, and turns to track number two called, "Salute Your Solution."

As the music starts to play, Tate begins to bob his head and dance around Alex's room to the fast beat of the song. He throws in so many dance moves that Alex, Cast, and Thompson all watch in amazement from her bed. Tate starts doing the running man, to John Travolta and

Uma Thurman's dance in the movie *Pulp Fiction* where they do the twist. He does some quick spins and shakes his hips around, trying to mimic Alex on the days he saw her practice her exotic dance.

Alex, Cast, and Thompson start to throw her boots, socks, and pillow at him while he's dancing to make him stop.

"Fucking goofball," Cast says as he laughs and throws Alex's other boot at Tate.

Alex tries to laugh, but her face is still sore. Instead, she watches the three of them as they pick on each other. Suddenly, she realizes that she may have been an only child growing up, but now she has three brothers. *They'll always have your back,* she thinks while feeling sad that Liam isn't there to see how close they've become as friends.

After they leave, she starts to feel better and tries to go for her morning run, but that's out of the question. She then tries to train with Brock and Decker but that's also too difficult. Finally, she decides to help Tate, Cast, and Thompson on one of their missions outside the wire. Maybe she'll get lucky and run into Liam.

As she walks to the SUV, she thinks about the call she got from him just before dawn to see how she was feeling. He wanted to know if the captain had tried to come back to her room.

She loves hearing his voice and wants him so badly that she can't stand it. She also wants to see him again before her mission on the day of the eclipse with the Shadow. That's only in a week and she doesn't know if she's going to make it out of the palace alive.

"I want to see you before the day of the eclipse," she'd said to Liam when he'd called her that morning.

"I know. I want to see you too, really bad," Liam said to her.

While Tate is getting the SUV ready and Cast is double-checking Thompson's gear, Alex decides to call Liam again right before heading out.

After it rings a couple of times, Liam answers and says, "Hey, my love."

"Hey, baby. I'm heading out with the guys right now to help them on one of their missions. Are you going out today?" she asks.

"Since I've gotten to this shitty compound, I've been on the road nonstop doing the lieutenant's errands. Text me when you get someplace and I'll try to make it out that way," he says optimistically.

"I will, but I gotta go now and I don't want to lose any more minutes on the phone," she says as she gets into the front seat.

"I love you Alex. Watch your back," Liam says.

Alex closes her eyes and smiles. "I love you more," she whispers so that the guys can't hear her and make fun of her the entire trip.

Alex hangs up the phone and places it in her cargo pocket.

"I luuv yuuu," Tate says mockingly as he leans in making kissy noises with his lips at her.

Alex pushes his face away. "Shut up Tate!"

"Yeah, shut up Tate," Cast says, as he mocks Alex while also making the same kissy noises at her.

"You dumb shits. Can we go now?" Alex asks while shaking her head with a grin on her face.

Alex notices how the roads this morning are packed with cars clogging up the highway, and there are so many people walking on the side of the road as well. She's seen this before, so it doesn't make her too nervous. She's just more vigilant while watching the road. They have two stops today, and the first one is to Bravo compound to pick up the medical supplies that Thompson requested. It's not too far from Charlie compound where Liam is now. Then they need to go to the city center to get to the main headquarters building to pick up and drop off some awards packages that Captain Goodfellow requested.

The drive to Bravo is typical. Tate follows the same route he always takes while Alex watches for any suspicious activity on the road. Thompson and Cast are in the back also looking out for anything off or suspicious.

Alex pulls out her phone and quickly texts Liam where they're headed and how long it's going to take them to get there so that he can try and make it there to meet up with her. She hasn't seen him since he was forced to move to Charlie compound by the captain, and all she can think about is kissing him.

After an hour on the road, they finally make it to Bravo in one piece. Tate parks the vehicle in the same spot he always parks it and opens the hood right away to make sure everything is okay with the engine. Thompson heads to the medical tent for the supplies, and Cast goes to say hello to his Army buddies.

Alex looks at her phone and doesn't see a response from Liam. She walks around the compound to see if he's also walking around but doesn't see him. Jabar's tent is nearby so she goes to say hello to him. She notices him behind the counter inspecting new rubies that have come in.

"Salam, Jabar," Alex says as she approaches the counter.

"Salam, my friend. You look happier today from when I saw you last," Jabar says.

"Yes, I found Liam and he's on Charlie compound. Have you seen him here today?" she asks hoping Jabar says yes.

Right before Jabar can answer, he looks past her and sees someone enter his tent.

"I see fate has rewarded you," Jabar says, smiling as he motions his head toward the entrance.

Alex quickly turns around to see Liam standing there, smiling at her.

As they slowly walk up to each other, Liam can see her lip is already starting to heal and her eye is no longer swollen from the fight she had with the captain.

They embrace for the longest time in silence before Liam lets go and looks into her eyes once again.

"I've missed you so much," he says as he gently caresses her bruised eye and cut lip.

"Me too," she says as she tries to think of a way they can spend some time together before she leaves the compound.

"Come on. Let's go find the guys and see how much time we can have together. Goodbye Jabar," she says as they quickly leave the tent.

They see the guys waiting by the vehicle when they come up.

"Oh shit. Look who it is, Sergeant Anderson in the flesh! What's up man?" Cast asks as he slaps his hand on Liam's shoulder.

"Hey, Cast. What's up, man. Tate, Thompson, what's up guys," Liam says.

"Cast, how much time do Liam and I have before we gotta head out to headquarters to drop off the awards packages?" Alex asks.

"About an hour. Come on, follow me," Cast says as he starts to walk toward the dorm rooms.

He takes them to a transient room that Cast uses from time to time when he can't make it back to Alpha compound before sundown.

"This room is private, and nobody will see you in here. Just keep it down, okay?" Cast says with a slight grin on his face.

Alex and Liam look at Cast gratefully as he walks away and heads back to the vehicle to wait with Tate and Thompson.

They both enter the small room, which consists of a twin bed and a dresser. Liam gently pulls Alex to him and kisses her hard on the mouth.

"I missed you so fucking much," he says and then continues to kiss her.

Alex's face is still in pain, but she doesn't care, she just wants him inside her.

The sexual tension that's been built up since he left makes them quickly start to take each other's uniforms off. Alex unbuckles his belt while Liam unbuttons her top. She manages to get his pants down while Liam gets her top and undershirt off.

As their mouths meet once again, she starts to stroke him below. Liam's already hard for her because he couldn't do anything but think about her for the past few weeks. He pulls Alex's pants down and gently flips her around. Then he bends her over the bed and enters her.

He hears her let out a satisfying moan as he slips inside her. He closes his eyes as he hears her moan again and again. Not wanting it to end, he continues to enter her over and over for what feels like the longest time. He watches as Alex grips the sheets with both hands as she begs him not to stop.

After some time, they're breathing hard, and their bodies are covered in sweat. Finally, Liam and Alex both let out a final gasp that leaves them both satisfied and exhausted with pleasure.

She flips over onto her back as Liam bends over to kiss her lightly on the mouth.

"I missed you," she whispers while caressing his hair and looking deep into his eyes.

"I missed you more," he says with a big grin on his face. Liam looks down at her bare breasts and notices she's wearing the ruby he got for her birthday. Without saying a word, he bends down and kisses her neck and then down to her nipple. He can feel her nipple harden in his mouth and can hear her breathe out with pleasure.

"Baby," she whispers lightly, as her eyes close and her head tilts back.

Liam stops kissing her and starts to take her boots off and then her pants. He wants her again and as he quickly climbs on top of her, he notices all the bruises on her body from the fight she had with the captain.

"What's the matter?" she asks as she can see the look of worry on his face.

"I can't. I mean look at all these bruises. Aren't you in pain?" he asks as he gently gets off her.

Alex sits up next to him and says, "It's okay. They'll be gone in a few days." She leans in to kiss him in the mouth. This is a lie, the pain is still there, but she doesn't want to ruin the moment. She continues to kiss him hard in the mouth as she climbs on top of him.

The feeling of her wet tongue and her breath in his mouth finally makes him give in as she takes control of him.

Straddling him, she slowly moves her hips back and forth with him inside her again as they continue to kiss. Their bodies are slick with sweat, and Liam can faintly smell her vanilla perfume. The sweet smell that reminds him of her during those lonely nights.

Feeling that sudden wave of ecstasy rush over her, she starts moving her hips faster. Arching her head back, she exposes her breasts and the ruby that nestles between them to Liam. She's on the verge of coming when she whispers his name.

"Liam."

Watching her completely take control of him, he lifts her, lays her on her back, and thrusts inside her.

She wraps her legs around him and pulls him in closer so she can kiss him in the mouth.

They hold each other close as Liam moves his hips faster and faster when suddenly, they climax and let out a sigh of release as they lay down to catch their breath.

As they lay there, breathing hard and looking at the ceiling, Alex smiles and rolls to her side and kisses his arm. She notices the sad look on his face, sits up on her elbow, and says, "Hey…what's wrong?

Liam slowly moves his head to look at her and says, "I'm scared for you. I want to go with you on the day of the eclipse."

"No, you can't. It's too dangerous," she says, shaking her head then gets up to put her uniform back on.

"I don't even know the ins and outs of the mission anymore because the fucking captain sent me away," he says with frustration.

Putting her boots back on and not looking in his direction, she says, "Liam, please don't do this. You're ruining a great moment."

"Can you at least tell me what the plan is? I need to know," he says as he stops her from getting dressed.

Alex looks into his worried eyes, gives in, and tries not to sound afraid as she says, "The plan is simple. Farid will take me to the safe house so that I can get dressed and ready. Then he will drive me to the palace where I will dance for the Shadow during the solar eclipse. Then I kill him."

Liam looks at her with concern at how calm she sounds while describing one of the most horrifying things a person can do. He kneels in front of her as she continues to lace her boots and takes her hands into his. Their foreheads touch as they sit there in complete silence. Finally, he says, "Alex, I know you can do this without a doubt in my mind. I'm just really scared of losing you."

"I know, baby," she says softly as she places both her hands on each side of his face. Looking back into his eyes, she says with determination, "I will come back to you. I promise." Then she gently kisses his lips.

Not wanting the kiss to end, he pulls her closer to him as she slides onto his lap. The kiss they share is long, deep, and slow. It lasts for what seems like an eternity.

It's Alex who finally breaks away and stands up, leaving Liam to look up at her from the floor.

"It's time for me to go," she says with dread as she holds her hand out for him to take.

Liam doesn't want the guys to see him upset so he tells her to tell them he said goodbye. She leaves the room and walks back alone to the SUV, where they're waiting for her.

The guys can see by the look on her face that she's sad and ready to make the last run over to the headquarters building and back to Alpha compound. They all know that this could be the last time she sees Liam before her mission with the Shadow and that she may never see him again. They don't say much when she gets into the vehicle and the guys refrain from making fun of her for being with Liam. They just leave her alone with her thoughts as they ride out the gate in silence.

Chapter 19
The Fate of a Friend

Alex looks out the window in silence while Tate drives on the outskirts of the city and to headquarters for their last run of the day. Cast and Thompson talk in the back seat with each other, knowing that Alex is thinking about Liam and preparing herself for her mission with the Shadow.

Tate watches Alex and notices that she isn't her usual cheerful self, but he still wants her to feel like she can talk to him.

"Alex…Are you okay?" Tate asks as he keeps his eyes on the road.

Not turning to look at him she says, "Yeah, why?" in a sad tone of voice.

"I thought you would be happy to spend some quality time with Liam," he says as his dimples start to show. He can see that his attempt to make her laugh isn't working.

Alex continues to sit there and think about what Liam said to her about the plan for the day of the eclipse. *I'm just really scared of losing you.* She starts to wonder if she's going on a suicide mission, never to return to him alive. She realizes that no one in her life has ever felt this way about her, except maybe her mother.

Lately, she's been thinking a lot about her mother and how she lost her to a car crash at such a young age. Alex wonders what her life would've been like if her mother didn't die. Her mind instantly flashes back to seeing her mother in the casket, wearing a white sundress with little pink and yellow flowers. She remembers the pastor reading a poem from an unknown poet that she later found and kept in her pocket all these years. *Why am I doing all of this?* she thinks to herself as the dust from the road billows in the air. *What am I trying to prove?*

"Hello…Alex, did you hear me?" Tate asks, raising his voice a little.

Alex turns her head to reply when suddenly she can feel the vehicle quickly shift to one side and a loud pop coming from the front left tire.

Tate tries his best to keep the vehicle on the road but hits the ditch going sideways.

"What the fuck!" Cast says from the back seat.

"Shit, we got a fucking flat," Tate says annoyed as he gets out of the vehicle to inspect the flat tire. He quickly opens the back and grabs the spare.

"Cast, get out and help him while Thompson and I lookout for anything that might come," she says as she grabs her M4 and positions herself five feet from the SUV.

It's a little over five minutes when suddenly Alex starts to hear rapid gunfire that's coming from over the ridge and in their direction.

They all stop what they're doing and land on the ground. Cast and Thompson find a small stone wall and lean against it. Alex quickly runs over to Tate and continues to help him with the flat tire. "Stay behind the vehicle, okay?" she orders Tate as he continues to quickly fix the tire.

"Looks like we ran over something that caused this flat. Maybe something those fuckers out there planted in the road, and who knows what else. I gotta call this in," Tate says as he pulls out his radio and asks Alpha compound for backup support.

"Alpha, this is Ghost 5. Come in," Tate says but only hears static. He tries again as he presses the radio receiver button down. "Alpha, this is Ghost 5. Come in."

Tate's having a hard time getting a signal, so he goes around the bend in the road and tries to get a better signal to call it in.

Alex follows him while Cast and Thompson fire back at the ridge in front of them.

Alex and Tate reach the other side of the bend where she can no longer see Cast and Thompson behind the stone wall, but she can still hear the gunfire going back and forth.

"Fuck. Why aren't they answering?" Tate asks while looking down at the radio and leaning against a burned-out tree stump.

Alex faces him and looks behind him to make sure no one tries to flank their position.

"Alpha, this is Ghost 5. Come in," Tate says again. Finally, he hears a man respond. "This is Alpha, go ahead."

"Alpha, we need back up. We're out here just past Bravo compound heading west toward the city. We got a flat and were taking on fire from the north ridge," Tate says out of breath.

"Roger that, Ghost 5. We're sending two vehicles in your direction. Hang tight," the man on the other end replies.

"I can't believe this is happening," Alex says out of breath as she watches Tate clip the radio back on his gear.

"Our guys at Alpha are coming to get us," he says, reassuring her because he can see the panic written all over her face.

"Don't worry Alex, we'll be o—"

Suddenly, blood sprays all over her face as she sees Tate's neck open up right in front of her. He instantly lands on top of her as they both fall hard to the ground. She can feel Tate's warm, thick blood from his neck pour onto her in big pulsating pools. She tries to scream but the shock of what's happening leaves her mouth wide open and no sound coming out.

"TAAAAAAATE," she tries to say his name as he lays there on top of her, lifeless.

Alex can hear quick footsteps and prays that it's either Cast or Thompson coming to help them. She manages to gently roll Tate's body off her and can see that his eyes are still open, looking off into the vast distance.

"No…no, Tate, no," she says sobbing while gently shaking him to wake him up. She knows he's gone but she doesn't want to believe it. Reaching over to hold his hand, she notices that his skin is already pale from losing so much blood and that his hands are ice cold to the touch.

As Cast and Thompson quickly approach, they see Alex is trying to shake Tate awake but nothing is happening. She can feel Cast pull her off him and take her back to the vehicle for safety while Thompson gently picks up Tate's body and place him on the ground behind the vehicle in front of Alex.

They look at her covered in Tate's blood. It's soaked through her gear, shirt and undershirt and feels hot and sticky on her skin. Using the water from his canteen, Thompson tries his best to clean her face with a wet rag, but Alex slightly pushes him away as she stares at Tate's lifeless body. Hot tears roll down her face and her voice is hoarse when she tries to talk.

"Who did this?" she asks as she continues to look at Tate's lifeless body in front of her.

"I don't know. A sniper maybe. That's why we're behind this vehicle," Cast says pissed off that someone murdered his friend as he watches for any oncoming vehicles to pick them up.

"Tate said they're coming. They're coming for us soon," she says out of breath as her hands start to shake from being in shock.

"We'll get him back to Alpha. Don't worry," Thompson says as he checks the rest of her body to make sure she didn't get shot as well by the sniper.

"Thompson, I'm fine. Stop…please" she says with exhaustion as she moves his hand away.

He reaches over and holds her tight as she starts to cry uncontrollably again. Thompson and Cast don't shed any tears yet because they're still in the angry phase of the mourning process. They watch as their good friend lays there in a pool of his blood and can see Alex break down as she places her bloody hands on her face.

They sit there for what seems like hours before two armored SUVs from Alpha compound come to pick them up. Cast and Thompson sit in the lead vehicle while Alex has Tate laying on her lap in the back seat of the second vehicle.

The driver is frantically talking to Alex, but she doesn't hear a thing he's saying. Tears come down her face as she holds Tate in her lap, and she watches him as his eyes stare past hers while holding his hand in silence. Her friend, her brother, is dead and there's nothing she can do about it.

They arrive back at the compound, and everyone has already heard what happened to Tate. Cast and Thompson quickly get out of the lead vehicle and run over to where Alex is. They gently pull Tate's body out of the vehicle and place him on the stretcher. Alpha compound doesn't have the capacity to hold deceased members, so Tate will be going over to Delta compound where the deceased are properly processed and sent home to the families.

Covered in Tate's blood, Alex does her best to not breakdown in front of everyone as her and the guys walk next to the stretcher as Tate is being carried off.

With their hands over their mouths, everyone from the compound can see Tate's blood on her. Even Captain Marcs, who's standing in the crowd, watches Alex softly cry as she holds Tate's hand. Thompson doesn't like everyone staring at her, so he gently tries to pull Alex away from Tate's body.

"No," she whispers as Thompson gently pulls her hand off Tate's to take her back to her room.

"Let me take you back to your room, Alex," Thompson says softly as he wraps his arm around her shoulder to guide her away.

"Wait." She reaches into her cargo pocket and pulls out a small piece of paper. The paper has the poem that the pastor recited on the day of her mother's funeral. She's carried that poem her whole life and now wants to give it to Tate.

"Please make sure this goes with him when they send him home," she says with tears streaming down her face and with sorrow in her heart.

Thompson takes the small paper and wants to see what's written on it. He looks up at Alex and gently asks, "May I?"

Alex nods as she watches Thompson gently unfold the paper. The poem was from an anonymous poet that seems to have experienced a great loss in their life. It reads:

I am no one…insignificant…small…unseen…

I am a grain of sand on a vast desert…

A small star in the night sky…

A drop of water in the open sea...

When burned to ash, I float away like dust...

Then forgotten forever.

Thompson gently folds the small piece of paper and looks up at Alex with tears flooding his eyes.

She's never seen him like this and knows that he feels just as broken as she does for losing such a good friend.

"I'll make sure his family gets this along with his things," he whispers to her.

Not wanting Thompson to do that alone she says, "I want to help you."

Thompson can't deny her help seeing as Tate was her friend too and the fact that she's still covered in his blood.

"Okay. Get cleaned up and meet me in his room in an hour and bring Cast with you too," Thompson says as he tries to compose himself to keep from crying.

Alex nods but before she looks away from Thompson, she sees Captain Marcs watching them from the crowd. *That son of a bitch*, she thinks as she glares at him in anger.

Thompson sees her expression and turns around to find that he too can see the captain watching them. His mind instantly remembers what he saw on the video camera earlier that morning of him beating the hell out of Alex. He starts to aggressively walk toward the captain because he wants to punch him in front of everyone, but Alex quickly grabs his arm.

"Don't," she whispers while she and Thompson look at the captain intently. "If you do anything, my plan was all for nothing," she whispers as she pulls him away from the crowd.

"Shit…sorry, I couldn't help myself," Thompson says as he takes a deep breath.

"I know, trust me, I wanna hit that bastard just as much as you do but not in front of everyone. Then it just looks like *we* are in the wrong and not him," she says while looking over her shoulder to see that the captain is gone.

Alex heads back to her room and slowly shuts the door. It takes every part of her not to break down again, but as soon as she sees herself in the mirror, she suddenly understands why everyone outside stared at her. She looks like she just stepped off the set of a horror movie with blood all over her. With her hands shaking uncontrollably, she's having a hard time unbuttoning her shirt. Tate's blood has already hardened in the seams and her undershirt is stuck to her skin from the soaked-in blood. Even her hair is saturated with it.

Alex slowly leaves her room and heads down the hallway and into the bathroom to take a shower. She turns on the hot water, closes her eyes, and stands underneath as it flows through her hair and down her body. When she finally opens her eyes, all she can see is Tate's blood going through her toes and down the drain.

No…no, she thinks as her heart starts pounding faster. She has a hard time breathing when suddenly, she pictures Tate's blood spraying on her face again and watching him fall onto her in slow motion. The images replay in her mind over and over like a broken record. *No…not again,* she thinks as she starts to cry but no sound comes. "Breathe… Just breathe," she says. After a few moments, she composes herself and spends the rest of her time cleaning blood from her body and her long, thick hair.

Before meeting with Thompson, Alex does what he asked and goes to get Cast from his room. After knocking a few times, she can hear

Cast inside and taking longer than normal to answer. When he finally opens the door, she can see that he too was crying before she got there.

She looks at Cast's red eyes and softly asks, "You ready?"

After a few moments, he softly replies, "Yeah, let's go."

They slowly walk to Tate's dorm room in silence, trying not to talk about the incident and stir up any feelings that will lead them to break down again. When they reach Tate's room, his door is ajar, and they can hear someone inside. Cast slowly opens the door and they both walk in to find Thompson putting a couple of cardboard boxes together.

Thompson looks over to Alex and says with a hoarse voice, "You look better," indicating that he no longer can see Tate's blood all over her.

She nods her head to him with watery eyes and does her best to not let the tears fall. This is not about her. It's about mourning their friend.

All three of them look tired and broken as they each take a corner of Tate's room and slowly pack up his things in silence.

Tate's room looks like a movie producer's studio. He has two full-sized posters on the wall of his favorite movies. The one on the wall next to his bed is Stanley Kubrick's1980 film *The Shining* with Jack Nicholson and Shelley Duvall. On the opposite wall, he has a poster of Quentin Tarantino's 1994 film *Pulp Fiction* with Uma Thurman laying on the bed in her black dress and heels while smoking a cigarette. Tate also has a ton of bootleg movies that he got from all the vendors at the surrounding compounds stacked on his nightstand. On the floor is a deck of cards laid out like he was practicing how to play Spades.

Alex finds the digital camera he had and turns it on to see all the photos Tate took of her and the guys hanging out. After their shifts were over, Tate would take pictures of them during card games and movie nights. She smiles at a picture of Tate attempting to ride a camel.

"Guys, look at this," she says with a sad grin on her face. "Remember this day?"

Cast gently takes the camera, smiles, and says, "Oh yeah, this was the day that the compound had the Fourth of July parade and when Tate rode the camel and couldn't hold on and fell right off."

"I remember that he complained about his arm hurting for a week. I told him to stop being such a baby," Thompson says with regret in his voice.

They all look at the photo together in silence when suddenly they hear Tate's door open to find Liam standing there in shock and out of breath.

"Liam?" Alex asks. She instantly starts crying as she runs to go and hug him. She doesn't know or care how he found out about Tate or how he got there so fast. She's just happy he's there, holding her. She can feel his body shaking and she can hear his broken breath as he tries not to break down uncontrollably.

Slowly letting her go he asks, "What happened? Who did this to him?" as tears come down his face.

"We think it was a sniper," Cast says. "We hit something on the road and the next thing we knew, we were being shot at by someone on the mountain ridge."

"I should've been there wi—"

Suddenly, they see the captain standing in the doorway, staring at all of them in anger.

Liam doesn't even flinch as he instantly grabs the captain by the throat and slams him into the wall.

"HOW DARE YOU FUCKING TOUCH HER YOU SON OF A BITCH!" Liam screams.

"LIAM NO!" Alex says as she tries to pry his hands away from the captain's throat.

She tries to move Liam's hand, but he won't budge, and she can hear the captain start to make choking sounds.

"Guys, make him stop!" she says to Cast and Thompson who were sitting back and watching Liam take on the man who beat up and sexually assault the love of his life.

It finally takes both Cast and Thompson to pull Liam off him. If they didn't, Liam probably would've killed the captain with his bare hands.

The four of them stand over the captain as he falls to the floor, gasping for air. Alex quickly positions herself in front of the guys to make sure none of them get the urge to kill him.

Standing over him, with her arms folded she asks, "Why are you here? Did you follow Liam to come here and cause trouble? Don't you think you've caused enough trouble?"

Standing up while clutching his throat, the captain replies angrily and stares at her with piercing eyes. "I came here because I need to know if *YOU* are going to continue the mission that you set out to do with the Shadow!"

Alex can feel the heat rise on her face as she becomes angry at the captain's comments. She slowly moves toward him with confidence and her eyes pierce right back into his.

"How DARE you come into this room and make demands of me after what you put me through this year! NOT to mention WHAT YOU DID TO ME IN MY FUCKING ROOM!" she says as she screams inches from his face.

He can feel her breath as she screams with fury and can see Liam, Cast, and Thompson move closer to him to continue what Liam started. Out of fear and being outnumbered, he puts his hands up and says, "I have some information you may want to know…regarding who killed Sergeant Tate."

Alex stands there silent as she studies his face to see if he's lying to her. She glares into his eyes and realizes that he may have something useful to say.

Stepping back, she asks, "What is it?"

Taking a deep breath, he says, "At my daily intel brief with the Colonel this morning, he mentioned a report where men with AK-47s ambushed a convoy from Delta compound. They confiscated everything, including the guns, ammunition, and one sniper rifle. Tate was killed by a sniper, right? Well, the men from Delta compound who were ambushed described the man who took the sniper rifle out of their vehicle. He has a scar that runs from his forehead down the side of his face."

The captain can see the look on Alex's face, which tells him that she knows who the man with the scar is. It's the same man who'd tried to ambush her convoy the day she went looking for Liam and when she threatened the man with her M9.

Alex suddenly feels the hard lump in her throat as her stomach drops. She'll never forget the scar on that man's face and the way he'd stared at her with those dead, psychotic eyes. Trying to play it cool, she replies to the captain. "What do you expect me to do with that information?"

With a slight grin on his face, Captain Marcs replies, "Oh, I haven't gotten to the best part. Those men have been doing these ambushes all over the country. Intel found out that those men belong to Asim Barzan Majid, more commonly known as the Shadow."

Chapter 20
Debts Paid

As Alex lays in bed, she can hear the morning call to prayer. She notices the sound of the man's voice is slightly off-key from what she's used to hearing every day. *He probably had a bad night*, she thinks as she continues to lay there, listening to him wailing on as she stares at the ceiling. Alex woke up hours ago, thinking about her mission today. The day has finally come, and she thought about all her training and everything she's experienced in-country, from the good to the bad. Mostly, she thought of Tate's death, which was already a week ago.

Throughout the week, she took the photographs of the dead girls and the Shadow off her wall since she no longer needed to look at them. She cleaned up her room and got rid of the vodka and cigarettes because she no longer used them to numb the pain. She didn't even listen to music because she needed her mind to be clear and ready.

The man finally stops singing and Alex rolls over to her side. She can see the warm, welcoming red glow of the ruby Liam gave her sitting on her nightstand. She reaches over and gently picks it up and holds it up to the morning light that's shining through her blinds.

The red glow gives her clarity in the fact that today she may accomplish something bigger than herself or that she may ultimately die. Mostly, her mind thinks about Liam and how much she's fallen for him. *No, you can't think about that now*, she thinks to herself as she quickly puts him out of her mind. *You need to focus.*

After a few moments, she gets out of bed and walks over to the full-length mirror to look at herself. She happily notices that her face is back to normal with no bruises or a cut lip. She inspects the rest of her body for any bruises or cuts but doesn't find any. Farid said that she must look perfect when presented to the Shadow.

Alex goes over the day in her mind and remembers that Farid will be arriving at the compound three hours before the eclipse to drive her to the safe house in the city. His wife, Fatemah, will be there to dress her and do Alex's makeup and hair.

She has no idea what she'll be wearing, but it doesn't matter. Her main mission is to show up to the palace, dance, and then kill the Shadow. For most of the year, Alex has been given intel on what the Shadow and his men have done to women and little girls from all over the country. The Shadow's men are just as bad as him, and if Alex is going to do this, she's going to make sure she does it right.

Standing in front of the mirror, she warms up on some dance moves and feels confident about taking him and his men on. To her, confidence and determination are going to get her through this day. She realizes that a person cannot have these qualities without first feeling pain and anger in their lives. All the anger she's felt toward the Shadow only fuels her confidence and determination in wanting to see him and his men dead. When she thinks about it, she almost feels sorry for the poor bastards. Almost.

After taking a shower and grabbing a quick bite to eat, Alex runs into Captain Goodfellow outside the chow hall.

"Good morning, Sergeant Foster. How are ya?" the captain asks in a bright and cheery mood.

"I'm doing okay ma'am. How about you?" Alex asks with her head down.

Captain Goodfellow can tell that Alex has a lot on her mind and wants to make sure she's okay.

"I'm sorry about Sergeant Tate. He was such a good person," Goodfellow says with sorrow in her voice. "I'm here if you want to talk, okay?"

Alex can feel the lump in her throat start to come up and tears start to form in her eyes but quickly controls herself. She doesn't want to talk about Tate today. It will only upset her, and she can't afford to lose her focus. Not today, so she quickly changes the subject.

"Ma'am are you going to watch the solar eclipse today?" she says, hoping Goodfellow doesn't talk about Tate or anything else sad.

"Oh yes, I made sure to get me a pair of those special glasses to wear so that it doesn't hurt my eyes. Do you want to sit with me when it happens?" Goodfellow asks as a kind gesture.

Alex looks at her apologetically and says, "I would love that, ma'am, but I have a mission outside the wire when the eclipse is happening." With a slight grin, she hopes Goodfellow thinks it's just another normal day of missions for Alex.

"Oh, well, that sucks. I hope you get to see it while you're out there in the shit," says Goodfellow.

Alex wishes she could've had Captain Goodfellow as her officer in charge. She loves how she doesn't have a filter and just says anything that pops in her head. Captain Goodfellow's comments always make Alex laugh plus, she's easy to talk to.

"Yes, ma'am. I'll be sure to try and catch a glimpse of it while I complete my mission," Alex says as she walks away to sit at the picnic table for a while to think. She goes over the plan in her head that Farid and Captain Marcs laid out for her. She no longer needs the captain's help, nor does she want it after what he did to her. She doesn't want to see him or even deal with the videotape until her mission today is over.

Don't worry. His time will come, she thinks to herself as she reflects back to that night. Alex still has the copy of the video of Captain Marcs punching her face and ripping her clothes off, but she doesn't want to focus on that right now. All she needs to think about is the mission, which is going to start in a few hours.

It's currently eight in the morning and Farid will be arriving to pick her and the guys up at eleven to take her to the safe house to get ready. Liam is supposed to meet them there as well to see her off. It makes her nervous seeing him beforehand, but she can't deny him that.

The last time Alex saw Farid, he mentioned that the total solar eclipse was going to start at precisely two thirty-five in the afternoon and is supposed to last for six minutes and thirty-three seconds. In her mind, that's plenty of time to dance, kill the Shadow, and then escape the palace hopefully unharmed. Farid also mentioned that the Shadow normally has ten to fifteen armed guards scattered throughout the palace when he throws these lavish parties. Knowing Farid, she's sure he will go over the plan again today before she gets to the palace.

According to Farid's last brief with her and the captain, there will be political figures from across the country with their wives, some performers like singers, and maybe other dancers as well.

The main event will be when Alex dances right in front of the Shadow, just as the moon makes its way in front of the sun, creating a dark shadow in the room. This will be Alex's cue to strike as the room gets dark, and everyone looks up to admire the eclipse. The instant darkness will disorient the guards, which will give her a better chance to escape out of the palace alive. By the time the six minutes and thirty-three seconds are up, Alex should be long gone.

The Shadow asked months ago for the best exotic dancer around the city and that's when Farid took that chance and showed a picture of only Alex's eyes to the Shadow. That's all the Shadow needed to see.

Alex was complimented on her eyes her whole life. She never understood why because to her, they're just her eyes and nothing special. To others that met her for the first time, they could never look away. It always made her feel uncomfortable, especially when asked if she wore contacts because to them, her eyes didn't look real.

Alex's eyes are big and bright where the outer ring is dark then it instantly goes from light green to light caramel specks surrounding the pupil. Depending on the time of day, the light caramel color will take over the green and make her eyes bright and inviting to look at. She remembers Liam spending the longest time staring into her eyes when she would talk to him. Most of the time she'd have to repeat what she said because he wouldn't be paying attention.

So, she has the eyes, the body, the dance moves, and the training on how to kill. *How hard could it be?* she thinks to herself. She continues to sit at the picnic table for an hour going over the plan in her mind. *I should go see Brock and Decker before I leave with Farid*, she thinks. She gets up and walks toward the back building and as she opens the door, Captain Marcs comes up behind her. Apparently, he was stalking her as she sat at the picnic table going over the mission in her mind.

"Nervous, Alex?" he asks her in a snide tone of voice.

Are you fucking kidding me? she thinks as she slowly turns around and looks at him with a back the fuck off look on her face. *I am not in the mood for his shit*, she thinks as she moves a foot away from him.

He can see the way she's looking at him and continues to taunt her. "Today is the day. Are you ready or not?" he asks demandingly.

Finally, having had enough of his bullying, she slowly moves toward him, glares into his eyes, and says, "And what if I wasn't ready? What are you going to do about it, Captain?" she asks in that Air Force sass he knows all about.

Standing there pissed off, he wants to hit her for the way she's talking to him.

Alex can see that she's getting under his skin, and decides to press further. "What are you going to do? Nothing. Do you know why you're going to do nothing? Because *you* are no longer in charge of me. *You* don't call the shots anymore, Captain."

At that moment, she can see two military police sergeants and Captain Goodfellow walking toward her and Captain Marcs.

"Sergeant Foster, please move away from him," says Captain Goodfellow in a stern tone as she looks Captain Marcs dead in the eyes.

Alex has no idea what's going on, so she does as she's told. She moves away from Captain Marcs and stands next to Captain Goodfellow.

"Captain Marcs, you are to report to the Colonel's office immediately. Sergeant Grant and Sergeant Brown will be escorting you there now," she says in a demanding and stern voice toward the captain.

He stands there in complete confusion but tries his best to not let it get to him that the J1 officer is telling *him* what to do.

"Why does the Colonel want to see me and why do I have to be escorted?" he asks her sarcastically, as if being summoned to the Colonel's office was no big deal to him.

"The Colonel will fill you in, Captain. Now go," she says as she looks at him with disgust.

As the two MPs escort Captain Marcs to the Colonel's office, Captain Goodfellow turns to Alex and looks deep into her eyes with pain and sorrow.

"Why didn't you tell me or anyone else Sergeant Foster?" Captain Goodfellow asks with concern.

Oh shit. What is she talking about? Alex thinks as she looks at Goodfellow with confusion.

Captain Goodfellow can see the look on Alex's face and decides to continue.

"I just saw the video," Captain Goodfellow says. "After we spoke this morning and I mentioned Sergeant Tate, I could see how hurt you were about his death. I then realized that Sergeant Tate handed me a small package before he left the compound on the day he died. When he handed it to me, he asked that I come and see you right after opening it. Unfortunately, I had gotten so busy that I didn't open it until after speaking with you this morning." Goodfellow shakes her head and has that same look of disgust she gave to the captain on her face.

Alex can see that Goodfellow truly worries for her and finally says, "I didn't tell you or anyone else because I was afraid of him and of what he would do next." But that was a lie. She isn't afraid of the captain. She's just waiting for the right moment to strike. Now it seems she doesn't have to do anything since Tate took that burden away from her. Alex no longer has to deal with the captain or even be around him or worry about him anymore.

Brock and Decker come out of the door to the back building as Captain Goodfellow and Alex stand there talking. They heard the commotion from inside and have come out to see what's going on.

Cast and Thompson see Alex and the rest of them standing outside and come over to see what's going on as well.

Alex sees them and instantly pulls them aside and whispers, "Tate gave Captain Goodfellow the video camera the day he died, and she just watched the video this morning. She also just had Captain Marcs escorted to the Colonel's office."

Both Cast and Thompson grin at the same time from what she just said.

"Damn, I wish I could've seen that asshole get escorted by two enlisted guys," Cast says.

Thompson agrees and then starts to think about Tate's motives for giving Captain Goodfellow the camera and not letting Alex do it. Then his face suddenly lights up as if he just solved a hard math equation.

"Oh, Tate, Tate, Tate. That boy knew exactly what he was doing," Thompson says with a proud smile.

"What do you mean?" Alex asks.

"He knew that if *you* turned in the video camera that it would've looked bad on you. But if someone else turned it in, that you would be the victim and Captain Marcs the predator. See the difference?" Thompson says.

Alex takes a minute to figure it out, but she starts to see where Tate gave her the advantage.

"Wow, Tate was looking out for me the whole time," she says as she regrets all of the times she made fun of him or told him to shut up. "I feel bad for the way I treated him sometimes," she says while looking at the ground.

"No, Alex. Tate was your friend, your brother and what do brothers and sisters do? They fight and mess with each other. But in the end, he cared about you and your well-being. Especially when the captain moved Liam off the compound. That pissed Tate off," Cast says.

Alex is astounded after hearing this. She had no idea that Tate was looking after her like that. The whole time she thought she was looking out for him.

As Alex, Cast, Thompson, Brock, Decker, and Captain Goodfellow walk back toward the chow hall, they can hear Captain Marcs yelling as he's being physically escorted to one of the vehicles by both MPs.

"IT'S A LIE. I WAS SET UP! GET YOUR FUCKING HANDS OFF ME NOW!" he screams as one of the MPs puts him in the back seat of the vehicle and slams the door in his face.

Alex slowly moves next to Captain Goodfellow as they all watch him in the back seat screaming. No one can hear what he's screaming at that point as the MPs get in the vehicle and drive him off the compound.

"Where are they taking him?" Alex asks Goodfellow.

"To the main headquarters building in the city to face the general," she says. "They might call you in to make a statement about what happened. If you want someone to go with you, please don't hesitate to ask me, okay?" Goodfellow says.

"Yes, ma'am. Thank you," Alex replies. She's grateful at how Captain Goodfellow stood up to Captain Marcs the way she did.

As Goodfellow walks away and back to her office, the guys, including Brock and Decker, come up to talk with her about what they've just seen.

"Holy shit. What the fuck just happened?" Brock asks.

"Captain Marcs got what was coming to him, that's what happened," Cast says with relief in his voice.

Alex moves closer to Brock and Decker to talk with them one last time before she heads out to the safe house with Farid and the guys.

"Thank you both for being so patient with me this past year. I couldn't have learned all that I have without you," she says.

"I have to admit, it was fun putting you in chokeholds and throwing you around the room. Well, until your ass got good!" Brock says with his big arms folded and a smile on his face.

"Yeah, you were ruff at first, but you finally came around and then you started to learn all the really good moves. Some of my guys are still hurting from how you kicked their asses. Now remember what to do if you get cornered, okay?" Decker says in a way a big brother would instruct her on how to beat up the school bully.

"Yes, I remember Decker. You freak'n seared that shit into my brain. I don't think I can ever forget what to do," she says as she laughs at all the times Decker yelled at her for messing up the moves.

At that moment, she sees the front gate open and Farid's vehicle coming through. Going from laughing to being serious, Alex slowly looks at Cast and Thompson. Everything that just happened with Captain Marcs and the laughs they just shared is over. It's time now to get serious and start getting geared up to leave the compound for the mission.

Everyone on the compound is starting to get ready for the total solar eclipse that's going to happen in a few hours. Alex and the guys go to grab all their gear to leave the compound and head over to the safe house. She quickly sends Liam a message on her phone that they're heading to the safe house within the hour. She smiles when she sees his reply: "Got it. See you there. Love you."

They do what they always do before leaving the compound on missions and check each other's gear to make sure they have everything. The only difference is that Tate isn't there to check Alex's gear and he isn't there to drive. Cast decides to drive, with Alex in the passenger seat and Thompson in the back seat, leaving one seat empty.

As they follow Farid to the safe house, Alex watches the road but doesn't say anything. She starts to get a little nervous that she's actually going to do this. It reminds her of how she felt the first time she jumped out of a plane. She trained for it and was pumped up and ready until it was time to jump and look down at the ground. She remembers how her stomach turned, but by that time it was too late because she had to jump.

They reach the safe house and quickly enter the back door before anyone can see them. The safe house is old and is two stories high with broken windows and very little plumbing. The street is narrow, and the people on that block stay in their homes for fear of being shot by stray bullets. Not even the children play outside since many have died at the hands of rebels that would drive in and murder anything that moved.

When Alex and the guys walk in, Farid introduces his wife Fatemah to them. He introduces her as his beautiful painter. She's around five-foot-five inches tall and wears a blue burqa with only her eyes showing. The rest of her body is covered from head to toe. Her eyes are dark brown and painted with black eyeliner. Her eyelids are covered with gold and pink eye shadow that shimmers in the light and is mesmerizing to look at.

"Come, come," Fatemah says in broken English as she waves her hand for Alex to follow her upstairs to one of the bedrooms.

Cast, Thompson, and Farid watch as both ladies walk up the old, noisy steps when Alex turns and says, "Let me know when Liam gets here."

Chapter 21
The Painted Lady

Both ladies reach the upstairs bedroom. Fatemah escorts Alex inside, closes the door behind them, and then locks it. She doesn't want to be disturbed while she works on Alex's costume, and she doesn't want anyone to see her before she's finished.

As Alex waits for Fatemah's instructions, she looks around the room. It's small and has two small windows that let in enough light for Fatemah to dress her. She notices all the makeup, hair items, and a big box of body paints with every color possible inside.

On the table, she sees a black crown that has five points coming out the top, with the middle one being the highest. Alex walks over and picks it up to look at it closer. It's made from metal with black lace and golden patterns that swirl within the fabric. The patterns of gold cover up the metal to make it look intricate and unique. The crown curves on each side and makes a point at the middle where her forehead will be and has a tear-shaped black stone that hangs there.

Alex notices that each of the metal points of the crown has a small handle attached to it. She can feel that something is lodged inside and when she pulls on the handle, a four-inch blade comes out. Each point on the crown has a hidden blade that's double-edged. The blades are so sharp that they can slice a single piece of paper with ease. She pulls out one of the blades and can feel how comfortable the handle fits in her hand.

Fatemah watches her intently and says, "You try," while motioning her hand toward the empty wooden wall that's ten feet away.

Alex takes the blade in her hand and swiftly throws it at the wall. She hears the blade make that satisfying sound that most precision knives have when making contact with wood. She smiles as she looks at Fatemah who's also smiling because she's impressed at how Alex threw the blade with such accuracy.

"Where did Farid get this crown? I have never imagined wearing something like this," Alex says with amazement as she inspects it closely.

"Farid made it by hand," Fatemah says as she motions her hands like she's building something.

"Wow, very impressive," Alex says as she continues to look at each angle of the crown. The blades sit perfectly hidden and when Alex tilts the crown upside down and shakes it, none of the blades fall out. She puts the crown on the table and looks in the big box full of paints.

"What's with all the body paint?" Alex asks, wondering what her outfit is going to look like and if she's going to be able to move in it as she dances.

"You wear paint," Fatemah says as she starts to mix the colors she's going to use on her.

Alex looks around the room and doesn't see a costume or anything. She realizes that the body paint is her costume. Wide-eyed and horrified, Alex looks at Fatemah with confusion.

What the hell? I'm not going to wear any clothes? she thinks in horror.

Alex scoffs and asks, "Wait, what?"

Fatemah can see the look of confusion on Alex's face, so she smiles, puts the bowl of the mixed paint down, and starts to slowly remove her blue burqa. As she removes the burqa over her head, she hears Alex gasp.

Alex is in shock to discover that Fatemah is completely naked underneath. The only thing covering her is body paint and Alex can't help but look at the breathtaking design.

Her whole body is covered in exotic flowers that turn into a huge cherry blossom tree. It wraps around her whole body and ends on her back in one massive tree trunk. The lines of the branches are perfect, and the colors of the blossoms are vibrant and pink and match her eye shadow. She slowly starts to move her arms and body, and it's as if the tree has come to life and the branches move as the wind blows.

Alex has never seen anyone do this. Of all the places in the world, she never thought she'd ever see something like this here.

"How did you do this?!" Alex asks in amazement.

"My sister. She painter like me," Fatemah says. "This for Afia, my daughter," she says as she points to the cherry blossoms on her body.

Alex remembers Farid telling her that the Shadow took his twelve-year-old daughter, Afia, and he and his wife never saw her again.

Alex continues to admire the beautiful cherry blossoms and suddenly feels sad about Fatemah and Farid's daughter. To lighten the mood she says, "You look beautiful, and your sister did a great job painting you."

Alex doesn't know what to say and is a little nervous going to the palace in nothing but body paint and a crown full of blades. *You can do this*, Alex thinks. She looks at Fatemah and finally says, "Okay, I'm all yours. I trust you so do what you have to do."

Alex has no idea how the body paint works so she watches Fatemah mix the paint colors. There's a lot of gold in one bowl and a lot black in another bowl. Then there are smaller bowls of turquoise and dark green with some deep blues and purples.

"How long will the paint stay on my body?" Alex asks her.

"Until tonight, then take off in shower," Fatemah says.

"Will it rub off or smear when I sit or dance?" Alex asks with curiosity.

"No. Paint sturdy," Fatemah says with a smile. "Take off clothes."

Alex does as she asks and starts to remove her uniform one piece at a time. She neatly folds each item, places them on top of one another, and puts them on the bed. Then she places her boots next to one another on the floor.

Alex stands there naked, in the middle of the room, where both windows shed the perfect amount of light for Fatemah to work. There are so many brushes and sponges for her to choose from but the first thing she picks up is a small spray bottle. It's called setting spray, and Fatemah puts light mists of it all over Alex's naked body, which will prevent the paint from smearing.

After a few minutes, she picks up a high-density medium-size sponge and dips it into the big bowl of gold paint. This is going to be the base color that's going to cover most of Alex's body. She starts with her legs, front and back and the bottoms of her feet. Then she moves up to her arms, shoulders, and backside. The gold is faint in color and gives Alex a delightful glittery glow about her.

Fatemah does some touch-ups on the gold paint to make sure she doesn't miss any spots then picks up the bowl of black paint. She uses a small paintbrush and outlines a choker that goes around Alex's long neck. Then draws a black line that goes from the side of the choker down to the inner curvature of her breast. The line continues down toward Alex's navel and then she mirrors the image on the other side of

Alex's body. She starts to fill in the outlined area with small scales like the scales on a snake.

When she finishes outlining the scales, Fatemah paints a replica of Cleopatra's Egyptian collar that looks like it drapes around Alex's shoulders and down to her breasts. She paints a blue scarab in the middle that's holding the sun over its head and adorns the bottom part of the collar that covers Alex's breasts with blue and turquoise stones.

Fatemah then picks up the blue, green, and purple paints and starts lightly filling in the scales she drew on Alex's torso and down to her hips. The scales make Alex look iridescent when she moves, and the color of the gold on her body and the black outlines make her look like she's wearing a costume.

She then paints on a black lacey thong. Around each of her legs, she draws delicate, subtle lines that give them depth before helping Alex put on a gold pair of four-inch thigh-high spiraled heels. The heels have thin, sparkly straps that wrap around each leg going all the way up to her mid-thighs.

Fatemah then goes over to a small dresser in the corner of the room and pulls out a thin shimmery belly dancer chain made of small gold coins that wrap around Alex's hips. The chain of coins barely covers her below but with the black thong Fatemah painted, it helps better conceal her down there.

She's finally done painting Alex's body front to back and now it's time to affix the crown on her head before she works on Alex's eyes. Her eyes are the centerpiece of this entire costume, so Fatemah wants to save that for last.

The hair is the easy part. All Fatemah has to do is put the crown on, then make multiple braids to attach to the inside so that it stays in place. After it's affixed to Alex's head, Fatemah asks her to move around to see if it comes off or shifts in any way. She watches as Alex moves her body and the crown stays perfectly in place. Now to work on her eyes.

Fatemah uses black paint and makes a thick outline of the Eye of Ra around each eye. The Eye of Ra is what the ancient Egyptians used to repel evil and restore harmony, which is fitting for Alex's mission. She uses eyeliner to bring out Alex's eyes then uses the purple, green, and deep blue paints to lightly fill the inside. Fatemah then affixes small golden rhinestones to the corners of each eye to help capture the light. She finishes by using a very light brush to put some gold flakes on her face. The look is very subtle and complements the rest of Alex's body.

Alex can't see herself from where she's standing, so Fatemah takes her over to the full-length mirror on the other side of the room. She can't believe her eyes when she sees the intricate details of the collar and the iridescent scales on her body. Alex starts slowly moving her body and can see how the scales move and make her look iridescent and mesmerizing to look at.

"Oh, wait," Fatemah says as she goes over to the table and picks up two gold snake arm cuffs that wrap around each of Alex's arms. She helps Alex put each snake cuff on and then turns her around to take one last look in the mirror.

"You are ready," Fatemah says with a smile on her face.

As they both head back downstairs, Farid gasps at the sight of Alex. The guys slowly get up and are speechless just as Liam walks through the door. He's standing at the bottom of the stairs as Alex slowly walks toward him. He watches as the scales on her body move in unison and can hear the sound of the gold coins dancing on her hips. As she reaches the bottom of the stairs, he looks at her from the intricate crown on her head then down to her bright green eyes.

"You made it," she says softly.

Everyone stands in complete silence. Finally, Farid waves his hand at the rest of them to go to the backroom to give Liam and Alex privacy. Fatemah hands Liam a long, black see-through veil to put on Alex before she leaves.

Not paying attention to everyone leaving the room, they look into each other's eyes. He starts to slowly look at her and his heart starts to race at how she looks in the body paint.

"You're so beautiful," he whispers as he raises his hand and holds it lightly to her cheek. He fixates on her exquisite painted eyes as he slowly places the long black see-through veil over her crown. It cascades to her feet, covering her completely from head to toe.

"Come back to me," he says as he watches her eyes gaze back at him from under the veil.

Alex doesn't want this moment to end, but she knows that time is ticking and she needs to go before it's too late. She moves toward the door, turns back, and says, "I will."

Chapter 22
The Party to Remember

The palace is frantic with servants running around trying to make everything perfect for Asim's eclipse party. It's a special day because there's going to be double the number of guests at this event compared to his previous ones. He stresses multiple times that he wants everything to be flawless.

"This party will be the one that'll be remembered for decades!" Asim says loudly while watching the servants get everything ready.

There hasn't been a total solar eclipse since before Asim was born. To him, everything must be perfect. This time, he's holding the party in the main ballroom. It's bigger and the ceiling is dome shaped with intricate carvings that open to the sky. When the sunlight hits in the afternoon, the carvings make stunning designs all over the room.

His black mahogany throne is in the center of the room for everyone to see. There are tables upon tables of food and drinks for all the guests to enjoy, and there are small alcoves with fancy couches and long see-through curtains in the corners of the room.

For the music, Asim requested an up-and-coming singer. The young man started his career by singing during the call to prayer. The people love his voice so much that he gets invited to perform at many rich gatherings all over the country. Today, he will sing, and the exotic dancer will dance to his voice for Asim.

I can't wait to see her eyes, Asim thinks as he remembers when Farid showed him the photograph of Alex's eyes. He's never seen such bright green eyes with light caramel golden specks in them. He remembers how he couldn't look away and told Farid, "You will fetch her and only her and if she is not good, you will pay the price my friend."

Asim walks past his throne with the seventy-inch-tall wing-back and instructs the guards to make sure everyone can see him in the middle of the room during the eclipse as the dancer dances for him.

"I must look like a king up there!" he yells at the guards.

Then he instructs them to make sure his dogs are locked in their cages in the cellar and to keep it guarded. When the guards comply, he leaves the room and heads up the double staircase to his suite.

The head guard instructs one guard to put the dogs in the cellar and guard it all day and then instructs the servants to make a platform.

"It must have two steps going up! Asim must be higher than the rest of his guests," he instructs.

The servants quickly work for an hour making a platform. It's made from flat sheets of plywood, then covered with an intricate black and gold Turkish rug made of silk and cashmere. There's just enough room on the platform for his throne and the dancer to dance in front of him.

When Asim enters his suite, he sees two naked girls waiting for him on the large round bed. He ordered his guards earlier to kidnap two young girls for him because he needs to be relaxed before the party starts.

The girls are young and look untouched by other men. Asim grows impatient and needs to get the tension out of him now, so he throws his cane on the side of the bed and instructs one of the girls to take his shoes and pants off while the other takes his shirt off.

"You, take it off," he says to one of the girls, but he quickly notices they're both afraid and look as if they've never done this before. Asim becomes frustrated by this and slaps one girl hard in the face. He looks at the other girl as if he's going to slap her and she immediately complies by taking his shoes and pants off. The girl he slapped cradles her cheek before coming back up and slowly starts removing Asim's shirt.

Fully naked, he lays on his back and grabs the girl with the red cheek by the hair and forces her mouth onto his erect cock. As he forces her head up and down, the girl begins to sob as she makes gagging noises with her mouth. The other girl is next to Asim being violently fingered using his other hand. As he comes into the girl's mouth, she falls off the bed and vomits on his floor. In a fit of rage from this sign of betrayal, he grabs his cane and hits her hard over the head, instantly knocking her out.

The other girl isn't so lucky. By that time Asim's in a full-blown rage and he grabs the girl on his bed by the hair and starts to violently punch her in the face.

She doesn't know how to defend herself and as Asim continues to pound her face, she lays there and takes every hit. By the time he finishes beating her, he leaves her there with a broken nose, a busted cheek, and a swollen eye. Some of her teeth had flown out of her mouth and onto the bed.

Asim finally calms down and calls two of his guards to clean up the mess in his room as he gets ready for the party.

"Take them downstairs. If they wake up, keep them quiet," he yells to his guards as they silently clean up his mess.

After his long shower, Asim goes into his large walk-in closet and picks out the Giorgio Armani deep blue silk suit that was handmade to his specifications and imported from Italy. The suit fits him perfectly and makes him look regal, even with the long, sleek black cane he walks around with. As he studies himself in the mirror, he marvels at his reflection and wants nothing more than to be respected like his father, but better.

Today is about my power, he thinks as he reflects on how clever he is for not inviting his father to the party. Asim made sure to not tell his father about the palace party. He wants this day to be all about him. The last party Asim threw, his father arrived, and all the attention was on him and not Asim. But not today. He made sure to tell his servants and the guards to *not* mention this party to any of his father's close friends. Not even Asim's younger brother or mother are allowed to attend because he wants all the attention for himself.

The guests are starting to arrive and are brought to the main ballroom with the dome ceiling. There's food and drinks and a harpist who's playing in the corner as the guests wait for Asim to arrive. Some of the men are wearing traditional Afghan clothes while others wear expensive, handmade silk suits that shimmer in the rays of light coming through the dome.

The women look extravagant in their velvet dresses with gold embroidered lace that lines the sleeves and around their necks. Some are even wearing the traditional colorful Afghan dresses with headscarves that cover their hair. Each of the pieces of fabric is adorned with small gold coins that clink when they walk, and their eyes are painted with dark eyeliner and adorned with jewels on each side.

As the guests eat and talk amongst each other, Asim is in his suite finishing getting ready before he is announced. He's standing in front of the mirror and goes over in his mind that today is the day he will convince the important guests to help him overthrow his father. *I will become a better leader than him*, he thinks as he smiles cunningly at his reflection.

Asim doesn't want this event to be like all the others he's thrown. Today is special, so he decides not to get the guests drunk from his concoctions of alcohol or get them high from his personal stash of cocaine. Instead, he wants them to be awake and see all that he has compared to what his father has. He wants to take over the political party because he knows that his father's time in the political scene is coming to an end. The only way to do that is to persuade the guests to help him overthrow his father.

He looks at himself in the mirror one last time before he heads down to the ballroom to be with them. As his head guard announces his arrival, everyone stops chatting and looks at Asim as he enters the room. They gaze at him in his deep blue Armani silk suit and can hear his cane hit the floor as he walks past them. This new attire makes him look fierce and authoritative, just like his father.

As he walks confidently toward the middle of the room, the only sound is coming from his cane hitting the marble floor with a hard clanking sound with each step he takes. When he reaches the platform, he makes it up both steps with ease, and he sits firmly on his massive throne. He then places his cane next to him and crosses his good leg over his bad one as he watches the crowd.

Each guest makes a point to come up to Asim as he sits on his throne to pay their respects. Normally, when a man approaches Asim, he would bring either his wife or lover, who would stand one pace behind him with her eyes down. This is because the men are afraid that if Asim catches a glimpse of a pair of beautiful eyes, then he will take her upstairs and rape her. He's known for doing this at not only his parties but any parties he attends.

It's getting close to the main event when the exotic dancer shows up. He's starting to get impatient and can't wait to see her and those eyes he'd seen only from a single photograph. Asim is sure in his mind that the rest of her will be just as good. Sitting there, ignoring some of the guests in front of him, he pictures those bright green eyes dancing in front of him on the platform and thinks of all the things he's going to do to her all night.

Thoughts of torturing and raping her go through his mind with such delight that a sudden feeling of euphoria hits him like a wave. *First, I will tie her by the wrists and ankles and spread her out, then I will gag her mouth*, he thinks. Feeling generous, Asim thinks that maybe he will allow his head guards to take turns and fuck her after he's done and then record it to watch later. This brings a smile to his face as he sits back on his throne and watches everyone eat, drink, and marvel in his presence.

Chapter 23
The Red Eclipse

Liam and the rest watch as Alex and Farid leave the safe house. With the black see-through veil on her, Liam can still see her bright green eyes as Farid backs the car out into the street and heads to the palace.

The ride is going to take forty-five minutes to an hour to get there and hopefully no one stops them on the road. To make this work, she needs to get to the palace in time for the total solar eclipse because every minute of that eclipse must count. For now, she uses this time to get her mind ready for what's to come.

Sitting in the back seat, she does her best to focus, breathe, and stay calm. The last thing she needs is to freak out at the palace and for the Shadow, or worse his guards, to pick up on her and kill her. She wants the Shadow to be relaxed and not see her coming. It'll be much easier that way if he isn't aware of her intentions.

As Farid drives her to the palace, she notices the road is deserted and dusty. In the distance, Alex can see the mountain range and nothing else. All the time she spent on the roads in this country, and yet Alex has never been on this road. She hopes that she'll make it out alive and back to Liam and her friends in one piece. For now, she can't think about that. She closes her eyes again and pictures the palace layout that Farid showed her when he last came to visit the compound.

Farid had told her that he'd visited the palace many times to bring Asim's mother fabric for the drapes in her room. The real reason he visited was to see the layout of each room and where everything was so that he could report back to the captain. Luckily, Asim and his guards barely noticed Farid since he was there for Asim's mother. He might as well have been another servant in Asim's eyes. This was a good thing because every time Farid had seen Asim's face, he wanted to kill him for what had happened to his twelve-year-old daughter, Afia.

As Farid drives, he looks in the rearview mirror and watches Alex in the back seat with her eyes closed as she slowly breathes in and out. He's never met a woman so brave as to face such a violent monster and his armed guards.

"You will be wonderful," he says as he watches her slowly open her eyes and give him a smile. "You remember what I told you about the room you will be dancing in, yes?" Farid asks as he watches the road heading to the palace.

Alex stays silent for a minute, recalling everything he's told her about the palace, and then finally says, "Yes, I'll be climbing the main stairs that lead up to the palace doors where two guards will be posted on each side. Then, I will walk down the main hall where there'll be two more guards posted by the grand staircase just before the main ballroom with the dome shaped ceiling. When I make my move and kill him during the darkness of the eclipse, I will escape out the back door of the ballroom, which leads to the kitchens, and then straight to the main garage. Then I'll go through the garage and out the back gardens where the big fountain is and find my way to the back gate."

"Yes, that is good Alex. But remember, there will be guards in the garage and the gardens," he says.

Alex thinks back to the day when Brock and Decker surprised her with five guys to fight all at once and she also remembers how she handled them all.

Looking at Farid she replies, "Then I'll kill them all."

As Farid gets closer, Alex can see the palace in the distance. It's all white and looks more like a castle rather than a palace. In the front, there's a massive staircase with fifty steps leading up to two huge double doors. At the foot of the steps is a large fountain with two massive marble horses, frozen in midair, with water rushing between them.

Farid parks the car in front of the fountain to let Alex out. There are two armed guards already waiting for them as they pull up. The guards see Farid and automatically know he's the man who's bringing the exotic dancer for the Shadow. Before one of the guards reach the door, Farid whispers, "I will meet you at the back gate for your escape. Good luck to you my friend and may God's angels protect you on your mission."

"Thank you for everything and if I take too long, it means I am dead," she says as the guard opens the door to let her out of the car.

Without looking back at Farid, she carefully steps out of the car, trying not to step on her long black see-through veil. As the light hits the veil, she notices the guard looking at her painted body and eyes in awe as she tries not to look directly at him. She manages to focus on the fifty steps that reach up to the top where two guards are placed at the huge double doors, waiting for her.

With each step up, the small gold coins that hang from her hips make a pleasant clinking sound. There's a slight breeze that suddenly makes her veil flutter to one side which reveals part of her leg. The gold paint and the shimmering stones from her high heels wrap around her leg and go up to her thigh, which leaves little to the imagination.

She finally reaches the top of the stairs as both guards open the double doors. She walks in alone and can see down the long, wide hallway with the double staircase going up on both sides. The floors are marble, and the walls are inlaid with gold wainscoting on each side. When she reaches the double staircase, Alex stops and looks up to see a massive crystal chandelier. The ceiling around it is painted with a mural of half-naked women with scarves that circle gracefully around the chandelier. The women seem to flow in exotic positions as they touch themselves.

"Come," one guard orders as he motions with his hand toward the double doors on the right side of where she's standing.

Alex can hear music playing and chatter coming from behind the doors. She's to be brought in five minutes before the moon makes its way in front of the sun and no sooner. The guard is telling her the protocol, thinking she understands Dari, but she already knows what to do. She's instructed by him to walk up to the platform, take her veil off in front of everyone and approach the throne where Asim is waiting for her. Then, once the music starts, she's to dance, and dance well or there will be consequences.

Her heart starts pounding faster, and her hands are slightly shaking from the adrenaline, but she immediately calms herself with a few deep breaths from under her veil. When the guard opens the double doors, Alex immediately sees the Shadow sitting on his black throne, watching her come into the room.

This is it, she thinks as she looks only at Asim and no one else. She thought by seeing him in the flesh that she'd run in the other direction. To her surprise, she steps forward, her eyes to his, with a slight cunning grin on her face.

She remembers what Farid told her about the protocol and slowly walks up to the bottom of the platform. Alex can feel all the eyes in the room watching her in silence as she walks past them. The only sound in the room is coming from her heels hitting the marble floor as her long, black see-through veil flows with each step. Her walk is seductive and with each step she takes, she feels more confident in her task.

The guests start to whisper at how they can see her painted body and intricate crown from under her veil, not to mention her painted eyes.

When Alex reaches the bottom of the platform, she watches Asim look at her intently from his throne. After a few moments of making him wait, she slowly bends down to her feet and lifts the veil. She takes her time going slowly up her legs, then to her hips, and then with one swift movement removes the veil over her head.

The room is completely silent as everyone waits for Asim to speak. Continuing to look into Asim's eyes, she gives him a grin. As the corner of her lip curls, she beckons him to come closer with an inviting stare. *Come closer, you son of a bitch*, she thinks as she keeps her gaze locked onto his.

Asim isn't used to women looking directly into his eyes for this long, mainly because they fear him, but he notices that Alex will not take her eyes off him. He's instantly in awe of her beauty and can't stop looking at her. Finally, he rises from his throne, grabs his cane, and goes down the two steps to see her eyes without breaking eye contact. He admires her perfect form as he gets closer to her.

I can't wait to see your blood hit the floor, she thinks. The pictures of those women and little girls she had on her wall for so many months, with their raped and beaten bodies, flash in her mind as he continues to circle around her.

He's now inches from her as he admires the artwork Fatemah has done on her body. The painted scales, the gold shimmer of her legs and arms, Cleopatra's collar that drapes around her shoulders and down to her naked breasts. To him, she looks like an exotic Egyptian goddess with nothing but body paint, small gold coins on her hips, and a crown on her head.

Asim circles around to her side and sniffs her neck, then moves up toward her hair to smell her vanilla perfume. He slowly walks behind her while Alex stands perfectly still for him. As he circles back in front of her, he finishes by staring into her bright green eyes. It's as if he wants to save the best part of her for last.

She stares right back and makes sure to give him a look indicating that she wants him to fuck her. Her heart wants to see his blood, but her eyes must tell the lie and give him what he wants.

One of Asim's men comes up and whispers something in his ear. He let Asim know that the eclipse will be starting in a few minutes. When Alex looks at the man, she sees the long scar that runs from his forehead and down the side of his face. He's the same man that tried to ambush her convoy the day she pulled out her M9. He is also the same man that stole the sniper rifle and killed Tate.

Alex does everything in her power not to take a dagger out of her crown and stick it right in that motherfucker's eye. *Don't look at him*, she thinks. She remains calm and waits for Asim to go sit on his throne.

After he reaches the top, he turns and watches everyone below then yells, "Allahu Akbar!" meaning God is great.

Everyone claps as Asim waves his hand toward the band and the singer so that Alex can start dancing.

The man on the Dhol drums starts playing first. He uses his hands and slowly beats the drums. Alex uses the rhythm of the beats to slowly move her hips. The gold coins clink together and the scales on her body move in waves as she rolls her hips seductively from side to side. Keeping eye contact with Asim, she raises her arms to the ceiling while her hips continue to roll slowly from side to side.

Asim curls his lip in a smile as his eyes move up and down her body. He watches as the painted scales move on her torso in unison with one another and listens to the satisfying sound of the gold coins on her hips. If she moves just quick enough, he can see her black-painted thong and the rest of her below.

As the drums continue beating, the singer begins to serenade everyone in the room with his booming voice. Some of the guests start to look away from Alex and over to the singer, which is what she is counting on. Alex uses his voice to continue seducing the Shadow by taking her hands and caressing her waist, then slowly moving her hands up to her breasts as she continues rotating her hips. Then she slowly starts to bend down into a squat pose and opens her legs wide, revealing herself to him.

As she looks up at Asim, she can see the room is slowly starting to get darker. *Finally*, she thinks as the moon starts making its way in front of the sun. *Get closer to him and then strike*, she thinks as she moves her body inch by inch closer to him.

The guests start to look up at the dome ceiling as the blue sky begins to darken. They can see the bright sun through the intricate designs and the moon starting to cover its light.

Time to move closer, she thinks as she moves toward the Shadow and starts her routine to give him a lap dance. First, she imagines the little wooden chair she practiced on for months in the training room. *The chair is a man*, she'd always told herself. She'd danced on, around, and in front of the chair as if it were an actual man.

The man continues to sing, and the drumbeats begin to get faster and faster. The room is now getting darker by the second. Alex turns her body away from the Shadow and forces his legs open so she can place her hips there. Rotating her hips slowly, she arches her body back and lays on him.

Asim is slightly surprised at how she's so willing to be this close to him, let alone lay on him without being commanded to do so. He takes his fingers and slips it under the gold coins and then into her, penetrating her over and over. The other hand makes its way to her breast as he finds her firm nipple and pinches hard while kissing her neck.

You motherfucker, she thinks as she ignores the pain of her nipple being pinched. *Keep going, just a little more*, she thinks. The room isn't completely dark yet. *Get on top and kiss him*, she thinks as she slowly twists her body over him as if she were a snake moving in for the kill. She manages to slowly roll her body over his silk suit, get on top and straddle him as she exposes her painted breasts in his face. She moves in closer to his mouth and slips her tongue inside without breaking away her gaze.

Asim enjoys every movement as she moves her hips back and forth with her tongue wrapped around his as their lips meet. *She's not like the others, she's not afraid*, he thinks as he takes his hands and grabs both of Alex's hips as she continues to rotate them back and forth. He's getting harder with every move of her hips on top of him. *Her vanilla perfume, her breasts, and her eyes*, he thinks as he tilts his head back. As the erection in his Armani silk suit rises with delight, the moon finally makes its way completely over the sun.

She can hear the guests murmur about how dark the room is. Even though her eyes have not adjusted just yet, she can still see the Shadow in front of her with his head tilted back enjoying his lap dance. *It's time*, she thinks as she moves both her arms above her head and toward her crown with the hidden blades. She watches as the Shadow is completely oblivious to what her hands are doing because his head is still tilted back in a state of ecstasy. Alex slowly takes out the hidden blade from the top of her crown and quickly slashes his throat open from ear to ear.

The Shadow's blood sprays all over her face and painted body. She can hear his mouth make horrifying gurgling sounds. She can feel him quickly try and grasp his throat to stop the bleeding, so she pins his hands back to let him bleed out. Inches from his face she whispers, "This is for all those little girls you raped and tortured, you son of a bitch."

As he hears her American accent, his eyes widen in horror. *How did this happen? How did she get here?* he thinks. He can start to feel himself weaken from the loss of so much blood. He watches her smile at him as the cold darkness falls over his body. Finally, the Shadow is no more.

You did it! He's gone! she thinks as slowly gets off the throne and down the backside of the platform. No one in the room is aware of what's happened. They continue to look up at the solar eclipse. No one notices Alex get off the throne except for one man. The man with the long scar on his face sees what Alex did to Asim and starts shooting at her with his AK-47. The sound is so loud that all the guests immediately fall to the ground and scream in horror.

Alex still has the bloody blade in her hand, so she turns and quickly throws it at the man. The four-inch blade finds its way into his torso, and he falls to the ground, dropping his weapon. As she runs to pick up the AK-47, both guards come through the double doors and see Asim sprawled out on his throne with his throat cut open from ear to ear.

All the guests start running toward the open doors and the guards start spraying bullets from side to side, killing half of them.

Alex runs behind the throne and peeks her head around it. *Fuck, fuck, fuck*, she thinks. She can hear some of the guests yell out in pain and watches as the guards start to put a bullet in each of their heads. Not knowing that Alex is watching them from behind the Shadow's throne, she quietly takes the AK-47 and aims it at the closest guard. She fires at his torso and as he goes down, she quickly fires at the second guard. The bullet hits his leg but doesn't kill him. Watching him reach for his weapon, she quickly runs up to him and puts a bullet in his head. Her stomach turns as she watches the blood pour out of the gaping hole in his head and onto the marble floor.

Alex checks the dead guards' bodies for ammo and finds that one of them has a Ka-Bar knife. This type of knife is used by the U.S. military so, he must have stolen it on one of the ambushes. As she picks up the knife and inspects it, the man with the scar on his face starts to wail in pain from the blade she threw into his torso.

He killed Tate, she thinks as she watches him writhe in pain. She slowly gets up with the Ka-Bar in hand and kneels beside him. She watches as he lays on the floor, moaning in pain from the wound she caused him. "You deserve to feel this pain," she says as she climbs on top of him. She pins his shoulders down with her knees and starts to carve the letter T in the middle of his forehead with the knife.

His piercing screams penetrate her ears and can be heard throughout the palace. As she carves his forehead, she can feel the knife scraping the bone. When she finishes, Alex looks at him and says, "T stands for Tate you motherfucker." She then takes the Ka-Bar and slices his throat open, ending his life.

Alex slowly gets up and sheathes the bloody blade between the laces of her thigh-high heels. She can feel his hot, sticky blood along with the Shadow's blood all over her face and body. As she makes her way toward the back door that leads to the kitchen, two more guards suddenly come through the door. She quickly rolls to the ground and starts shooting the AK-47 at them.

The bullets go flying past them and only hits one guard. The other guard starts shooting back in her direction.

She suddenly feels her arm burning but doesn't have time to look at it. Pulling another blade from her crown, Alex throws it with such force that it sinks into the guard's forehead. To her surprise, the blade going into his forehead made the same satisfying sound as when she threw the blade at the wall back at the safe house.

She stands there silent, waiting to see if any other guards come busting in. The room is a blood bath with dead guests in fancy clothes all over the floor, five dead guards, and the Shadow in the middle of the room. Alex looks down at herself and says, "Jesus." To her, she looks like Death covered in blood.

She takes a quick moment to breathe before leaving the room and notices her arm. It seems that one of the bullets grazed her right arm and the skin is slightly open and bleeding. *Fuck*, she thinks as she goes over to the black veil she wore earlier, rips off a piece, and wraps it around her arm to stop the bleeding.

Suddenly, she hears loud footsteps approaching from the double doors, so she quickly picks up one of the dead guard's AK-47s and runs behind the throne again. Alex has the perfect vantage point from behind there since the damn throne is seventy inches tall and is made from black mahogany.

When the two guards enter, she's able to shoot one perfectly between the eyes. The other guard panics and starts spraying bullets out of his AK-47, not knowing where Alex is hiding. Many of the bullets hit the Shadow's corpse making him look even more grotesque. Luckily, none of them hit her.

She waits quietly while the guard continues to spray the entire room with bullets. She figures the fool is bound to run out of bullets at some point, which will give her the right moment to attack. Peeking around the throne, she fires three bullets right at his torso, instantly killing him.

Alex hears silence as she waits to see if any more guards are coming in the direction of the double doors. *Stick to the plan*, she thinks as she slowly heads to the back door toward the kitchen. She double checks the AK-47 she's holding to see if there're any bullets left and only sees one in the chamber. *Fuck*, she thinks. She quickly checks the rest of the AKs on the floor. Each one she checks is empty. She still has the small blades in her crown and the Ka-Bar knife on her thigh.

There's only one smaller door behind the throne that leads to the kitchen, so Alex quietly makes her way to it. She opens it slightly and moves quickly to the side of the door to make sure no one can fire at her from the other side. She doesn't hear any movement, so she slowly tiptoes down the hall toward the kitchen with the Ka-Bar ready in her hand.

As she continues down the hall, she hears loud barking coming from the door on her right. To her, it sounds like it's coming from below. The door has a padlock on it and as she puts her ear closer to the door, she can hear crying but not the crying from dogs; it sounds like a little girl. *What the fuck? Who's down there?* she thinks.

Alex tries to hit the lock with the end of the Ka-Bar, but the lock doesn't budge. She remembers the two guards she killed coming out the door that led into this hallway, so she runs back into the main ballroom and checks both guards for any keys that may open the lock. Rummaging through the two guards' pockets, she finds a bundle of keys and runs back to the locked door. When she finally finds the right key, she opens the door and notices a set of stairs leading down to a cellar.

"*Shit,*" she thinks and instantly covers her nose and mouth. The air is pungent with piss, shit, and an unrecognizable odor she's never smelled before.

Chapter 24
The Cellar

Alex struggles to find the light switch. She slowly walks down the stairs with the Ka-Bar in one hand while her other hand covers her nose and mouth. She can hear dogs bark but they don't approach the stairs, so they must be tied up. As she reaches the bottom of the stairs, the cellar opens wide. There are five steel dog cages along the right wall and five larger steel cages along the left wall. There's a large tarp on the back wall that's bulging like there's too much of something trying to be covered.

When she looks over to the left wall with the larger cages, her mouth opens in horror. Despite letting the smell of the room get into her mouth, she stares in shock. As she slowly walks closer, the dogs viciously growl and bark at her with such intensity that the sound of them hitting the cages makes her jump a little.

Looking at the cages in front of her, she sees that each one has at least seven women and little girls that are dirty and beaten. In one of the cages, the women and children are all standing on one side. On the other side of the cage is a dead woman that looks as if she'd starved to death.

The guards didn't take her body out of the cage and put her with the rest of the bodies that are under the tarp at the back of the room. Alex realizes what the odd smell is: it was the smell of rotting corpses under the tarp of all the women and little girls that either died from starvation or from the Shadow himself.

Alex continues to stand there, frozen at the sight of these women and children. She looks at the state of them and how they've been sleeping on a dirt floor and forced to lay in their own piss and shit. They have bruises all over their faces and bodies and look sick and malnourished. Many of the girls look no older than twelve years old. She watches them as they look at her with blood all over her painted body and the crown on her head in awe.

As Alex steps closer, they all look at her with wide eyes and gaping mouths. None of them say a word except for one little girl who looks up with her sunken eyes and says with a thick accent, "Help."

Alex finally snaps out of it and starts trying each key to see which one will open the first cage. She can feel her heart beating through her chest as the dogs continue to bark. Each key she tries doesn't seem to fit and she can feel the women and children start to panic. Suddenly, one of the women screams, and out of pure reflex, Alex rolls her body away from the cage.

A guard comes from behind her and tries to hit her over the head with a crowbar. Instead, he hits the cage, and the women and children quickly move back against the wall.

Alex quickly gets to her feet and grabs the Ka-Bar from her thigh. She watches his moves and notices by his stance that he wasn't expected to fight a woman. She swiftly crouches low on his right side and slices his rib cage while swiping his legs from under him. As he hits the ground face first, Alex lifts his head and finishes him by slicing his throat open.

As his blood pools heavily on the dirt floor, the women slowly come back to the front of the cages to stare at her and what she's done. From the way they're looking at her, she wonders what she must look like by now. All the blood from the Shadow, the man with the scar, and all the rest that she'd killed are all over her face and painted body.

She continues to try the keys. Finally, the right key opens all the cages. They come out one by one but are too afraid to go up the stairs. Alex goes first and puts her index finger to her mouth letting them know to be quiet as they approach the door at the top of the stairs. She can hear rapid footsteps going up and down the hallway that runs from the main ballroom to the kitchen where she needs to go. Slowly opening the cellar door, she peeks out looking in both directions to see if the coast is clear.

She can hear a few guards in the kitchen area and decides to leave the women and children there to go fight them head-on. Alex turns around, looks at the women intently, and says in a whisper, "Stay here."

They nod their heads in agreement as they watch the painted, bloody lady leave them and quietly shut the door. Crouching on the stairs, they stare at the door frame, worrying she won't make it back. The only movements they can see are from the shadows running back and forth from under the door.

Suddenly they hear a man screaming in pain and bodies hitting the walls. They flinch all at once as pots and pans hit the marble floor in a loud crashing sound. Bodies dropping to the floor and then the painted lady screaming in agony. Abruptly, the noise stops, and the only sound left is of their rapid breathing. *Did the bloody lady win or did they kill her?* they wonder as they stare helplessly at the door in fear of who's coming for them next.

They hear footsteps slowly approaching, but the door doesn't open right away. A woman at the top of the stairs looks in horror at the shadow under the door as the rest of them hold their mouths closed. The shadow under the door is very still as the doorknob slowly turns. To the women's relief, the painted lady is alive. However, she has blood running down the side of her head and looks like she's about to pass out.

One of the guards hit her on the side of the head with a frying pan just before she lodged the Ka-Bar into his stomach. One of the women notices her thumbs are covered with blood and another substance she doesn't recognize on them. The substance is from Alex blinding a guard when she pressed her thumbs into his eye sockets and used all her weight to crush them from within.

One woman holds Alex up so she can catch her breath as they slowly walk towards the kitchen. After a few minutes, Alex starts feeling better, despite her head feeling like she got hit with a wrecking ball. She leads them toward the kitchen and past the carnage Alex caused as she fought and killed the guards.

She motions them all to stay back so she can scope out the garage. When she enters the garage, she instantly notices the expensive cars ranging from a Maserati, a Ferrari, and a couple of Lamborghinis. They're lined up in a row with other expensive vehicles. She finds the switch that opens the doors and flips it.

The garage doors spring to life and open at the same time, revealing the gardens that lead to the back gate. She needs the back gate to open, so she flips all the other switches on the wall and one of them works.

With the gate fully open, Alex hears a vehicle coming through and tells them all to get down.

They don't understand English. However, they know the universal sign of someone motioning them to hit the ground, so they start to hide behind the cars and wait for Alex's instructions.

The solar eclipse is long over, and Alex can feel the sunlight hit her face as she looks to see that it's Farid behind the wheel. Fortunately for Alex, the guards that were supposed to man the garage and the back gate ran off when they heard all the gunfire.

He waited for me, she thinks as she sighs with relief.

Farid quickly comes out of the vehicle and says, "I was worried because it was taking too long." Looking at the blood on her face, body, and the side of her head, he slowly reaches toward her and takes the crown off. Despite the sun beating down on them, he can see her body slightly shaking.

"Oh, my friend," Farid says with sorrow, realizing the horror she went through in that palace. "Wait here," he says as he quickly runs back to the vehicle and pulls out the bag she'd packed at the safe house. It contains a T-shirt, sweatpants, and a pair of her sneakers.

"Here are your clothes. Now quickly put them on and we will go," he says.

"I forgot I packed this," she says as she quickly puts her clothes on. Suddenly, she hears Farid gasp.

All the women and little girls start to slowly come out from behind the cars and into the sunlight. They hold their hands up to their foreheads because they haven't seen the sun in a very long time.

Farid watches in shock as they slowly come forward. Alex then turns to Farid with exhaustion in her voice and says, "We have to help them and get them the hell out of here."

"How are we going to get them..." he says as he suddenly stops and peers into the crowd.

"No, it can't be," he says in a whisper.

He watches as a young woman with a dirty and beaten face walks toward him. He doesn't want to believe it because it's been so many years.

"Afia?" he asks in a whisper as he slowly walks toward her.

She looks to be fourteen or fifteen years old as she walks forward in ragged clothing, a scar on her lip, and a broken eye socket from being repeatedly beaten.

"Papa!" she says as she cries softly and falls into Farid's arms.

Alex watches them embrace and remembers when Farid told her that Afia was only twelve when she was kidnapped by the Shadow's men. She's now the same height as Farid and Alex notices how thin and frail she looks from being malnourished all those years.

Farid places both hands on his daughter's face and can see the pain and suffering she's endured all those years. Feeling guilty for ever thinking she was dead, tears stream down his face. All those times he'd visited the palace, his daughter was there the entire time, right under his feet.

"Farid, we have to go," Alex whispers as she tries to figure out how to transport them back to the safe house.

One of the women touches Alex's arm to get her attention then points toward the far end of the garage. Sitting there, plain as day, is the five-ton cargo truck that the Shadow's men stole on one of their ambushes.

Alex and Farid run over to the vehicle and look inside. The truck is massive and looks like it's in good condition. She remembers her training on how to repair these five tons, and luckily, they don't require a key to operate.

"Farid, start putting the women in the back of the cargo bed while I get this thing started," she says. She climbs in the driver's seat and tries to remember all the gauges and switches. Farid starts guiding the women and children into the back of the truck one by one. Alex closes her eyes to see if she can visualize how she turned on the vehicle during training. It comes back to her as she flips the top switch to turn the battery on, and then turns the second switch just below it to turn the engine on. She hears a satisfying beep and then the engine roar to life.

The truck is loud and bounces a little from the large engine rumbling under the hood. She checks all the gauges, just as Tate taught her when they'd looked at one on Bravo compound. Then she makes sure the pressure gauge for the air brakes is working properly. *Thank God for that,* she thinks with relief.

She looks out the back window and sees that Farid has about half of the women and children on the truck. She gets out to help him and sees all the luxury cars lined up in a row. Alex realizes that she doesn't want to leave the palace as it is. *I need to burn this place to the ground*, she thinks.

"Farid, when you're done loading them in the back, call Liam and the guys and let them know that we're heading to Alpha compound instead of the safe house. This truck is too big and will draw too much attention on those back roads. Also, tell Thompson to get all his medical supplies and to be ready for when we get there," she says as she helps him load a young girl into the back and then heads toward the garage.

"Alex, where are you going?" he asks loudly so she can hear him over the engine.

"I need to do something inside. Take the truck to the gate and wait for me. I should only be a few minutes," she says as she turns and runs back into the palace.

Alex quickly makes her way past the garage and into the large kitchen. The bodies of the three dead guards she fought earlier are lying there lifeless. She looks at one of them and remembers how she kicked him so hard that he hit the refrigerator, leaving a huge dent on the door. Then she finished him by breaking his neck. She had to use one of her hidden blades from her crown to slice another guard's femoral artery in his groin area. As he bled out, she finished him by using that same blade to slice his throat open.

The third guard surprised her with a frying pan to the side of her head. Luckily, Alex heard him coming and deflected most of the blow. However, it still hit her pretty hard. After they threw each other around the room, Alex managed to stab him in the abdomen with the Ka-Bar then pinned him to the ground and stuck both her thumbs into his eye sockets. She wasn't sure at the time if that killed him or the knife to the gut.

She quickly looks around the kitchen and notices all the high-quality equipment that looks like it belongs in Gordon Ramsay's restaurant. There're a few high-end refrigerators and multiple gas stoves that line up in a row. There's a long island so that the cooks have room to prepare many dishes at once. Then she sees the large toaster on the counter that can fit six slices of thick bread all at once. *That's it!* she thinks.

Alex has an idea but wants to get something before she leaves the palace. She runs back down the hallway, past the cellar door, and back into the main ballroom where she danced and then killed the Shadow and his men.

As she enters the room, the sunlight is coming through the dome ceiling and making intricate designs on the floor. She doesn't remember looking at the room much because her focus was on the Shadow. The room already smells like metal from the pools of blood from the carnage that took place.

It's eerily quiet as she slowly walks past the man with the scar on his face and over to the Shadow's corpse. Sprawled out on the black throne, she watches as flies land in his gaping mouth and the open wound on his neck that she inflicted. She looks at his eyes, which are rolled back in his skull. From the smell of him, it seems he relieved his bowels when he died.

Alex quietly looks at him and the rest of the room in silence. Suddenly, she sees that his cane is still placed at his side. "There it is," she says as she goes over and picks it up. She notices that it's unscathed by the horror that happened in the room. She holds it in her blood-stained hands and slowly pulls the twenty-two-inch custom blade out of it. Alex can see her reflection in the shiny steel and all the blood that's all over her face and neck. She didn't know she looked this bad when she went into the cellar to rescue the women and children. *No wonder they looked at me like that*, she thinks.

Suddenly, she hears the loud horn of the five-ton truck going off from outside the back gate. She quickly sheathes the blade and takes the cane with her. Alex runs back into the kitchen and turns on all the gas stoves, letting the gas seep out into the room. She then takes a recipe book that's laying on the counter and rips a bunch of pages out of it, rolls them up, and stuffs them into the large toaster. Alex pushes the lever down to start the toaster and runs out of the kitchen leaving the doors of the garage wide open.

Farid hits the horn again and Alex comes running out of the garage and down the driveway as fast as she can. The women at the end of the cargo bed hold their hands out for her to grab as Alex lunges herself onto the back of the truck. She manages to pull herself in as one of the girls knocks on the back window to let Farid know to start driving. Out of breath, Alex lays on the floor in exhaustion and looks up at the sky while holding the Shadow's cane in her blood-stained hands.

Suddenly, a very loud explosion comes from the back of the palace, and Alex and the rest of the women watch as black smoke comes out the roof and fills the garage. They drive away and watch flames violently take over the palace with no one there to stop it. One of the women smiles at the sight and then says, "Allahu Akbar." Alex remembers the Shadow saying that right before she danced for him but didn't know what it meant.

"What does that mean?" Alex asks the woman, but she doesn't answer since she can only speak in Dari.

"She said, 'God is good,'" another woman says to Alex with a smile on her face.

How can God be good after what I saw today? she asks herself. She turns around and watches as all the women and young girls look back at her with admiration and gratitude. Alex leans her back against the cargo door as the sun and wind hit her face. She watches as the moon parts ways with the sun to continue its journey around the planet. Her body starts to ache, and her head still throbs from where she was hit. *It could've been worse*, she thinks as she pictures all those dead men in that palace. But instead, she has to live with the fact that she murdered them all and their blood is literally on her hands.

Alex wants nothing more than to fall asleep and wake up with this day having been a dream. As she sits there thinking of her actions, tears start to fall down her face. She continues to hold the Shadow's cane in her hands, picturing his distorted face with his throat split open. She can hear the screams of all the men she killed, and she can feel the sticky blood that's all over her face and body, which reminds her of the day Tate died.

As Farid continues driving down the road toward Alpha compound, Alex suddenly feels someone touch her. She slowly opens her eyes and finds that one of the women is gently holding her hand.

The woman looks at her and with her eyes, she tells Alex that everything's going to be okay and that she did the right thing.

Alex gets the message, closes her eyes once again, and breaks down into tears as the woman reaches over and hugs her. She looks at all of them and can see how this one day can't compare to the years they'd spent in that cellar and under the roof of that madman.

After a few minutes, she stands up, slowly walks down to the front of the cargo bed, and holds onto the side, looking at the open road with the mountains in the distance. *How many palaces were like this one? How many women and children were trapped under the same roof of men like the Shadow?* she asks herself. She realizes that after today's mission, she's now become a completely different person. The blood on her hands is a witness to that and she instantly thinks back to the first day she sat in Captain Marcs' office when he showed her those photographs. She stands there and wonders if she could go back to that day, would she have made the same choice?

Turning her head back to look at the women and children she saved, she answers her own question. The dust from the road brushes her cheeks as Farid drives quickly back to Alpha compound. Alex can only think about Liam and how she can't wait to see him. She closes her eyes, imagines his lips meeting hers, and lets the warmth of the sun and the light wind caress her smiling face.

Chapter 25
The Return

Liam gets a frantic call from Farid over the radio to have him and the guys meet them at Alpha compound and to bring Fatemah there as well. He hears Farid's voice, and the first thing Liam asks is if Alex is alive.

"Yes, my friend. She is alive!" Farid says. "Please go to Alpha compound and get the medical equipment. We will need a lot."

"Farid, why do we need a lot of medical supplies. What happened? Is she hurt?" Liam asks. He hears a loud horn from the other end of the radio go off.

"We have many people with us, and they are hurt, and they need our help," Farid says out of breath.

"What people, Farid? Is the Shadow dead?" Liam asks loudly while holding the radio in front of him.

"Alex is here. I must go my friend. Meet us in one hour!" Farid says.

Liam does what Farid asks and tells the guys and Fatemah that they're to go to Alpha and wait for Farid and Alex to show up with a lot of injured people.

"Come on, everyone. Get in the SUV. We gotta head back to Alpha compound now. You too, Fatemah," Liam says with panic in his voice.

"What the fuck is going on!" Cast says as he quickly throws his gear on.

"Is she alive?" Thompson asks, also putting his gear on.

"Yeah, and it sounds like many others will be coming with her, so we need to be ready to help them," Liam says as he finishes putting his gear on and heads out to the SUV.

Cast takes the driver's seat while Liam jumps in the passenger seat and Thompson and Fatemah sit in the back. The back alleys in the city are tight and narrow, and Cast isn't used to driving in such tight corridors. Tate, however, was a pro at it. He slowly makes his way through and does his best to not draw attention to them.

Come on, baby. Please make it back to me, Liam thinks as he keeps his eyes peeled on the road for anything that might be a threat.

Cast finally makes it to the main road and hightails it to the green zone. They reach the main entrance of the compound, and the gate guard instantly recognizes Cast and lets them in.

Liam quickly gets out of the SUV and looks for any sign of Alex or Farid, but it looks like they haven't made it back yet.

"Thompson, go get all your medical supplies and bring them back here. Cast, stay with Fatemah," Liam says as he runs to the J1 office.

"Where are you going?" Cast asks as he watches Liam take off.

Liam doesn't have time to answer as he makes it to the J1 office to look for Captain Goodfellow. As he comes flying into the office, he sees that she's helping someone out-process to go home.

"Ma'am, I'm sorry to interrupt but can I speak with you?" Liam asks out of breath.

She can see the look of panic on his face, excuses herself from her customer, and pulls him aside.

"Sergeant Anderson, I haven't seen you in a long time. What's going on?" she asks out of concern.

"Ma'am, Sergeant Foster will be arriving shortly with many injured people. Can you help us when they get here?" he asks hoping she won't see how Alex is dressed when she gets back. A naked, painted body with a crown full of blades isn't the proper attire for someone stationed at a deployed location.

"Sergeant, what do you need?" she asks with full compliance.

"Sergeant Thompson is getting the medical supplies and we'll need help with administering medical attention," Liam says.

"Absolutely, I'll get some people together to help," she says without question.

"Thank you so much ma'am. Please meet us by the front gate," Liam says as he quickly leaves the J1 office and heads back to the front gate to wait for Alex and Farid to show up. His mind races with what to expect when they arrive. *Is Alex hurt? Did she accomplish the mission?* Before he can think of anything else, he hears a loud engine approach the other side of the gate and instantly knows it's them.

"Guys, get ready!" Liam says over to Cast and Thompson.

The gate opens and the M923A2 Turbo five-ton cargo truck comes slowly into the compound with Farid behind the wheel.

"Let them through!" Liam says to the gate guards.

Liam, Cast, and Thompson start to see women and little girls stand up and look down at them as they approach the vehicle. Their faces are dirty and many of them have broken eye sockets and dirty cuts on their bodies.

Liam is trying to find Alex in the truck but there are too many women coming off at one time. He sees Farid help a young girl in her teens and takes her toward Fatemah.

"Farid, where's Alex?" Liam asks but is interrupted when Fatemah sees the young girl and realizes it's her daughter Afia.

Liam doesn't want to bother them, so he goes over to Cast and Thompson. They're already helping the women and little girls get cleaned up, looking them over for any cuts and broken bones. Captain Goodfellow and a few of her crew also come and help clean them up.

Getting a sudden feeling of panic in his chest, Liam tries to figure out where she is. *She probably jumped off the truck before anyone could notice her*, he thinks. No one besides Captain Marcs and his team is supposed to know about Alex's mission.

Liam quickly runs to her room and notices that the door is partly open. He slowly approaches and can hear someone breathing hard and struggling with their clothes. Slowly opening the door, he sees her leaning against the wall by her bed, covered in body paint, blood, and nothing else.

"Liam," she whispers. Sobbing, she reaches out to him.

He quickly goes over to her and holds her close. He doesn't care about the blood getting on him because he's just happy to see her alive.

"Shhhh, baby. It's okay," he says as he lightly touches the side of her blood-stained face. "I thought I lost you," he whispers. Without saying a word, he gently lifts her into his arms and carries her to the shower down the hallway.

Alex wraps her arms around his neck and looks deep into his eyes as he carries her to the place where they made love for the first time.

As they reach the bathroom, Liam gently puts her down by the sink and turns the hot water on in the shower. He then kneels in front of her and slowly removes the belly dancer chain with the little gold coins that dangle from her hips. The blood is dry, and the coins stick to her skin as he gently pulls it off her in silence. From the ordeal she went through at the palace, Liam can see her body shake as he's kneeling in front of her. Remaining silent, he picks her up again and carries her into the shower, placing her under the hot water. Not caring that his clothes are getting soaked, Liam stands in front of her and lightly caresses the side of her head to wash the blood away. He cleans off the rest of her body and watches as the body paint and blood run down the drain.

Liam notices a piece of cloth covering the wound on her arm. He gently removes the cloth and can see a perfect line of blood from where a bullet grazed her. *Jesus*, he thinks as he slowly runs his thumb over it to wash the dried blood away and watches Alex flinch from the pain.

Liam looks into her eyes and can't believe she's standing in front of him, alive and unharmed. She has a cut on her head and a grazed bullet wound on her arm. *It could've been worse*, he thinks, but her eyes tell him a different story when she looks back at him. *She looks different*, he also thinks and realizes that she's seen things that no one should ever see and live to talk about. Liam instantly feels bad and doesn't know what to say to make her feel better. He never wanted this for her, and now that he sees her in this state of shock, his eyes suddenly fill with tears.

Finally, he says, "I'm so sorry baby," knowing those words alone can never mend what happened to her. The entire year, he's been there for her after every training day and encounter with Captain Marcs, and all he can say to her now is I'm sorry.

"Shhh, baby. It's okay. I made it back to you like I promised," she says softly as they hold each other there, hoping the hot water will wash away all the pain they went through that year. The worry that every day could've been the day they died on the road or got separated from one another gets washed away.

When they finally go back to her room, Liam reaches out again and embraces her for the longest time in silence. He thinks about how he almost lost her and how he hopes everything is going to be okay from now on. He can feel her body shake and wonders if it's from being cold from the shower, or if it's from the shock of killing the Shadow, his men, and then making it out alive.

As Alex stands there in Liam's arms, she thinks about how it's finally all over. The training, the dancing, the constant stress about the mission of killing the Shadow. She can't believe she survived it all. She thinks about the girl she was when she arrived there eleven months earlier, and the girl she's now become.

Alex opens her eyes, and she sees the reflection of herself in the mirror on the opposite side of her room. She notices how her bright green eyes stand out from the traces of black paint that remains on them. There's also some dried blood on her eyes from when she sliced the Shadow's throat open. Alex then shifts her gaze at the Shadow's cane that's leaning on the mirror. Suddenly, she feels like he's in the room, watching them as they embrace. *He can't hurt you or anyone anymore*, she thinks as she continues to stare at it.

As Liam continues to hold her, she gazes at the cane again. It stands there alone, helpless and without its master. She took the Shadow's cane before destroying the palace because she needs a reminder of the evil she faced and overcame.

It's at that moment that Alex realizes that she didn't just kill the Shadow. She killed the shadows that lived within her mind. All those years of being afraid and not knowing who she was lifted the moment she killed him and his men. Her father's face is gone from her mind, and Captain Marcs' abusive behavior is no longer a threat to her. When she found and saved all those women and children in the cellar, she knew that her life had changed forever.

Holding Liam tighter, Alex continues to look at the cane and then to her reflection in the mirror. *How many more are out there?* she asks herself. She pictures the cunning grin the Shadow gave her right before she danced for him. Then she pictures seeing the flies landing in his mouth and the slit in his throat. *Could I do it again?* she asks herself, contemplating if she still has the courage to face the darkness of men again and the shadows that live within them.

Epilogue

As the snow falls and the brisk air from the winter wind blows, Alex sits on her windowsill, enjoying the quiet morning alone. She watches the snowfall in silence while holding the ruby Liam gave to her in her hand. The one-bedroom apartment she's renting is not much, but it has everything she needs and is just outside of Seymour Johnson Air Force Base in North Carolina. After she returned from Afghanistan a year ago, she requested to be assigned there so she could be closer to Liam.

He's stationed at Fort Bragg, which is only an hour away from her. He makes sure to come and see her every weekend. For Alex, it feels nice to have her own place where they can be together without worrying about roommates bothering them.

It's been a year since she returned home, and even though the scenery has changed, her thoughts always go back to her time over there. Her apartment is small, and she doesn't own many things. However, she did put a few pictures up of her, Liam and the guys together. Her refrigerator has pictures of her time in Afghanistan and of the happy days she remembers with Liam and the team. One of them is a picture of Tate during one of the bazaars of him attempting to ride a camel. Cast, Thompson, Liam, and herself stood in front of the camel Tate was on while the picture was taken.

She looks at Tate and how happy he was in that photo with his big grin and dimples on his cheeks. It always makes her smile when she sees this picture. Today, however, her mind instantly goes to the momentwhen his blood sprayed on her face from the bullet that entered his neck that instantly killed him.

The walls start to close in on her and her heart starts beating faster as she drops the photo of Tate on the floor. She starts to breathe hard and cry uncontrollably as she holds her hand to her chest. It suddenly feels like she's back there again, laying on the ground with Tate on top of her bleeding out.

"No…no…please, not again," she says as tears flow from her eyes. She's on her hands and knees on the cold floor trying to get the images of Tate out of her mind.

"Breathe…just breathe," she tells herself as she slowly takes control and gets up from the floor.

Once, when Liam came for the weekend, Alex had one of her nightmares of the Shadow. He was chasing her in the cellar full of the dead bodies of the women he'd raped and murdered. In her dream, no matter how fast she ran he was right behind her. She could hear the choking sound his throat made when she'd sliced it open, and she could smell the blood in the room. Liam would help her when she woke up screaming and calm her down by holding her until she fell asleep again.

He begged her to go and speak with a professional about possibly having post-traumatic stress disorder. When she went, they taught her calming exercises so that if she started to have a panic attack, she would be able to control it. The panic attacks happened to her many times when she first returned home. She would call Liam to hear his voice, and he would calm her down over the phone. He would tell her to slowly breathe in through her nose and out through her mouth. After some time, her panic attacks lessened.

Slowly breathing in and out, she suddenly hears her phone ring and knows it's Liam. Before answering it, she takes a few more deep breaths and does her best to get Tate out of her mind.

"Hello?"

"Hey baby," Liam says.

Wiping the remaining tears from her face she says, "I miss you. I can't wait to see you this weekend." she says.

"I know I can't wait to see you too, but I called because I have to tell you something," he says with hesitation.

Alex can tell through the phone that whatever he has to tell her isn't good.

With dread, she asks, "What's going on?"

Liam takes a minute to respond and then says, "It's about Captain Marcs." He waits for her to say something.

For the past year, Alex did her best to get that man out of her thoughts. After the trial, where he was found guilty of rape on multiple accounts from his past, she didn't want to ever speak his name or hear about him ever again.

When she returned from Afghanistan, an Army Judge Advocate General officer called her for her testimony in the case against Captain Tyler Marcs. When Captain Goodfellow handed over the video camera of Captain Marcs attempting to rape and physically abuse Alex, she didn't know that there were other witnesses of the captain's behavior over the years with many other women.

The JAG officer that worked the case against Captain Marcs found dozens of rape and physical abuse testimonies throughout the captain's career. It was the video camera that Tate handed over that put the nail in Captain Marcs' coffin. When Alex had to watch the video again in court, chills ran up and down her spine, not to mention the fact that the captain was there and stared at her with apologetic eyes.

When he was found guilty and sentenced to time in prison, Alex never thought to see such a man cry and plead in front of everyone the way he did. He screamed bloody murder and had to be carried out of the courtroom by two armed men. It wasn't a good sight to see. However, Alex figured that she'd been through worse, and to see him found guilty only made her realize that men like him never triumph.

She feels her stomach drop. "Liam, what's going on with the captain?" she asks.

"He's dead. They found him in his cell where he hung himself with his bedsheet," Liam says with disgust in his voice. "I'm sorry. I know you don't want to hear about him anymore."

Alex sits down in shock that he's actually gone. She can't tell if she's happy that he's dead or sad for the guy for taking his own life.

Suddenly feeling relief, she replies, "No, I'm glad you told me. I needed to hear that."

Changing the subject he says, "I can't wait to see you this weekend."

"Me too. I miss you. The snow is starting to pass, so you should be okay getting here," she says.

"Yeah. Even if it's bad out, I'm still coming to see you. We can curl up on the couch and watch movies all weekend. How does that sound?" he asks.

Thinking of Tate again at how much he loved watching movies, she picks up the picture of him that fell to the floor, smiles, and says, "Sounds good to me. I can't wait." She then places the picture of Tate back on the refrigerator and slowly smiles at it.

"Sweet dreams, baby. I love you and I'll see you soon," Liam says.

Alex closes her eyes and smiles. Saying I love you to him makes her feel instantly better. She's so lucky to have found him during the most pivotal time in her life.

Smiling she whispers back, "I love you more."

After they hang up, Alex turns the TV on because sometimes it's too quiet in her apartment. She flips the channels and stops on CNN when she hears the announcer read a report of the troops that are still in Afghanistan. They show quick clips of the country and of many troops gearing up and getting deployed to go there. In the same segment, they show an Afghan political figure who's yelling at the camera.

The CNN announcer mentions how the Afghan political figure is on a manhunt for the person who killed his son, Asim Barzan Majid. They show a picture of Asim's face and Alex's heart starts to pound faster and harder. The picture shows the same cunning grin he gave her on the day of his death. CNN is now showing quick clips of the palace on fire and how nothing remained from the explosion Alex had caused.

Sitting there in shock, she turns the TV off. Suddenly, all the memories of that day come flooding back to her mind. She tells herself that she's safe now and that no one in the palace lived to see her kill the Shadow. Alex gets off the couch, goes to her bedroom, and opens her dresser drawer. She pulls out a long black cloth and unwraps it on her bed. Laying there is the long, sleek black cane that belonged to the Shadow. As soon as Alex touches the cane, she sees the Shadow's cunning grin on the day she'd danced for him.

She holds it in her hands and slowly removes the blade listening to the sound of the metal scrape against the sheath. She looks at her reflection in the shiny steel and remembers how powerful she felt the day she returned with all those women and little girls. Anytime Alex feels scared or unsure of herself, she holds the cane of the evil man she killed. She is now a confident, powerful woman who stops at nothing to see good prevail over evil.

The shadows in her mind will always, in one way or another, be there. It's how Alex fights the shadows that makes her the person she's become. If she didn't take the risk and face the captain head-on, then he'd still be out there abusing women. If she'd decided to walk out of the captain's office the day he showed her the photo of the Shadow, who knows how many women and young girls would've died in his wrath.

Good will always prevail over evil. If there's evil left in the world, the good will always be there to stop it. No matter the cost.

CPSIA information can be obtained
at www.ICGtesting.com
Printed in the USA
LVHW010752050422
715318LV00007B/408

9 781662 918490